"Vividly written, with characters the reader will come to love as friends, *The Sound of Wings* is a compelling debut novel of great emotional depth. Highly recommended!"

—Loretta Nyhan, author of *All the Good Parts* and *The Other Family*

"Grab a cup of tea, curl up on the couch, and get ready to get lost in Suzanne Simonetti's charming and heartfelt debut. Can't wait for the next book by this talented author!"

—Terry Lynn Thomas, *USA TODAY* best-selling author of *The Betrayal*

"A lyrical debut reminding us that behind every polished exterior there can be secrets and hidden truths. The women at the heart of this story transform as they battle demons, from the ones existing in real life to the ones they carry within. Through the passages of time and self-discovery, they form an unlikely alliance that brings them to a place of healing and growth."

—Tammy Hetrick, author of *Stella Rose*

"In *The Sound of Wings*, Suzanne Simonetti weaves together the stories of three women and their unusual bonds, which grow as they each confront their pasts and the secrets they keep from the ones they treasure most. You don't want to miss this heartfelt tale of love, sacrifice, and friendship! Beautifully written—and that cover! Put it on your list today."

—Gina Heron, author of *Buried Beneath the Lies* and *What's Left Between Us*

The Sound
of Wings

The Sound of Wings

A NOVEL

SUZANNE SIMONETTI

She Writes Press, a BookSparks imprint
A Division of SparkPointStudio, LLC.

Published 2021
Printed in the United States of America

Print ISBN: 978-1-64742-044-4
E-ISBN: 978-1-64742-047-5
Library of Congress Control Number: 2020922433

For information, address:
She Writes Press
1569 Solano Ave #546
Berkeley, CA 94707

She Writes Press is a division of SparkPoint Studio, LLC.

For Joe:

You will always hold the other key to me.
It's in your hands, my love.
It always was.

Prologue

Goldie

CAPE MAY, NEW JERSEY, 2014

He's back again.

Goldie shivered. The sun dipped beneath the treetops, curtaining the air with a chill. She wrapped her cardigan tight around, crossed the threshold of the rickety gate, and entered the butterfly garden. She ambled her way through verbena, aster, and clover, pausing just long enough to inhale the sweet scent of the Joe Pye weed.

And then . . . she could smell the scotch. Like a hard pinch to the nose.

Simon.

Goldie's husband had been gone for thirty years, yet somehow, his scent grew ever stronger. Lately, she wondered if it was just her weary and aging mind playing tricks. But no. He seemed so real. She could feel him, smell him. Why now? Why was he back?

Look.

Goldie spotted the monarch right away. Patrick. Her precious

1

father-in-law. He loved her more than he loved anyone else—even more than his own son. Simon knew it. And he hated Goldie for that. Hated them both for all the hours they toiled away in their butterfly garden—their own special place, where they shared dreams, stories, laughter while troweling the earth. Recently, she found herself retreating there if only to feel Patrick's warmth. His love. And what she felt she needed more than ever: his protection.

As she continued her walk, Goldie's vision slipped back out of focus. The butterfly garden became a blur. Her head was foggy, her thoughts random. When was the last time she had a good cry? She was out of tears. It had been four decades since she watched Patrick take his last breath. Goldie became awash in a fresh wave of sadness. A longing for what was. For what she once had. She knew there was a sense of freedom to be had in succumbing to such anguish. Sitting in the eye of your pain as it draws you down onto hands and knees. A healthy episode of unabashed bawling when your spirit feels as though it may just split in two. Over time, sorrow that has been silenced for too long eventually infects even the good parts—Goldie could see that now.

He called her Little Birdie for her maiden name, Sparrows. Even amidst a crowded room, Patrick made her feel as though she were the only one who existed. Goldie had lost her own father the year after he returned from combat in World War II (which coincided with her birth). Growing up without a father affected her in ways she would never fully comprehend, no matter how long she lived. She yearned for the love she'd seen her friends receive from their own dads. As a child, she would watch families at the park or at the diner and fantasize about joining the pack. How it must feel to have a complete family with both parents standing by. Her mother was old-fashioned. Widows did not remarry in those days. Goldie never spoke of it, but she longed for her mother to meet someone. Someone who could take her to the roller rink, bowling, to a drive-in movie.

Years later, a stroke of good fortune had brought Simon Knight into her path. She thought of him as her well-to-do, strikingly handsome "Knight" in shining armor with a degree in business administration who, serendipitously, came with Patrick: the most caring and lovable father imaginable. When the time came for Simon and Goldie to wed, it was Patrick who escorted her down the aisle. She was bound to Patrick by law—not by blood. However, that did not prevent him from taking her by the arm and featuring her in front of his fellow board members of the Duke University Medical Center. He introduced her as "my daughter." Overcome by the gesture, Goldie never paid any mind to the perplexing glances or hushed voices as she passed by: *A daughter? I thought Dr. Knight only had the one boy.*

Patrick taught her that a group of butterflies was called a kaleidoscope. Goldie thought it magical how he was able to command the attention of so many colorful creatures who seemed to trust him, know him, longing to be near him as much as she did.

"Remember to look for the monarchs."

They both loved the monarchs with their bright orange hues and black piping like a spider's web.

"In many countries around the world, they believe that butterflies are, in fact, departed souls," Patrick had told her. "The butterfly represents the soul's freedom upon death. In ancient Greece, the word for butterfly is *psyche*, which means soul. The Greeks believe butterflies are the souls of people who have passed away.

"Same thing is true in Russia, where their word for butterflies is *dushuchka*, derived from the word *dusha*, meaning soul. In Mexico, there is a small town where monarchs migrate every year. It happens to coincide with a Mexican holiday known as the Day of the Dead. The town celebrates the butterflies because they believe they are the souls of the deceased returning."

Goldie's eyes would widen, encouraging him to continue.

"The Irish believe butterflies to be the souls of the dead waiting to pass through purgatory."

As she walked the length of the garden, she could hear him, now.

"The brushfoots are back!"

The two spent an inordinate amount of time together on their own in the elaborate six-bedroom home Patrick had gifted the young couple for their wedding. With Simon struggling to make a name for himself as an accountant, he would leave well before dawn to tackle his one-hour commute to Virginia Beach and return long after suppertime, leaving his father and wife to their own devices. Goldie would spend the day in her home studio throwing pottery to be auctioned off at the church raffle and for sale at the local craft shop in town. Semi-retired Patrick would spend his mornings puttering around in his vegetable garden and following up on conference calls with fellow board members. Come midday, they would meet for lunch on the veranda to swap progress reports over a medley of fresh garden greens from Patrick's harvest and Goldie's tuna noodle casserole. She had acquired all sorts of knowledge being Patrick's sole companion, from everyday tasks like how to write a check to the proper way to arrange pocket cash.

"It's imperative to keep the small bills on the outside of the stack to camouflage the ol' Grants and Franklins at the center," he told her. "Although a person should never pull out his money for counting in front of onlookers. That would be in poor taste."

Sometimes Patrick's lessons were more sage in nature, and Goldie would tuck them into the figurative vault for safekeeping. He prided himself on knowing how to skillfully identify a liar behind an artificial smile and unctuous demeanor. He surreptitiously pointed out one of his fellow board members who had been known to skip out on his wife. He shifted on his feet, with a wily grin and darting eyes at every female who crossed his path.

"It's in the eyes, Little Birdie. The eyes will reveal all. But first, you must be willing to see."

For years, Goldie grappled with an unidentifiable hole. It wasn't until meeting Patrick that she knew what she had been missing. In his presence, she found peace. Sitting by his side, she felt comfort. Hearing his stories and pranks from yesteryear brought her giddiness and joy, like spending time with an old best friend. Learning from his great wisdom, Goldie discovered new things about herself and the world. She had finally understood what it meant for a young girl to bask in the shiny moonbeams of a father's love, strength, and utter devotion.

Meeting Patrick was a rare and precious gift, one that she cherished with every breath she took. But he was long gone. And with him, all the love he gave had been taken away. Stripped from her like clothing from a baby's back. What had she done to deserve such pain? Was this punishment for loving too much? Feeling too much? Why? Why was Patrick taken from this earth, where he was so hopelessly loved and desperately needed by Goldie? He always felt more like family than any other person she'd ever known—including his son, her own husband.

Right before he closed his eyes for the last time, he squeezed her hand.

"Remember to look for the monarchs, Little Birdie."

And just like that, Patrick had left her. The father to whom she should have been born. Torrents of excruciating pain coursed through her as the sorrow she carried in her heart manifested in her body.

With the lack of sunlight, her vision was particularly uncooperative as the pathway and nearby objects fogged over. Goldie ascended the uneven stairs, taking careful, deliberate footsteps.

Upon reaching the landing, she was struck hard and fast by the wafting scent of scotch.

Simon.

The heavy front door squeaked as it swung shut. Goldie secured the deadbolt and pressed her back up against the smooth pine. Her heart thumped against her ribcage. She took a moment to catch her breath. All she could hear was the sound of her loafer ticking against the floor.

Why now, Simon? Why are you back?

1

Jocelyn

For the first time in her life, Jocelyn found herself wishing the days of summer would pass swiftly. Willing any such time away wasn't common practice for a writer with an encroaching deadline, but she was a mother first, and there was nothing more unnatural or jarring than being separated from her child for an entire summer. Her baby. William James. Her darling little *Billy goat*, as she'd been calling him since the day of his birth six years earlier. Billy was visiting his father, Trevor, at the summer home he shared with his wife, Hannah, and their five-year-old twins in Ocean City, Maryland.

Reaching for a tissue, Jocelyn caught a glimpse of herself in the mirrored picture frame that held a photograph of Billy dressed in his miniature tuxedo and red bow tie: the world's most precious ring bearer. She had been adamant about including him in all aspects of her wedding to Bruce Anderson just seven weeks earlier. From the time she was a schoolgirl, she could picture herself shining as the bride, sailing through the air and waving to the crowd as if from a float in the Thanksgiving Day parade. But on that day, it was Billy who stole the show and the hearts of nearly every person in the room as he marched up to the dance floor during the best man's toast. Bruce's best friend, Craig Green, raised his glass and noticed Billy, who had managed to hoist himself up onto his toes, reaching for the microphone.

"You got something to say there, little buddy? The floor is all yours." Craig placed an encouraging hand on the back of Billy's collar and lowered the microphone to his mouth.

"My name is Billy Stevens. And my mommy is the most beautiful bride in the whole world."

The raucous sounds of tipsy guests gushing with delight filled the room. Craig smirked, nodded toward Jocelyn, and raised a palm to hush the crowd.

"She reads me lots of stories before bedtime and plays lots of fun games with me like Candy Land and puzzles and hopscotch, and she also lets me eat cookies on school nights . . . but only sometimes. I love you . . . BYE!"

Off Billy ran, back across the dance floor to reposition himself in front of the ice sculpture at the vodka station. A moment later, Jocelyn felt Bruce cradle the side of her face: a strong but gentle hand calloused from years of building homes. He leaned in and planted a tender kiss on her cheek. A loving husband and a son. Her two men: one big, one small.

But there was another man in her life. One that she would always have to contend with, and that was Trevor. The day he retrieved Billy for the summer, it felt as though she'd had a limb severed from her body, but Jocelyn was in no position to protest. Their custody arrangement had been more than reasonable and agreed upon from the start: they shared joint legal custody, while Jocelyn maintained physical custody. With the full year of wedding plans and family outings, she had monopolized Billy. They both knew it. As the spring ended, Trevor approached her with the idea of taking Billy for the summer. He would enjoy all the sun and sand he could stomach in Ocean City and get to spend time with his half siblings as well as Grandma and Grandpa Stevens in a seven-week-long itinerary that would include all sorts of excursions and family gatherings in the northeast corner.

Billy loved spending time with his daddy. And Trevor's wife, Hannah, couldn't be sweeter or more jolly if she were dipped in chocolate and covered in crushed candy cane. The first time they met, Hannah pressed her palms together and bowed. She was wearing a gold-and-black kimono jacket with crimson clam diggers and shiny ballet flats. You'd think she was Asian, yet her dirty blonde hair and grass-green eyes showed every bit of her Caucasian-ness. Trevor told her Hannah was from a mixed background—her late mother an Ashkenazi Jew, her father Christian, neither practicing—so Hannah's sense of religion was somewhat watered-down, if not nonexistent. In their brief exchange, she more or less told Jocelyn her religion was yoga. Jocelyn didn't care if she worshipped the Maharishi, so long as she didn't take drugs and was able to properly care for Billy. As Jocelyn later learned, Hannah Stevens raised the bar and then some, far exceeding all her motherly expectations.

Hannah was the type of woman who turned child-rearing into a sport. Jocelyn would never forget the time Billy had returned from a weekend visit at Trevor's. He kept haranguing Jocelyn for a cinnamon castle made of Belgian waffles. Where does one find a batter mold for such a feat? She could only imagine how many new incredible meals and crafty projects Billy would be exposed to after spending an entire summer with this woman. Jocelyn wasn't crafty. She was a writer through and through. Her cool ideas were only super neat in theory. When she tried to sketch a tree, it wound up looking like a Tootsie Pop. It was near impossible to feel anything other than second best around a mother like Hannah. How was one to compete with that? Of course, Jocelyn knew better than to compare herself to anyone, be it other mothers or other writers. And yet she just couldn't help herself. Every new person held a new benchmark, a new level of achievement to which she had to aspire. She was worlds from where she thought she'd be as a writer at this stage. But then, she hadn't been banking on all the changes to her plans, sketchy as they may have been back then.

All it took was one booze-soaked foolish night of unbridled lust to alter the trajectory of her life. Her dealings with Trevor were steamy at first, albeit devoid of any sort of real love. Their tryst was short-lived, ending before it started in many ways. Despite her reckless behavior, she had escaped with her little Billy goat, so there were no regrets. She had always known she'd become a mommy one day and quickly learned to ignore the reproachful glances and whispers from the older, more pious members of her family, who would never warm to observing their responsible, straight-A, English-lit-grad-turned-published-author give birth to a son out of wedlock. Jocelyn liked to look at the brighter side of things and knew so long as she had to be tied to an ex-lover for the rest of her life, there were far worse options than Trevor Stevens. He had come from good stock, after all, and negotiating on behalf of Billy's best interests was of the utmost importance to both Jocelyn and Trevor. And yet she could not free herself from the off-handed remark he had made about wishing for more time with Billy and the possible need to reassess their custody arrangements. As a writer of fiction, her imagination took her to all sorts of dark corners. Was Trevor just teasing—or was there more to that?

Jocelyn's debut was released the year before she had Billy. In addition to a handful of scathing reviews—*one-dimensional characters, convoluted storyline*—she also received high praise—*compelling plot, unforeseen twists*—and encouraging feedback from a few reputable book critics. So while her story about four lifelong best girlfriends fumbling their way through post-college life didn't make it onto any of the bestseller lists, Jocelyn had made a decent amount of connections and earned support from the literary crowd, and now there was buzz and anticipation over her second release.

In the months before her wedding, she sent her literary agent, Jeannie Ball, an outline and one hundred pages for her next novel. Jeannie had secured a second book deal with the publisher, and Jocelyn needed to turn in a completed manuscript by the end of August in order to receive the second installment of her advance.

Jeannie had a convivial, welcoming air about her, and Jocelyn couldn't have landed a more fitting agent to champion her work. Jeannie was also a Virgo, fastidious by nature. She didn't take deadlines lightly. All Jocelyn needed was a strict daily schedule that she could follow. And she would.

She sat staring at the words on her laptop, lost in thought. Much as she needed to be working, she could not spend one more second at her desk, where she hadn't accomplished a thing all morning. She headed for Billy's room, curling her body around the oversized dolphin on his bed. It had been a gift from a family friend and the first stuffed animal in his nursery. It was torn and tattered from years of use and being dragged to the park, but held the lingering scents of her sweet boy: a homey combination of baby shampoo and graham cracker crumbs she allowed him to sneak into bed during story time. She stared up at the glow-in-the-dark stickers peeling from the ceiling and walls. At night, Billy's room looked like the bottom of the ocean: an oasis full of seahorses, octopus, jellyfish. He was fascinated with sea creatures, wishing to be fully immersed in the underwater world. Jocelyn was sure to foster his interest and love for the deep blue. By the time Billy turned three, she got a better handle on juggling her role as mom and writer and penned a children's series about sea animals.

Standing in front of the tall dresser, she trailed a loving finger across the row of children's books bearing her own name in block letters across the bindings. Billy cherished the series, named *Adventures and Friends by the Seashore.*

For the past three mornings, her ritual hadn't faltered: waking to the sound of the harp at five on Bruce's iPhone; sharing a cup of coffee on the front porch with her new husband; listening with enthusiasm to the details of his latest home construction; making a show of gathering her writing materials; waiting for the sound of Bruce's truck to turn the corner onto Pittsburgh Avenue; heading straight for Billy's room to catapult herself onto the bed and subsequently weep into his pillow.

Jocelyn didn't want to bog him down with her strife. Men were different animals. Bruce didn't have any children of his own from his first, short-lived marriage. He'd grown up never knowing who his father was. His late mother, Daisy, was a bit of a free spirit and never shared the details of what happened to Bruce's dad. Jocelyn figured Daisy had wound up pregnant by some random stoner musician breezing through town back in the seventies, but she dared not share such sentiments with her husband.

Determined to make something of his life, Bruce put all the youthful energy of his twenties into building his contracting business for home construction, turning himself into one of the most formidable bidders on Cape Island. Jocelyn was fortunate to have found Bruce on his way up. His ambition inspired her to focus on her own endeavors and bring what she could to the table, like the pending second payment on her advance. Her husband worked hard, and her family was relying on that money. Bruce had been pulling his weight for their family, and Jocelyn needed to collaborate in this effort.

By sheer will, she peeled herself from Billy's comforter to spend the afternoon testing out a few new recipes for the charity event she was throwing the following Saturday night at their home to raise money for the homeless mission. In addition to some of the town's most prominent business owners, she'd encouraged Bruce to invite all of his clients—past, present, prospective. His business was thriving, and he and the crew had just completed their crowning achievement: a six-thousand-square-foot harbor-front home with three main decks on each level, two porches coming off the master and guest suites, and a wrought-iron spiral widow's walk leading to a crow's nest situated at the top of the house. The construction served up a panoramic view of the Cape May Harbor. To the left, the fleet of commercial fishing boats stationed at Fisherman's Wharf at the Lobster House. To the right, the US Coast Guard training base. The owner of this masterpiece was Abe Axelrod, Esquire—a criminal defense attorney from Maryland—and his new wife, Krystal. It was only a three-minute walk from Jocelyn and Bruce's twenty-two-hundred-square-foot attached home on the next block over. Bruce adored Abe, who paid him handsomely for the project, which took two years to complete from the first day they broke ground to the moment the last doorknob handle had been installed.

Jocelyn needed to rally her laser-beam focus now more than ever and had her sights set on only three things: her deadline, the charity event, and making it through the summer without Billy while maintaining some semblance of sanity.

I think I can, I think I can . . .

Only the mother of a six-year-old boy would unwittingly channel the will of the little engine that could.

Whatever it takes, she thought.

She sat at her computer, fingers resting on the keyboard, reviewing what she had written the day before.

"She was losing him. . . ."

Jocelyn thought of Trevor's flippant remark about custody. A chill ran through her as she recognized with startling clarity how pep talks from protagonists were woven into her story to foreshadow what would likely follow later in the plot—the hero's tragedy.

2

Krystal

Sighing in disgust, Krystal pushed herself back from her vanity, rising from the cushioned satin chair. She smoothed her palms down her expertly waxed thighs and turned to inspect her posterior in the full-length mirror. Krystal's self-approval was reliant on her current state of mind, and discovering a patch of grey hair just moments before such an inspection did not bode well. Instantly, she felt flabby, her skin saggy, and she vowed to do a few extra sets with her hand weights the next morning while tacking an additional mile on to her run.

What was the purpose of a magnifying mirror? To punish girls who obsessed? Krystal bristled at her choice of words. *Women. Not girls.* Surely, her female counterparts saw themselves in a worthier light by the age of forty-four. A vision blossomed: on her next beach run, she would smash the mirror up against the jetty, allowing its broken parts to be carried off by the tide. These judgments pervaded her mind while she scorned the stark white hairs sprouting from the edge of her blond hairline. She hadn't noticed them earlier that day, but this magnifier was like a curious child or elderly relative, always willing to point out the unbidden and painful truth.

Krystal entered the massive walk-in closet attached to her brand-new bedroom. She paused to marvel at the massive space with its endless rows of gowns and clothing, shelves stuffed with shoes and purses, climbing thirteen feet to the ceiling next to the remote-controlled skylight. She gazed at the designer labels, still unable to comprehend how such fancy brand names had found a home in her closet: *Valentino, Prada, Fendi.* Oddly, she preferred to stick with what had always worked for her and seemed to recycle six articles of clothing into different combinations. She had certainly come a long way from the Villas, living in a shoddy two-bedroom cape infested with pests. Krystal's late father would have been able to park his clunky old flatbed Chevy in her new closet. She could only imagine what her parents would think of their daughter living with such spoils.

"Just who do you think you are? Some silly princess of England or something?" She could almost feel her dead mother's wrath, see the lit cigarette dangling from the corner of her scowling mouth.

Her father's disdain would have been directed at Abe, Krystal's husband. Her father had always abhorred men with money.

"Mr. Big Shot Fancy Pants," he would have said. Krystal was almost glad he hadn't lived long enough to have the opportunity to snicker at Abe with his polished Italian shoes, pressed silk shirts, and gold rope chain, featuring a Star of David.

Krystal's father was a simple man who hadn't sought anything more than what he considered to be essentials: beer, cigarettes, tins of beef jerky, and a roof over his head. He'd worn the same construction boots for thirty-five years, which he repaired like a patchwork quilt with gobs of silver construction tape. As the existing tape became frayed, he'd replace it with fresh pieces.

Naturally, her father's philosophy on finances and what he considered fitting apparel had extended to his wife and daughter.

Krystal's mother lamented over the lack of personal items and money, blaming everything from the expense of having to raise Krystal to her lazy husband to the government to the neighbors. Other than her everyday sneakers, Krystal was permitted two extra pairs of footwear: her Sunday dress shoes and a sturdy pair of flip-flops for the warmer months.

When Krystal was a child, her mother had a way of spewing venom and making her feel guilty for everything, including her natural-born beauty. She always felt as though the stork had dropped her on her parents' porch from some foreign land, as she hardly resembled the two people who had supposedly created her. Often compared to a young Marilyn Monroe, Krystal was buxom and shapely. She was bubbly, naturally blonde, and loved to laugh—a stark contrast to her mother's concave chest, hunched posture, mealy brown bob, and general air of malcontent.

It wasn't until Krystal was old enough to secure a babysitting job that she could buy herself a few new pieces of clothing. Where most parents encouraged their kids to find part-time work, Krystal's mom was plagued with resentment for not only her daughter's uncontrolled, blossoming independence but her ability to make her own money. More often than not, her mother would fall victim to a series of harrowing and debilitating headaches, rendering her unable to drive Krystal to her after-school jobs.

It had taken years of therapy for Krystal to identify how her mother's anger and jealousy were mere reflections of her unfulfilled, dissatisfied existence. While in therapy, she had noticed a quote by Vietnamese philosopher Thich Nhat Hanh on the wall that resonated ever so strongly for her: *People have a hard time letting go of their suffering. Out of fear of the unknown, they prefer suffering that is familiar.*

Her mother was attached to the miserable life she had created with Krystal's father. It had all become so clear long after her parents died.

Lightly touching a pale pink blouse, she contemplated what to wear for the charity event next Saturday night at the Andersons'. Bruce Anderson had designed and built their dream home. For the last several weeks, he would sheepishly call Krystal, asking for permission to bring potential clients to their home. Krystal hadn't minded. She quite liked seeing the reaction on strangers' faces as they examined the all-glass walk-in refrigerator with its rainbow of fresh produce, and the wine bar built into the oblong granite island with seating for ten. Holding the blouse against her complexion, Krystal knew immediately mauve wasn't a flattering color on her, as it clashed with her bronze tan and platinum hair.

The day before, she had attended a ladies luncheon at the yacht club. Abe had been encouraging her to get involved with charities and mingle with the other women from this circle.

"Why wouldn't they all want to make friends with the most precious creature around?"

Abe's blind adoration of Krystal was sweet to a fault. Like many men, he couldn't grasp the tricky dynamics among women and how catty they could be to newcomers. Krystal tried desperately to fit in, but she stuck out like a poppyseed jammed between two front teeth. The other ladies didn't seem to know what to make of her. She was determined to keep trying until she befriended at least one of the women. In her heart, she felt as though she was letting Abe down if she wasn't accepted by the crowd. He hadn't known it, but the whole proposition dredged up a heap of uncomfortable memories of high school that haunted her still.

Krystal Boors is such a whore, those hateful girls would chant. All because she had slurped two wine coolers and let Ricky Kramer feel her up in the basement of his friend's house during the Super Bowl. Had she known that rumors would fly like hornets in a school full of hormonal, jerky teens, she would have been more careful in her decisions. It irked her that their words bothered her even now. She once cried to Abe about it, how cruel the kids could be, how jealous the other girls were of the attention she received from boys, and how even after all these years, their words had never left her. He reminded her that people only had the power over you that you gave them and that most of those girls were insecure around the prettier ones.

"Come on now, sweetheart. High school is long over," Abe had said, casually.

While he never had anything but the best intentions, Krystal still felt like a fool.

"And how is the queen of Cape May Island?"

Abe entered the closet, placing a large hand on her bare shoulder and covering her neck with a flurry of kisses.

"Trying to figure out what to wear to this thing next week," she said, turning to face her massive husband. Abe was only six years older than Krystal but appeared to be more like twelve. Having lost most of his hair by the time he was thirty, only a modest patch of tarnished hair remained at the base of his head like a soiled ring around a bathtub. Abe had always enjoyed the good life, which included fine cuisine, and he sported a substantial girth as evidence of his culinary indulgence. He tried desperately to lose weight before their wedding and managed to take off seven pounds by walking every morning and giving up his nightly ritual of German chocolate cake paired with Ben & Jerry's Hazelnut Fudge Core. Unfortunately, he was just one of those people whose body didn't allow him to let go of the weight without a battle. Abe returned from their honeymoon to St. Tropez with the seven pounds he'd dropped and an additional five. None of that mattered to Krystal, who fell in love with his tender, generous heart. To her, Abe was her hero, and that made him the sexiest man alive.

"Sweetheart, you could wear a body bag and shave your head and still be every man's first pick," he said, sealing his words with a kiss on her cheek and handing her a chilled flute of champagne.

Krystal needed to steady her hand as the weight of the Baccarat stemware pulled her arm down like one of her plastic dumbbells. She still wasn't used to the exorbitantly expensive, heavy French crystal she received for her bridal shower.

Abe retreated from the closet, dropped his terry cloth robe onto their California king, and headed to the master bath. Krystal smiled to herself; he was sort of like her child in many ways. She wondered how he had managed to come so far without the warmth of a steady lover by his side.

Plopping in front of her vanity and raising the weighty flute to her lips, she thought back to the day they met, the day Abe was visiting the lighting store on Route 9 where she had worked since graduating from Atlantic County Community College. He was being led by an eager woman with the exuberance of a perfumed sales lady at a department store. She was well-dressed, perfectly coiffed, around sixty, and carried a Gucci bag on her dainty arm. A forest-green Jaguar was parked out in front. Assuming the woman was another overzealous wife, Krystal tried to hear her spiel as she shepherded Abe from room to room, and thought she heard the words "statement piece" several times.

When the two turned the corner to the front desk, Abe stopped walking as soon as he saw Krystal. The woman kept blathering on and on about two buffet lamps, but Abe's attention was rapt as he locked eyes with Krystal. It took a few moments before the woman realized she had completely lost her one-man audience. Luckily, she wasn't his wife but an interior designer.

Abe had only to visit Krystal's minuscule studio apartment once before insisting she pack a bag and stay with him.

"What are all these?" he asked, opening the cabinet beneath

her kitchen sink and discovering the ever-growing collection of bottles and cans she'd been saving for the five-cent refunds. His gaze swept the room and landed on her face. She realized the look he wore that night wasn't one of pity or disdain but wonderment. Behind his eyes was an acknowledgment, a reverence.

Immediately, Abe made some calls, and with the finesse of an attorney straight out of a John Grisham novel, he was able to get her out of the lease, as well as recover her security deposit. A month later, he presented Krystal with a three-and-a-half-carat emerald-cut diamond.

Aside from all the lavish gifts, Abe had brought the art of hugging into her life. Krystal hadn't been hugged as a child and was able to determine with the help of her therapist that she had been starved for affection. For Abe, showering her with love came naturally, and she knew no man in the history of the world who gave better hugs.

Krystal could hear Abe humming a tune as he finished showering. She examined herself in the mirror, inhaling deeply, sucking in her belly, turning to the side, examining the curvature of her profile, and contemplated who would be in attendance that evening, knowing this was a different crowd from the yacht club. New faces. New women. New snap judgments about her appearance. One of her biggest fears was that someone would recognize her from high school.

The bathroom door opened, allowing a puff of steamy air to billow into their bedroom. Abe stood cloaked in a silk bathrobe like a shah exiting a steam room at the royal spa. Watching him dab the towel at the few remaining strands of hair at the back of his head, she imagined what he would think if he knew the truth of her humiliating past. All those mean pranks from her fellow cheerleaders. Krystal had always been the target, the butt of all their jokes. Some thoughts never seem to release their grip, no matter how much time has passed. No matter how worthy and righteous her husband told her she was. No matter how clean and pretty her new surroundings.

Krystal tried to hush the words rattling around her head: *High school is never over.*

3

Goldie

Spilling the flywheel with her foot, Goldie observed the startling contrast of her creased and trembling hands against the smooth clay. *No room for error on this one.* The unwelcome thought lingered for a beat, poking at her self-doubt, and she knew it must be quelled before proceeding. Nearly fifty years of throwing clay had taught her the dangers of placing too much importance on any one piece; her hands would furl beneath the torch of self-imposed scrutiny, shooting a brush fire of crippling tension up her arms and through her torso. Goldie's creativity was best served when she was able to silence the ego and stifle judgment, losing herself in the motion, textures, and soothing sounds of human hands on wet clay. And yet, disparaging thoughts kept snaking their way in. This piece was to be auctioned off at the charity event in the home of her longtime friend and contractor, Bruce Anderson, and his new wife, Jocelyn. This mermaid, whose dazzling tail measured twenty-three inches from tip to tip, would serve as the harbinger to her fellow business owners of her unwavering talent and resiliency to keep her small business afloat. Her creations had always piqued all sorts of interest among her peers, but this one needed to send a direct message: Goldie Sparrows still "had it," and Little Birdie Studio wasn't going anywhere.

She was preparing to adorn the fanciful mermaid with a wide bronze medallion at the end of a ropy chain and cuff bracelets for each of her dainty wrists, similar to the ones Wonder Woman wore on that TV show from the seventies. She was trying out a crafting medium that was new to her, using metal clay. It consisted of very small particles of metals such as silver, gold, bronze, or copper mixed with an organic binder and water for use in jewelry-making, beads, and small sculptures. Metal clay had the capability to be shaped just like any soft clay, by hand or using molds. After drying, she would fire the clay in her kiln. Once the binder burned away, the pure sintered metal was all that remained.

As she continued to work, a stream of freezing-cold water trailed her bare back like an uninvited hand. A sharp inhale caught in her throat, forcing the sleeping cat on her lap to dash across the room.

"Goodness! Pardon me, Laverne," she said. One of her cats had taken cover under the wooden bench next to her sister, Shirley. For cats born of the same litter, the two were vastly different from one another. While Laverne required constant contact and reassurance like an insecure lover, Shirley preferred to go it alone, requiring few attachments and a healthy dose of autonomy—much like Goldie. And much like her mommy, the hands of time had been slowing Shirley down lately.

Spring gave way to summer with a jolt. The temperature inside her home studio was warmer than expected, and the ice from her homemade shoulder pack turned to water within minutes. She removed her foot from the pedal and scooted to the sink in the washroom. After rinsing her hands, she peeled back the surgical tape holding the makeshift ice pack that she had jerry-rigged to her upper arm. Gently rolling her head from side to side, she pulled her left arm taut across her chest for an extra stretch. *Darn rotator cuff.* How could such a simple move like tying a smock behind her back cause such agony? A move she'd been making nearly every morning for decades. She let the healing water cascade over her arthritic hands, feeling both pity and gratitude for her swollen digits. All those years. All that sculpting. Her most precious instruments had paid the price.

Little Birdie Studio, located on Carpenters between Decatur and Ocean, opened at noon and closed at six from November through May. With tourist season now in full swing, the store was open from nine to nine, daily. The twelve-hour days had never been much of a bother in the twenty-nine years of running her Cape May business. It wasn't until this past January—on the eve of Goldie's sixty-sixth birthday—that everything changed. Looking back, she could see how that bitingly raw morning was to foreshadow what she would face in her studio a few short hours later.

Reaching the end of the long staircase, she noticed a puddle of water gathered just beside the front door. Much as she loved her Painted Lady built after the Great Fire of 1878, the leaky roof was only one of the many parts in need of repair. Once she made it through the parlor to the kitchen, her vertigo ignited on the uneven floor boards. She shuddered to think of what Bruce Anderson's estimate was going to be for the repairs. She'd already used most of her savings for her retirement on refurbishing the studio.

Goldie's walk to work was fairly quick and pleasurable from Easter through Halloween, but the winter proffered an ample buffet of unforgivingly frigid mornings. After the ten-minute walk, she reluctantly removed an embrittled hand from its mitten to insert the key. To her shock, the bolt was already unlocked. The studio lights were on. Someone was inside. A burst of adrenaline coursed through her veins as her heartbeat sprang to life. Ever so carefully, she opened the aluminum door and, against her better judgment, entered the building. She placed her bag onto the checkout counter. A noise filtered out from the back room. . . . The glass carafe was placed back onto the burner of the automatic coffee maker. A moment later, footsteps . . . and then, a silver-haired woman entered from the back. She saw Goldie standing there in silence and nearly spilled half of the brew down the front of her fuzzy pink cashmere sweater.

"Oh my! You scared the wits out of me!" It took her almost a full five seconds to realize she was staring at Gloria Eagle— her business tenant for the last seventeen years. In all that time, Gloria had never beat her to the shop. Goldie opened. Gloria closed. That was the way it had been since the inception of their arrangement.

"I could say the same. . . ." Goldie was exasperated and pressed a shaky palm to her chest, unable to form words between her racked nerves and the thoughts pestering her consciousness. What on earth was Gloria doing there so early, and why hadn't Goldie been able to immediately place the one person she'd spent most of her time with for years, and what did that mean?

"I suppose you're wondering why I'm here." Gloria was dabbing her blouse. "I don't think I've been up this early since Bernice was just out of diapers." She paused, as if waiting for feedback.

Goldie said nothing as she plunked down onto one of the carpenter stools and waited for Gloria to elaborate.

"Well, the thing is . . . I tossed and turned all night. Simply awful. Brought back a lot of memories of those grueling years of hot flashes and night sweats. Remember those dreadful things?"

She resisted the urge to scoff at Gloria's rhetorical question, wondering when her old friend would stop sauntering and arrive at the point.

"I need to be closer to my daughter and grandbabies." Gloria released her words in rapid succession, as if they might become jammed on the way out.

Befuddled, Goldie flipped through the dusty Rolodex of her cloudy, panicked thoughts as she tried to remember where Gloria's daughter lived.

Visibly irritated by Goldie's hesitation, Gloria inhaled deeply and threw her shoulders back. She seemed to grow three inches. "I already found a small community right outside of Tallahassee, and I have to move in by the end of March."

She couldn't have been more stunned if an armed perpetrator wearing a Richard Nixon mask had entered, commanding her to clean out the register. Gloria must have taken Goldie's silence for disdain and added, "I'm sure you will have no problem finding someone who can rent the tables."

And just like that, after nearly two decades, Gloria was leaving. Of course, Goldie knew better than to take such a decision personally and would never begrudge Gloria her desire to be near her family, but losing Gloria's rent for her novelty item section of the store was cause for concern; she would have to find ways to cover expenses and bring in more revenue with her current resources and services—not a place a woman of her age wished to find herself.

Goldie had been brainstorming ways to add to her cash flow. Her first inclination was to start a series of pottery classes to draw a crowd and generate interest in the shop. She had taken out a modest ad in some of the papers and other publications and distributed flyers at the B&Bs and restaurants throughout the town. She decided to offer a series of summer sessions as a test run. So far, she had signed up three local women and two tourists for the class, which would begin the following Sunday. It was a start.

"Morning! Pretty boy. Good boy, Malcolm." Her ten-year-old African grey parrot cawed as Goldie passed by his cage. She paused to make sure he hadn't been plucking his feathers as he sometimes did if she wasn't paying him enough attention. He was a chatty sort who loved to mimic, and once he got a word stuck in his craw, there was little she could do to extract it from his vocabulary. He was a beautiful bird with a rich charcoal-grey coloring and wine-stained tail. Greys could be sensitive and needed much care and attention. Goldie had become so consumed by her mermaid she had let her other duties, like doting on Malcolm, fall by the wayside. She made a mental note to pick up a fresh pomegranate from the farm stand as a surprise afternoon treat.

She marveled at the stunning olive dish—with feet, decorative handles, and two small bowls on either side, one for pits, one for toothpicks—she had thrown last week for Bruce's new wife. She hadn't met Jocelyn yet, but Bruce crowed over her proficiency as a hostess, in addition to her skills as a novelist. Jocelyn's specialty seemed to be hors d'oeuvres and cocktails. Bruce mentioned that one of Jocelyn's favorite treats was assorted olives from the Seaside Cheese Company in West Cape May. Once Goldie had learned of Bruce's color scheme for their new kitchen, she meticulously selected the hues to match the glazes. She went out and purchased a brand-new quality spray gun and compressor to replace her old one and chose red earthen clay for the bowl. With precision, she had to alter the form, once leather-hard, by slapping the base on a board to cause the end to turn upward and the shape to become oval. The lively feet and handles were created by pulling looped wire tools through slightly stiff clay. The colored transparent glazes gave the jade green dish a slick and shiny surface. Goldie never would have gone to such great lengths for such a piece had it not been for Bruce's wife.

Her breakfast tradition with Bruce Anderson at the Salt Water Café had started by happenstance. While it certainly wasn't uncommon to see the same faces at the same places at the same times throughout Cape May, the two seemed to bump into one another with startling frequency. Goldie would position herself near the windows of the café so she could look out onto the marina while treating herself to a large bowl of their home-made cabbage soup. Bruce sat just a ways down at one of the larger tables, where he would thumb through the contents of his metal clipboard and gobble down a large crab omelet while tapping away at his calculator. At that time, he was between marriages and known around town as not only the most eligible bachelor on the island but a self-made thirty-something with striking good looks. After several run-ins and good-morning pleasantries, the two got to talking—much to Goldie's surprise and delight. After a few chats about her home and growing concerns on preserving its integrity and beauty, Bruce designed and constructed an outdoor shower made of teak wood with a wrap-around bench and stone walkway leading to the side of the old Victorian. The project took nearly four months. The animals adored having Bruce around—Brutus, the seventy-pound boxer, nearly toppled him over with his overzealous greetings of body slams while Laverne wound in and out of his legs—and it was clear to see they were just as sad as Goldie was when it was time for him to go.

Immediately, she hired Bruce to replace the linoleum flooring with ceramic tile, replace old fixtures, and brighten the walls with a fresh coat of paint. It had been almost two years since the completion of that project. Meanwhile, their breakfast meetings continued. But as Bruce's wedding date neared, his appearances at the café seemed to wane and then eventually ceased once Jocelyn moved in with her little boy. Goldie not only understood but felt pride in seeing Bruce shed the skin of bachelorhood and embrace this new role in much the same way he approached his business—with determination, responsibility, and honor. A man's family should come first, and she could only imagine the ever-growing demands on him as a new husband and father.

A month earlier, she had unexpectedly bumped into Bruce at the café. Now sporting a shiny band of gold and with a fresh spring to his gait, he appeared as though five years had been shaved from his age. After a warm hug, the two sat down for a long overdue catch-up. Goldie gently lifted Bruce's hand to take a gander at the ring.

"She must be one pretty special lady to brighten a man's face like sunshine."

Bruce was enamored with his new wife, who he said was busy working on her next book. He held the door for Goldie as they exited the café and meandered over to the charter boats docked at the marina.

"I don't know what I did to deserve all this," he said. "Gotta be someone looking out for me."

Oh, how she wished she could tell him all that she knew of his past. Alas, too much time had gone by. He had lived a good life and landed better than she ever imagined he might; there was simply no need to overturn the applecart. Not now.

Just then, as if on cue, the sun peeked from behind a cloud with a wink. She wondered if Bruce noticed it too.

"For a poor guy like me to be swept up by a talented, beautiful wife." He shook his head gently in disbelief. "And she's got the perfect kid. There's so much I want to teach him and show him. . . ." He closed his eyes as the emotion of the sentiment lodged in his throat. "I just want to make her proud, you know? I want to measure up. She could have had any guy with her brains and beauty. And Billy, he deserves the best."

You are going to make some lucky child very happy one day, Little Birdie.

Even all these years later, Patrick's words never left her. He would often remind her just how much he had always longed for a daughter of his own.

"I was one of six Knight children. We were all boys . . . except for the five girls. When you're the only boy raised in a house brimming with dolls, pigtails, high-heeled shoes, and hair rollers, you grow accustomed to having girly stuff around. My old man would hem and haw over the frivolity and utter mayhem that comes with having five willful and energetic daughters, but the truth was . . . that ol' bastard enjoyed every second of the giggles and silliness my sisters brought to our home."

It was peculiar for a man—especially one from Patrick's generation—to openly profess a desire for a daughter. He was nothing if not candid with Goldie.

Having been such a young bride, her thoughts on babies were stowed neatly at the back of the drawer of her life's desires. Always so consumed with her artistic endeavors and time-swallowing projects, she gave little consideration to much else. Patrick was the one who planted the seed of having a baby in her head. The adoration she carried for her father-in-law overwhelmed her at times, and she often wondered if there would come a time when she could express her gratitude and return some of the happiness he had brought to her life. The prospect of giving Patrick a grandchild filled her with excitement. After their chat, she felt a pull to become pregnant. She would sit back and listen to Patrick in all his animation while her mind fashioned the infant she would one day place into his loving arms, its delicate and tender head sleeping soundly over the great big heart of a loving grandfather. Unfortunately, the webs of time were spun too quickly for her to fathom, and she never did get the opportunity to present her sweet father-in-law with a grandchild.

A baby had never been meant for her in this lifetime—she knew it was a buried pain she might never come to terms with before she left this world. She reminded herself it was enough to see Bruce overjoyed with fatherly pride. Meanwhile, she would try to keep her concerns at bay. And only wished for Jocelyn to be as fantastic as Bruce believed her to be.

That morning, she joined Bruce in his reverie and closed her eyes. She conjured words in her mind to whomever might be listening from the aether: *May this overwhelming sense of happiness always be borne of truth. May the gift of a father's love, which was stolen from him before birth, rain down in buckets of pride and devotion upon this new young boy in his world. May the harmony now orchestrating this new marriage remain free from the ugliness of betrayal—and deceit—for the rest of his days.*

Drying her hands with a warm towel, Goldie resumed her position at the workstation. She tried to steady the craft knife in a wavering hand and cursed herself for indulging in an extra cup of coffee after lunch. One would think after innumerable nights spent staring at the ceiling with her heartbeat thumping in her eardrums against the backdrop of Brutus's unabashed snoring, she'd have learned to cut herself off from caffeine well before midday. She tightened her grip on the tool. The pink fled from beneath her skin as the blood drained from her bent knuckles while she struggled to keep still. Panic set in. The decorative finials for the mermaid's base should be leather-hard—firm to the touch, still damp, prime for crafting—but they were already a step beyond that. Any drier and the clay would harden and remain in its hideously deformed state forever. She examined the blueprint she'd sketched for the design. Maybe she could forgo the decorative finials she had wanted to place along the perimeter? No. They could not be compromised. The harder she gripped, the more her hand shook. It was no use. She had no control over the knife. In utter frustration, she slammed it hard against the table, startling herself nearly as much as her lap company, who had taken cover on the far end of the room.

"Forgive me, Laverne. . . ."

Resisting the urge to cry took almost as much energy and stirred almost as much pain as the act of crying itself. She hadn't permitted herself to weep openly in years. It was like trying to avoid scratching an old scab; once she started, she wouldn't be able to stop until the crusty flesh was ripped wide open, spilling fresh blood from the gaping wound. She raised the knife to examine it more closely. This was one of her new ones. Had she purchased a lemon?

A rush of hot air prickled the back of her neck. The sour smell of scotch scorched the inside of her nose.

Simon.

For every year he was dead, his presence seemed to gain power, arriving at her lowest points. There was nowhere for her to hide. His voice poked her eardrum like a hard finger to the sternum.

That knife is perfectly fine.

She dropped the knife, which bounced off the floor, coming within a centimeter of her foot. She wrapped both hands around a glass of water, spilling most of the contents down the front of her apron. Her shoes became saturated as if she had tripped in a rain-filled pothole. Her eyes lost all ability to focus, betraying her desperate need for stability. There was no escaping Simon's words.

The knife is not the tool with the problem, my darling.

4

Jocelyn

NIGHT OF THE CHARITY EVENT

"Hey, baby. You feeling any better?" Bruce asked gently.
Jocelyn was in deep thought as she put the finishing touches on her individual peach and blackberry cobblers. Feeling remorseful and slightly ashamed from her earlier episode, she spooned up a generous helping of fresh whipped cream infused with mint and stretched her arm toward Bruce. His mouth slowly dropped open like a baby chick's as the head of the spoon disappeared.

"Mmmm." He smacked his lips. "Not only a writer but a chef too." He retrieved a bottled water—his third in ten minutes—from the refrigerator and headed upstairs. She smiled to herself.

Last summer, Bruce had collapsed on a job site and was rushed to the ER. It turned out his blood pressure had plummeted from dehydration. His doctor sent him for all sorts of tests, but he was released with a clean bill of health. Jocelyn was proud to see Bruce following through on maintaining safe levels of hydration and grateful that she didn't have to nag him about it. There had been an awkward moment in the hospital when Bruce was faced with having to answer for the missing half of his family's medical history. He never spoke of the father he never knew, and Jocelyn never brought him up. When they first met, the few times she had asked a couple of questions, Bruce's expression had steeled, his mood turning somber.

Earlier that afternoon, Jocelyn decided to spend one hour on her book before cleaning the kitchen and making herself presentable for her guests. What she had discovered—but had forgotten—while penning her debut novel is that one of two things can occur in those rare instances when a writer finds herself with only a brief window of opportunity in which to work due to time constraints: either a miraculous key to the plot is uncovered like buried gold in a locked chest *or* a calamitous oversight is found like a tumor in a seemingly healthy breast. In Jocelyn's case, it was a prodigious inconsistency in her timeline and certainly not an issue she should be tackling this close to deadline. The blow was staggering, but she didn't have the luxury of time to spend fixing it. There were seventy-five people coming to her home in just four hours. With her insecurities aflame, she felt the pang of missing Billy and called Trevor's mobile even though she knew they were off on a family excursion. He answered after the first ring.

"I got held up at work. Hannah dropped the kids off at camp."

"*Camp*? What camp?"

"The twins attend a local camp over at the convention center in the mornings. We signed Billy up. He's been three times already and made a group of new friends. He loves it so much he practically begged me to send him again next year."

"Next year? He's not coming back next year," Jocelyn said.

"What do you mean he's not coming back? Of course he is."

"He may come for a visit, but he's not staying for the whole summer again. This was unusual circumstances."

"Yeah, well, I've been meaning to talk to you about that."

"About what?"

"I don't want my kid to think of me as his part-time dad. It's important that Billy knows he has a home and family here too. With me and Hannah."

"What are you driving at?" Jocelyn could feel the adrenaline release as her panic kicked in.

"I want more time with my son."

"You have him for the whole damn summer!" She wanted to scream. Billy had been taken from her for weeks, and here his father was asking for more.

"I have him for the summer because you kept him from me for months with all your wedding plans and all your . . ."

"All my what?"

"All your other stuff. Look, I don't have time to get into this with you now."

"We had an agreement. Papers were signed. I can't see why you're trying to change things now."

"Let's just talk about this another time."

"There's nothing to talk about! We had a deal."

"Yeah, well . . . deals can change."

"What the hell is that supposed to mean?" Jocelyn hated how hysterical she sounded. She never had an easy time wrangling her impulsive behavior, but right then, she needed to spew.

"As usual, you are overreacting. Do me a favor and save the melodrama for your new husband, because I refuse to deal with this shit."

Trevor's words set Jocelyn off into a tirade. She'd never remember all the jabs, but she vaguely recalled a few aimed at Trevor's stalled career and Hannah's laissez-faire parenting style. "Did you hear me? Are you there? Hello? HELLO?"

Jocelyn found herself screaming into the phone. She removed it from her ear to look at the screen. *End of Call.*

He had hung up. She paced the kitchen feeling as frazzled as one of her thwarted heroines. She missed the good old days when people would slam the handset down onto the base, letting the raucous clatter indicate the unceremonious end to the conversation—somehow that seemed more dignified than being left to scream into a phone with no one on the other end.

Jocelyn called Trevor repeatedly only to be met with his voice mail. "*That bastard,*" she muttered through clenched teeth.

"What the hell is going on?" Bruce said as he entered the kitchen, taking furtive glances all around as if they had an audience. "I could hear you freaking out all the way from the driveway. And so did the mailman and some lady walking her dog."

"Sorry." Jocelyn forgot she had raised the window by her desk earlier for some fresh air. The blood drained from her extremities, taking her energy along for the ride. Her hands began to tremble. "He let his *wife* enroll *my* son in some camp."

"He who? Trevor? Sweetie, Hannah is just about the safest person in the world to trust with Billy." Bruce grabbed a water from the refrigerator and leaned up against the granite peninsula he'd installed for Jocelyn's wedding present. He was always showing his love, from leaving a twenty-dollar bill by her purse with a note (*Your adoring husband insists that you take an afternoon lunch break with some crab cakes at the Harbor View*) to swapping out the quartz-composite countertop for granite in the tropical-brown pattern she had always adored. Despite all the thousands of sweet gestures he made on her behalf, they were currently overshadowed in the light of his glowing praise for Hannah. Jocelyn was terrified that Trevor would take her to court to fight for more custody. She felt embarrassed. What did it say about her as a mother to have his father looking to take Billy from her? The tears were unstoppable.

"Oh, baby." Bruce wrapped his arms around her as she cried into her hands. "What is this really about? I know you miss Billy. Heck, I miss the little guy myself. I was looking forward to taking him on the Thunder Cat Dolphin Watch and to see Vinny Babarino."

Babatunde was Billy's favorite Bengal tiger at the Cape May County Zoo, but since he had difficulty pronouncing its name, Bruce playfully renamed the tiger after John Travolta's character in the hit series *Welcome Back, Kotter*. The sentiment made Jocelyn sob harder, thinking of how Bruce had never had such experiences himself and how he was missing out on sharing such treasures with Billy.

"Honey, I promise you. Billy is in the best hands possible. I'm telling you, the first person in the world I'd ever pick to care for him would be Hannah Stevens. That woman knows what she's doing. Anyone can see that. I'm sure the camp she put him in is great. She's got the whole mother bit down to a science."

Jocelyn loved Bruce. More than anything. And she knew he was only trying to make her feel better. But in that moment, she had the urge to slap him right across his chiseled, stubbly face. He wasn't getting it. Not that she could articulate her thoughts. Like a dreary March sky, her mind was a cloudy, dismal mess. Maybe if she never mentioned anything about Trevor wanting more custody, it would just go away. If she didn't shine a light on it, then it wasn't real. Jocelyn hurried from the kitchen to her bathroom, rebuffing her husband's pleas for her return.

"What is this really about?" Bruce's words commanded her attention like a grab of the arm. She closed her eyes.

I want more time with my son.

Why would Trevor bring that up now when he had the whole stretch of summer with Billy? Trevor had always been used to getting his way. She knew better than to take these words lightly. Then there was Hannah: world's greatest supermom. Anyone would pale in comparison. Jocelyn had never met any woman who relished motherhood as much as Hannah. She made it all look as simple as tying a shoelace or kissing a boo-boo. Hannah found her true calling through motherhood and approached the role as though the kids had served her with a great honor by having been born. She didn't treat them as if they owed her something or as though she'd sacrificed her own personal happiness for their mere existence.

"I could have pursued a career like some of the other girls my age. Instead, I had you and your sister."

Jocelyn's eyes popped open at the memory of her mother's words. Unlike her mom, Jocelyn chose a career path. By the time she reached her late twenties, most of her girlfriends were picking out wedding dresses and swooning over the four Cs—color, clarity, cut, carat—of their diamonds, and Jocelyn was scribbling short stories and patching paragraphs to form plots. Then Billy joined the party. And Jocelyn was terrified. Not because of how her son would fit into her life but because of how she would fit into his. Terrified she could never be the kind of mom this sweet little boy so desperately deserved. Jocelyn was always convinced her mother's resentment had been embedded in her genes.

That afternoon was the first time she allowed her emotions to go unchecked in front of Bruce. It wasn't a good look, but she supposed that's what marriage was all about: bearing not only the tender underbelly of your unmade face, soiled hands, and morning breath, but also the dark alleyways of your untamed thoughts and unsightly mannerisms in front of the one person who had agreed to wipe the dribble from your chin should that odious day ever arrive. That was the way of the world. The magic of the first date would cast its romantic spell over the union, lasting for a string of months, leaving you with a sense that the majesty of the sunsets and delicacy of birdsong were created solely for the two of you. If the spell was potent enough, you'd find yourselves hand in hand at the altar on the precipice of the rest of your love story with the one person who swooned at your quirky laugh, indelible talents, and incomparable humanity. As time pressed on, stripping back more layers from your persona, another version of yourself would emerge. A version far closer to your true essence. A version you wished to keep hidden away from the world.

Jocelyn was a tad more social than Bruce. Perhaps it was all that time she spent alone cramped up at her writing table searching desperately for the right words and the proper order of those words. She tap danced up and down sentences, cartwheeled over and around paragraphs, cutting and pasting from chapter to chapter in a dizzying array of concepts, plot points, and dialogue.

Back in grad school, she'd read Phillip Roth's *The Ghost Writer*, the first of the Zuckerman Unbound trilogy. The protagonist was a promising young writer who found himself in the home of his idol and mentor, E. I. Lonoff, who said, "I turn sentences around. That's my life. I write a sentence and then I turn it around. Then I look at it and I turn it around again. Then I have lunch."

Jocelyn was now keenly aware of the acute reality behind these words. The delete key had become both friend and foe. Hour after hour, day after day, all those months spent staring at her monitor, her fingers hovering over the keyboard, her sore bottom planted to her chair. At the end of it all, she had to trust that her time spent in solitude had not been in vain. She made a decision to enjoy the evening before her because she knew she would spend the next several weeks ascending the mountain of her incomplete manuscript.

The outreach program was an important mission dedicated to providing succor for the less fortunate. The effort focused on the provision of food, clothing, housing, and internet access for job searches. As with most of her events and gatherings, Jocelyn had intended to keep the guest list to a reasonable number, her budget modest, the accoutrements understated. And once she moved from the planning stage to execution, the party had increased exponentially in size, cost, and flamboyance.

When Jocelyn was a little girl, she'd spend hours cooking on her Hasbro Play 'n Make Kitchen for her dollies. As she got a little bigger, she'd position herself at the kitchen table, pretending to scribble away at homework while sneaking peeks of her mom in action. Once she was out on her own, she began dabbling with new food and recipes. She couldn't leave a bookstore without a full stack that included a classic, bestseller, new release, and cookbook. When she wasn't at her desk dreaming up new stories and characters, she would spend all day in the kitchen allowing her creativity to explode in culinary delight. Her specialties were appetizers, light desserts, and refreshing cocktails. Her shelf of cookbooks, while lovely, became mere references to spur her imagination. She began recording all her recipes in a spiral-bound notebook she'd had since college and was able to trace each recipe back to a momentous time in her life—whether good or bad. She would purposefully leave out a key ingredient that she forced herself to commit to memory just in case the notebook fell into the wrong hands.

The soufflé had risen perfectly. The turkey cocktail meatballs had browned to perfection, and the dipping sauce—her own creation involving mashed figs, caramelized Vidalia onions, and melted gorgonzola—was the best batch she'd ever mixed; the juice from a medium blood orange and a shot of sweet Vermouth were the secret ingredients not written next to this recipe. Despite the monumental setback with her timeline and her screaming tantrum with Trevor, the evening was starting to shape up.

Jocelyn worked with the two servers she'd hired for the night on the finishing touches, while Bruce paced the kitchen guzzling bottle after bottle of water. He had this annoying new habit of crushing the empty bottles like an accordion between his two gigantic hands before tossing them into the recycle bin on the other side of the room as if he were shooting hoops. He claimed it "saved a ton of space." The sound of the crushing plastic only heightened her already frayed nerves.

"Sweetie, please go outside or something. You are making me nutso over here," she said, adorning the colorful pitchers of her specialty cocktail with fruit skewers.

Bruce stopped his pacing. He looked at her with the open eyes of a child and said nothing, which said it all: she had trampled his feelings.

"Oh, honey. How about you go relax and help yourself to a beer? Or maybe I can fix you a whiskey sour. Would you like that?" Jocelyn said gently, not realizing she was using the same tone she would with Billy until one of the servers eyed her suspiciously. Bruce scratched his head and blinked. If Jocelyn didn't know better, he could be Billy's age.

"Nah, I can do it," he said, heading toward the sliding glass doors that led to the tiki bar set up on the back patio.

"Can I have a kiss?" she said, trying to palliate his wounded pride.

Her wonderful new husband. Rugged and strong with the sensitivity of a boy. She was reminded of her great fortune feeling his lips pressing to hers as she ruffled her fingers through the underside of his hair. Men like Bruce were in low supply and high demand. Jocelyn would never have believed his type existed if she hadn't been lucky enough to marry one. Bruce cradled her to his chest. His fingers trickled down her back: a prelude of how they would cap their evening. She searched his eyes as if standing before a wishing well, wondering at what point in their marriage she could shed the cloak of self-doubt that she'd never be capable of reciprocating her husband's love and loyalty in the way he so deserved.

The Axelrods were the first to arrive. Abe Axelrod was known for his large personality, which was as robust as his bank account—and midsection. Jocelyn hadn't had much interaction with him save for a passing wave, but he'd found the direct route to her heart: the day before, Abe had handed Bruce a $10,000 donation check for the cause.

Bruce's affections for Abe lay elsewhere. Abe had an appetite for many things in life from boating and golfing to reading and dining out to making loads of money. Bruce idolized Abe in the way of a younger brother and loved to share some of his tales and life advice with Jocelyn. His latest success story and newest passion was his wife, Krystal. When Jocelyn heard Abe had married a local girl from a certain section of town, she was ashamed to admit the first hideous thought that came to mind was "gold digger." (And she was sure not to share such a disparaging sentiment with Bruce, who had come from meager beginnings himself.)

As if reading her thoughts, he said, "I've had many dealings with Krystal over the past year while Abe travels and whatnot. She's a real nice girl. Make sure you give her a chance."

Bruce perked up as soon as Abe entered. Jocelyn was slightly perturbed by the feeling that arose inside her from the shadows: jealousy? She couldn't think of one girlfriend she had ever felt so close to. At least not in many years. She supposed that went with the territory of replacing real-life people with imaginary ones and forgoing social engagements to spend her nights dancing around her kitchen in boxer shorts and tank tops in the pursuit of her creative impulses both at her desk and oven. Watching the men who were from starkly different worlds made her realize what she was missing. Abe treated Bruce as though the two used to pull off stunts together back in prep school. He'd already hooked Bruce up with his next three gigs: one homeowner looking for a screened-in porch area on the deck; a young family looking to blow out the back of their house for a movie room; an older couple looking to make their ranch wheelchair-accessible for their daughter, who'd soon be returning from Afghanistan without the company of her left leg—Abe would be covering the full cost of that last project.

"It sure is a pleasure to finally meet the woman behind this fine man," Abe said to Jocelyn, shaking her hand.

"I don't know how to thank you for your very generous donation," she said.

Bruce tapped Abe on the arm. "I want to show you something." The two men slipped into a huddle at the island over Bruce's iPad.

Jocelyn noticed Krystal in the dining room eyeing the breakfront that housed pictures of their friends and family at the wedding. She was quite striking, but close-up Jocelyn became distracted by her over-application of makeup, which seemed not only extravagant but unnecessary. Her shiny black leggings, immodest cleavage, and five-inch snake-skinned pumps were reminiscent of the eighties. Jocelyn wondered why Krystal felt compelled to garner attention with such a dated, unpolished ensemble. Especially considering the wardrobe she should be able to afford with all that new money. But watching Krystal trail a tender finger down a framed picture of Billy filled Jocelyn with shame for judging this woman on her appearance.

"He sure is a handsome little guy. Look at that great big smile. You can tell he's well- loved," Krystal said wistfully. "The happy ones always are." Her voice trailed off as did her attention while her eyes continued to hop along the line of framed photographs. Jocelyn wished she could follow Krystal to wherever she had drifted.

Slinking an arm through Krystal's, she guided her through the kitchen past Bruce and Abe. "We girls are going to grab ourselves a *real* drink at the pool bar," Jocelyn said.

"Hey, wait a second. You're gonna leave me alone with this guy?" Abe said.

"Have fun, ladies!" Bruce called to their backs.

The patio was already brimming with guests. Jocelyn had made it her business to greet each and every one while introducing Krystal. There were many items being auctioned off, from paintings to gift certificates to event tickets offered by restaurants and cafés, local farms, wineries, artists, photographers, even the Mid-Atlantic Center for Arts. Some of the parishioners from the local churches offered handmade baby clothes and quilts for bidding. Jocelyn was overwhelmed by the turnout and generosity of her townspeople. Krystal seemed awestruck by the wide array of offerings.

"I should have made something for the auction," she said to Jocelyn, fidgeting with her halter top.

"Honey, you did quite enough already," Jocelyn said, realizing she had thanked Abe for the check but not Krystal. "Forgive me. I didn't properly thank *you* for your extreme generosity. You have helped many people in need who are struggling desperately to survive." She gave Krystal's hand a squeeze.

That's when Jocelyn saw the enormous mermaid that Bruce had picked up from Little Birdie Studio earlier that day. Three spotlights were positioned on her to highlight the intricate details of craftsmanship. She felt the slightest bit guilty for wishing to outbid the others for the magnificent piece.

"Wow. That is absolutely stunning," Krystal said.

"It really is."

"Who made that?"

Jocelyn plucked one of the business cards from the table and handed it to Krystal.

"Goldie Sparrows. She's the owner of the pottery studio in town. She's wildly talented and a good friend of Bruce; he just adores her."

Krystal nodded, taking it all in. Jocelyn escorted her to the tiki bar once the crowd of guests had thinned out.

"I'm a Prosecco drinker, but I wouldn't mind something a little stronger tonight. Would you like to try a batch of my signature cocktail?"

"Sure!" Krystal's enthusiasm was genuine and contagious.

Jocelyn ladled a generous serving into two goblets, handing one to Krystal.

"Here's to the success of your new book," Krystal said. "I can't wait to read it."

"Oh, you're sweet. It'll be a while before that happens. I'm getting ready to submit my first draft. But when the time comes, I'll send you an ARC."

Krystal's smile changed to a look of polite confusion.

"That stands for Advance Reader's Copy. You'll get your very own version. Writers give them to fellow authors and book reviewers. And sometimes, to friends," she said, smiling.

Krystal seemed pleasantly shocked, as if she'd just discovered a fistful of cash in an old handbag stashed in the back of her closet. Jocelyn formed the distinct impression that Krystal wasn't accustomed to kindness from other women. She knew how catty her fellow females could be. Especially with someone as overdone and underdressed as Krystal, the type of woman who automatically turned heads, gobbling up all the male attention in the room.

"This is really delicious!" Krystal said, pulling the glass from her lips for a closer look at the cocktail. "What's in it?"

"Hmm. My recipes are sacred," Jocelyn said, winking.

The drink was her own secret blend of vodka, grapefruit-flavored seltzer, a shot of Cointreau, and a splash of orange juice, along with a skewer with a strawberry, an orange slice, a hunk of kiwi, and a large blackberry.

"I call it Over the Rainbow. I wore out my DVD of *The Wizard of Oz* when I was pregnant. It was one of my feel-good flicks. After Billy arrived and I was able to drink again, I invented the cocktail. Spending time in the kitchen helps me decompress and forget about life. It offers me a place to express my creativity without the pressures of deadlines and book reviews."

Krystal listened wide-eyed while she sipped. She would need a refill momentarily. The only thing Jocelyn loved as much as fan mail from readers was seeing people enjoy the recipes she'd crafted.

"Looks like you need a refill. Go easy. These can sneak up on you."

Off in the distance, Jocelyn saw Goldie Sparrows approaching. She never felt all that comfortable around the woman. Part of her always felt as though she was being judged, or something; she was never quite certain how Goldie really felt about her. Goldie and Bruce had a bond all their own, an inexplicable connection. The few times Jocelyn and Bruce had run into Goldie, the two greeted each other like old friends. Jocelyn knew how much Bruce missed his mother, Daisy, and she suspected he found solace in this newfound alliance with Goldie, who seemed innately concerned with Bruce's well-being.

Jocelyn turned to retrieve an empty goblet from the bar to offer Goldie a glass of Over the Rainbow. While Krystal and Goldie became acquainted, Jocelyn tried to drum up an endearing, sentimental toast. She hoped her words would be memorable in a way that solidified the special bond between women.

To old and new friends alike. . . . Not "old." She didn't want to make Goldie uncomfortable by highlighting the marked differences in their ages. *To the sweetest things in life: hearty food, successful endeavors, creative passion, and strong cocktails to wash away all the . . . all the . . . cobwebs?* Jocelyn had spent far too much of her time chanting nursery rhymes to a six-year-old. She'd wing it. Toasts sounded more natural on the fly, anyway.

As she turned back around, the warm July night air was suddenly replaced by a thick fog of awkward confusion. The color had drained from Goldie's already fair complexion. She seemed out of sorts: With them physically, but not mentally.

Jocelyn was relieved to hear Bruce's voice coming from the rear. She cast a sideways glance at Krystal.

What the hell just happened here?

5

Krystal

NIGHT OF THE CHARITY EVENT

Eighteen months earlier, Krystal had been introduced to Bruce Anderson. It was the weekend before they broke ground on the plot of land that was to become the Axelrods' new home. Bruce's sandy blond hair and blue eyes gave him the appearance of a young Robert Redford. His boyish charm delicately veiled his unassuming magnetism. Unlike most single men in their prime, Bruce lacked that flirtatious, sexual energy Krystal was all too familiar with. The one that rumbled like thunder behind a scrim of wily grins and shifty eyes. If Bruce found Krystal to be attractive, she never would have known it. He made no untoward glances and certainly none that lingered for more than a beat. There were no conspicuous tactics like the flexing of a muscle or forcing humor to make her giggle. Their interactions were as perfunctory and innocuous as a handshake. Most men meeting Krystal for the first time took one look and automatically placed her upon some unreachable pedestal. But she had learned over the years that with those death-defying heights came an inevitable crash to the ground. Bruce was the first straight man who looked at her as anything other than an object of desire. He was deferential, including her in every aspect of the decision-making during construction. If Abe opined on a topic concerning the house, Bruce made sure to ask Krystal what she thought. She and Bruce came from similar blue-collar backgrounds, and she'd have bet her brand-new harbor-front home that Bruce hadn't played any sports in high school; she suspected he had had one, if not two, after-school jobs—just like her.

Abe's connection to Bruce had been different. As a budding entrepreneur, Bruce was thirsty for knowledge. And as an established and successful businessman with strong ties, Abe had much to share. The two hit it off like long-lost brothers, which was surprising given the disparities between their backgrounds and social standings. Females were naturally drawn to Abe with his charismatic, approachable manner, which made him formidable to most men whose personalities (and coffers) paled in comparison. And yet Bruce wasn't intimidated by Abe's wealth or power, as he regarded their interactions with a genuine and childlike curiosity.

A few weeks back, Krystal had just returned from her morning beach run when she bumped into Bruce on the deck.

"That husband of yours is a good guy. I only wish I had the smarts he has," Bruce said.

"You're just as smart," Krystal said.

"Thanks, but it's not the same. Men like Abe know how to make money. *Real* money." Catching his brief departure from formality, Bruce straightened his posture. "I just mean—"

"I know what you mean. You don't have to explain," she said gently.

"The thing about Abe is . . . he's an open book. He tells me about his philosophy on life and why he thinks the way he does.

He gets it. Life, I mean. And he's a nice guy. A really nice guy. Where I'm from being rich and friendly don't exactly go hand in hand."

Krystal nodded and smiled reassuringly, which seemed to set Bruce at ease.

"I heard you just got married," she said. "Congratulations!"

"Thanks! Jocelyn is great. And I have a son now. Did Abe tell you?" His excitement was touching.

"I heard. That is so wonderful."

"Yeah. Billy keeps me young. I'm blessed. What can I say?"

Krystal offered more felicitations and began to excuse herself when Bruce added, "And by the way, thanks for making Abe so happy. Nice guys deserve a good woman."

It was in that moment she realized the depth of his affection for her husband, which warmed her. He saw the goodness in Abe. And she was able to see the same goodness in Bruce. She only hoped his new wife was able to see and appreciate what she had.

As they headed for the Anderson's on foot, Krystal caught Abe stroking the few remaining strands of hair at the back of his head. Inside the house with the air-conditioning on full blast, she'd been perfectly comfortable in the outfit she was wearing— but once the door opened and she hit that wall of humidity, Krystal tugged at her leggings, which fit her like a second skin. She wished there were a way to absorb some of her husband's self-assuredness with each of his long, even strides along the pavement. She struggled to keep up as her heels snagged on pebbles and twigs in an awkward dance with the sidewalk. She pictured how challenging the walk home might be after several cocktails and wished she could slacken her bra straps, which were cutting off blood flow to the muscles in her neck, now taut as wires.

"Why so fidgety?" Abe asked.

"Sorry." She wiped her brow, dismayed to feel the back of her hand painted in a thick coat of perspiration, and resisted the temptation to kick off her heels and sprint back to the house to refresh.

Later, the street would be lined with cars, but as usual, Abe and Krystal were the first to arrive; her husband preferred having one-on-one time with the host and made a habit of arriving at least fifteen minutes early to most functions. She started down the driveway toward the front door, but Abe gently guided her in the direction of the back gate; he thrived on familiarity and prided himself on knowing the tiniest details of people's lives. She could only imagine how he had managed to learn what door the Andersons used to enter and exit their home.

The backyard looked like a tropical oasis, a reminder of the first vacation Abe had taken her on, a Club Med resort in Turks and Caicos. A string of American Redbuds at the far end of the yard were decorated with white twinkle lights. A kidney-bean-shaped pool sat in the middle of the landscape, with a small waterfall pouring in illuminated water in a rainbow of colors. A makeshift tiki hut with a roof of fronds was set up as a bar station. Krystal noted the faux rocks along the pathway with music streaming from them. Having spent three years on the arm of Abe Axelrod, she'd been exposed to the upper echelon of home decor and ambiance and knew if she were to ask him what he thought of the setup, he'd use one of his Yiddish terms, saying it was a bit on the *schlocky* side.

She spotted Bruce across the patio. Behind him stood a pretty brunette in a tea-length chocolate-brown dress and cork wedges. She sported a professionally layered choppy bob with caramel highlights accentuating her crown. Lean and sculpted shoulders spoke of a well-balanced diet and fitness regimen—either a swimmer or a yogi, Krystal presumed. Her demeanor was pleasant and welcoming, her style fresh and tasteful.

Krystal was unable to keep her insecurity in check and immediately wished she had worn a less revealing top to conceal her cleavage. And what should she say? She'd never been much of a reader and wasn't sure of the protocol when speaking to a published novelist. Would most people have brought a new copy of the author's book and asked for an autograph? She knew that some celebrities found such requests irritating and this probably wasn't the appropriate place or time, but Krystal wasn't sure what was expected and kicked herself for not thinking of it before *that moment*. She continued to observe in silence; as Jocelyn smiled, the corners of her eyes creased into little hearts. Warmth emanated from her soulful brown eyes as delicately as her designer perfume lacing the air.

Just then the sliding glass doors opened, breaking Krystal's concentration. Two young women in matching black-and-white uniforms, carrying trays of food. As they approached, one face came into focus: Tammy Frill. She was a former backstop on the cheerleading squad, and one of the meanest girls in high school. As if her perspiration weren't bad enough, Krystal's body temperature spiked.

The cheerleaders were scattered on the cold and smooth gymnasium floor after practice, playing a game of Truth or Dare. It was Krystal's turn in the hot seat—she chose a dare.

"What are you doing here?" Tammy said, the same cruelty from their youth flickering in her eyes.

"Bruce Anderson built our home."

Tammy stared down at Krystal, who remained seated, cross-legged. It was Tammy who would be the one administering the dare.

"I can't wait to see this new pad of yours," Tammy said. "What time again? I'm working the day shift, but I'll ask my boss if I can leave early."

They were timing her. Krystal would have to raise her shirt for a full ten seconds or it wouldn't count. A few moments later, she was unable to see anything but the fibers of her tightly knit sweater. Her nipples hardened in the damp air. She didn't know it at the time, but that first piercing whistle sound would be what haunted her most of all in the days to come.

"Any time after six thirty is fine," Krystal said.

She was having a gathering with some old friends to show them the new house. Her friend Amber had asked if it was okay for Tammy to tag along.

Sensing her hesitation, Amber had said, "We should leave the past in the past. Don't you think?" The question caught Krystal off guard, and she reluctantly (and foolishly) agreed to let Tammy come.

Several of the football players had been hiding behind the bleachers, waiting for Krystal's big moment. With cameras. It was a setup. Tammy's wicked laughter trumped even the boys' that afternoon.

"Heard you got a bunch of things to show us. Something about shells? Jewelry? I never knew you were so crafty," Tammy said.

Krystal could read the words broadcast across her dirty smirk: *You're not fooling anyone with that fancy husband and huge mansion. I know who you are and where you're from. You belong right here, next to me wearing one of these uniforms, carrying trays of coconut shrimp and handing cocktail napkins to a pack of phony rich people. You're just a wannabe. You know it. I know it. And so does every person here. You could never be one of them.*

As Tammy strode back to the house for more trays, Krystal looked to her left and right, as if Abe might miraculously show up beside her in support as he had in times past at precisely the moment she needed him. No such luck. He was to remain at Bruce's side for a large chunk of the evening while showing his protégé the ins and outs of how to play host and work the crowd.

Krystal was on her own for the time being. All she had to do was saunter over to the tiki hut and score a drink to trim the edges from her fraying parts.

With each swallow of her pink champagne, the heat and angst from moments earlier began to abate. The twinkle lights danced in greeting, thanking her for being there. A prominent couple passed by, but not without acknowledging her first.

"Good evening, Krystal."

Three simple words and her confidence was building as she grew more enchanted with every sip. The din of hushed voices mixing with gentle laughter became an elixir. Steadily, she became immersed in the hypnotic atmosphere, watching in awe as Jocelyn floated from guest to guest. Krystal could hardly wait to jump online to order every book and read every word Jocelyn had ever put in print.

Meanwhile, guests continued to spill onto the patio. After two champagnes and a plate of food, Krystal became aware of her belly bloat as her waistband tightened across her abdomen. She'd put enough mousse in her hair to maintain its volume, yet she always had the feeling she needed more. Balancing her near-empty champagne glass in one hand, she reached for her compact to apply more lip gloss, noticing her liquid eyeliner puddling in the corners. She needed to head into the house but waited until Tammy Frill was occupied with her duties to avoid getting tangled in her web.

There was not a blank wall to be had in Jocelyn's hallways. Nearly every square inch was covered by framed photographs. The powder room off the kitchen was occupied, so Krystal meandered into the living room to bide time. The room smelled of baked apples and pumpkin pie from the Autumn Harvest Yankee candle burning on the mantel. Krystal thought she was the only one who enjoyed the scents of the fall year-round. The only light in the room other than the flickering candle was a

Tiffany floor lamp stationed in the corner, illuminating a wall of bookshelves. She was taken by the collection of impeccable hardcovers and recognized many of the names: Austen, Brontë, Updike, Hemingway, Dickens. English teachers were always her favorites in high school, and they had inspired her love of the subject. Yet between bussing tables and babysitting, she had never developed the habit of reading for leisure. For years, she would jog by coconut-scented people scattered up and down the shoreline, planted in beach chairs, feet tucked beneath the wet sand, novels perched on their thighs, and wonder about this elusive world of words in which they seemed to be suspended. How did it feel to be in one location physically as you drifted in your mind somewhere else through a story world? She had always been so focused on working up a good sweat that she hadn't realized until now that she wanted to join their club of beach readers. Her Law of Attraction studies taught her she shouldn't exert too much energy wishing for any one thing, which only kept her in the energy pattern of not having it; she needed to embrace the feelings of already receiving what she desired, as opposed to concentrating on the lack of it. So there Krystal stood in the Andersons' living room, trying to conjure the pride of being a well-read woman with the ability to converse with other readers about a myriad of topics and books and stories and characters who'd made everlasting impressions. She was so enthralled by the notion of this new hobby that she could hardly wait to wrap her arms around it.

Only a handful of guests remained scattered around the backyard working on the remnants of their cocktails. Tammy looked haggard and less than humored by these inebriated stragglers. Krystal couldn't help but be amused: she had been on both sides of the fence. When it came right down to it, no group of people—regardless of financial status—was exempt from their fair share of boozehounds.

As Krystal stood by the tiki bar waiting for Jocelyn to retrieve more drinks, a woman approached. She had a long, flowing crinoline skirt and matching top with delicate beading along the neckline. Her silver hair cascaded down her back, braided at the midsection. Her flat metal earrings were as big as serving platters and reflected the light and images like hallway mirrors. As she neared, Krystal could see her own reflection framing either side of the woman's angelic face.

"What an enchanted evening," she said to Krystal. There was a relaxed, casual way about her. She approached as if they were already well acquainted.

"You own Little Birdie Studio," Krystal said.

"Either that or there's another wild-haired woman running around town wearing my pantyhose." She laughed. "My friends call me Goldie." She offered a toothy smile, and her skin was the color of pale pink seashells. "Come to think of it, my enemies call me Goldie as well."

Her laughter was so boisterous Krystal couldn't tell if it was coming from a general air of jubilation or an excess of liquor. She had the distinct impression Goldie was just acting on her unpredictable and mysterious nature. She felt at any given moment that Goldie could do one of two things: wave her hand and cast a menacing spell or break out into a dreamy chorus of "Kumbaya."

"My partner of many years has left me . . ."

Krystal didn't know if the "partner" she was referring to was a man, a woman, or an imaginary friend. With someone like Goldie Sparrows, it wasn't easy to tell.

"I am so sorry."

"Oh, that's quite all right. Change is good. It's the only real constant we have in life, you know." Goldie's attention began to falter as she seemed to be contemplating the meaning behind her own remark.

"I hear your shop is on Carpenters."

"For the last twenty-nine years. Just opened up for in-house pottery classes."

"That sounds like fun," Krystal said. "I would love to come see what you do."

Goldie's eyes fogged over like sea glass. Her smile deflated. She appeared to shrink two inches. Her hands flew to the back of a chair as her feet did the mambo. The bottom of the chair lightly tapped the cement pavers of the patio. Goldie's eyes alternated between wide open and squinted slits as she tried to regain her focus.

Krystal was about to ask if she had said something wrong when Jocelyn turned around with a full glass of Over the Rainbow for Goldie. She seemed as taken aback as Krystal by the sudden change in demeanor.

Goldie Sparrows no longer seemed to be standing there. Someone or some*thing* had taken her place.

6

Goldie

NIGHT OF THE CHARITY EVENT

In the years following Patrick's death, Goldie sought refuge from her immeasurable grief in the butterfly garden. As she slipped further into the depths of her own solitude, she needed to retreat to the one place she could still feel his presence. Her safe place. Away from Simon after he started becoming more emotionally removed and hurtful. Sometimes, it seemed as though Patrick's soul had vacated his body and descended upon their beloved garden just to be with her.

Her favorite was the red-spotted purple, which looked like those old T-shirts she would tie-dye back in the sixties. The rainbow of soft tones and blue pastels seemed surreal on the gentle, peaceful creatures. Patrick's two favorites were the painted lady, resembling a sting ray with matte-grey-and-orange coloring and two blood-orange spots for eyes, and the red admirals, black with red trim and white specks on the tips of the wings.

"Remember to look for the monarchs."

The Sound of Wings

The first spring after Patrick died, Goldie was visited by more monarch butterflies than she had ever seen before. She knew it was him. Her Patrick. Coming for a visit to remind her that he would be watching, just as he had promised.

Of all the many flowers and plants in the butterfly garden, Goldie was most taken with the *Buddleja davidii*, known as the Black Knight. He was the darkest flower of all the buddlejas, almost a grape violet. Patrick positioned him behind the black-eyed Susan with her vibrant petals of yellow orange.

"Will you look at that. . . ." Patrick said, mesmerized by the stark contrast of the sunny yellow against the midnight blue and how brilliantly the two complemented one another in aesthetic harmony. "Her natural beauty emanates against the protection he provides." Patrick waved a hand over the stunning array of flora that, to him, had been so much more than mere flowers and plants. "She wields grace and elegance as he towers overhead in reverence with a quiet yet commanding presence. I suppose it's no secret the Black Knight remains my favorite of the lot. We share the same name, the name of *Knight*—a solid English name in which I take great pride."

Goldie was able to recreate Patrick's garden when she moved to Cape May. There was only one secret addition, her precious belladonna berries. A member of the nightshade family, it wasn't a customary plant to have in a butterfly garden, but Goldie had her own reasons for keeping her there.

Mrs. Knight had fallen ill during Simon's early childhood and lost the battle to heart disease several years before Goldie entered their lives, when Simon was still in high school. She remembered the few times Simon had opened up about the devastating loss of his mother. He was so tender and vulnerable. Goldie was overcome with love for him, wanting only to protect and heal his broken spirit. Once, after a long dinner and several tumblers of scotch, Simon came undone and sobbed against her breast like a child. The next day, he would make dark jokes about his unchecked display of emotion. When she tried to tell him that it was okay, he tickled her until she spilled onto the floor in peals of laughter, sufficiently changing the subject.

When it came to Patrick, the story was slightly different. Simon never shared his feelings about his father with Goldie. But she could see how desperately he sought his father's love and approval. When the three had dinner, Simon would boast about his expertise at work. He would cut his coworkers down to size, claiming they were "stupid and incompetent." As a doctor, Patrick's professional pursuits revolved around science and patients. He knew nothing about the business world, which held no interest for him. He listened and nodded patiently, but Goldie could see Simon become antsy and start to fidget with his food at his father's lack of enthusiasm—which could be taken as apathy—for his son's endeavors.

One evening, Simon stormed off from the table following a newlyweds' quibble. He had been griping about his coworkers earning higher salaries. Patrick rightfully suggested his son return for additional schooling if he wanted to earn more money. Goldie's mistake was opining in agreement with Patrick. Enraged, Simon transferred his pent-up frustration over his father's lack of approval onto Goldie as his arms flailed about in a tirade before his dramatic departure from the table.

"Sorry about that, Little Birdie. I'm the one he's sore at, you know. You didn't do anything wrong. That boy can be his own worst enemy sometimes. Letting his emotions get the better of him and carrying on like that. No sense of reason. He's just like his mother."

Goldie had always suspected there was more to the story of Mrs. Knight. Until then, an opportunity to question Patrick about his late wife had never presented itself.

"What was she like?" Goldie asked.

"Let's just say she wasn't an easy sort. Best I don't share too much. Simon can be hypersensitive where his mother is concerned."

Goldie saw Simon in her peripheral vision. He was eavesdropping from the hallway and scowling at his father. When Simon's eyes moved to her, his air of contempt remained. She wondered what she had done. Why was he so angry with her? All for agreeing with Patrick on his good advice?

"Give him time," Patrick added. "We men are missing the gene for patience and maturity that come naturally to you gals. Eventually, he'll wise up. We all do. Well, most of us, anyway."

She remembered being filled with hope by Patrick's words. Her Simon would return to her. This was a temporary episode.

As Goldie headed for the Andersons', she glanced at her watch. It had only been ten minutes, and she already missed her animals. She longed to be back with them, back at her flywheel, back where living didn't require so much exhausting human interaction. She always preferred the company of animals, plants, and clay to that of people, feeling most like herself when she was alone. Examining the untouched canvas before her, she'd sit in silence with her sketch pad as seeds burgeoned beneath the rich soil of creativity, rendezvousing with the hidden potential just moments before the unfolding. She imagined her exuberance was like that of Michelangelo as he peered into the opaque, untouched slab of marble and saw the David winking back at him.

Goldie let herself in through the unlocked front door of the Andersons' home. Easing her way down the hallway, she likened the experience to taking a dip in the ocean at the onset of the season—a slow and steady progression leading up to full submersion. Rounding the corner, she had a full shot of Bruce standing in front of the Viking range, his smile matching the gleam of the stainless-steel hood overhead. She was gratified to see this confident, well-adjusted, and successful man standing in the treasured kitchen he had renovated for his new wife.

Look at how far you've come, she thought. *How safely you've landed.* She only wished she could properly and openly express the magnitude of her pride in all that he had accomplished.

"There she is! Now, the party can start."

Bruce's spirited reaction to her arrival instantly made Goldie feel as though she were the guest of honor. In that moment, she wasn't able to properly divulge how she felt, but in the days and weeks ahead, she would relive that once-in-a-lifetime, glorious moment as she basked in the sunshine of Bruce Anderson's unexpected adoration.

He took the heavy package from her arms and tenderly kissed her cheek, a dollop of honey. The olive dish for Jocelyn had turned out more spectacularly than Goldie had anticipated. The richness of the blue and green glazes covering each of the four finials allowed the bowl a certain sophisticated elegance. On the bottom of one of the feet, Goldie had carved her initials and the year. She was proud of the piece, which could easily retail for well over $100.

"Jocelyn is going to love this. I mean, no matter *what* it is," Bruce said. His clumsy mannerisms in speech were overshadowed by his endearing boyish charm. "I'll keep it on the dining room table so you can give it to her yourself."

"The *Axe* is back!"

A robust man with a booming voice came barreling into the room. He was smiling at Bruce like a wily bandit until he noticed Goldie standing there.

"Pardon me. Didn't realize we had company."

"Abe, come on over here. Let me introduce you to one of the most talented women on the island. Or anywhere, for that matter," Bruce said.

While they'd never been officially introduced, Goldie

recognized Abe Axelrod from his pictures in the newspaper. As one of the richest transplants in all of Cape May County, he was known for three things: making money, and lots of it; his altruistic tendencies toward the downtrodden; and his proclivity to consume.

"Enchanted," Abe said, extending an open palm as if rolling out a carpet.

"Likewise," said Goldie.

"I told Goldie all about your house, Abe. I probably bored the poor woman to death with details."

"Nonsense. Don't be silly. I love hearing about your work. You know that by now," Goldie said.

"The mermaid looks unbelievable. I put it on the center table with nothing else around it. You have to go look. Jocelyn was salivating when I brought it home. She had me set it up with extra lighting," he said.

Goldie was so grateful when Bruce offered to pick up the piece for her earlier that day. Normally, she'd never trust anyone to handle one of her babies, but this was Bruce, and she couldn't think of anyone in this world she trusted as much.

Bracing for the onslaught of mindless chitchat, Goldie headed toward the party out back. As she made her way toward the stairwell, she was nearly trampled by a horribly rude, disgruntled server who impassively held the door. Goldie carefully crossed the threshold to begin her descent down the wooden steps leading to the patio, all while feeling the young woman's impatience radiating like the stench of the city dump in July.

Goldie looked her in the eye before clearing out of the girl's path.

"No one stays young forever."

"What?" the young woman said, emitting a puff of foul cigarette breath from her cheaply glossed lips. Her name tag read *Tammy*.

"Easily negotiating an unfamiliar stairwell in a dimly lit environment is a luxury one never considers until the day she discovers what a formidable challenge such an endeavor may pose."

Goldie examined the body language emanating from Tammy's young yet weathered face. Her lanky body retreated, slithering back to the swamp from which she came.

It's called compassion, you heartless twit, she thought.

Releasing her unstable grip from the railing, Goldie raised her head and faced the crowd. There stood her neighbors and fellow business owners. Her "friends" in the weakest sense of the word. Sadly, Goldie had done a fine job of isolating herself. She couldn't blame them, really. She'd always been a bit of an enigma to them. She knew it. If this wasn't the home of Bruce Anderson and for a good cause, she would never have ventured beyond the comfort zone of her own four walls.

At the buffet table, she helped herself to a paper plate and scanned the food, trying to avoid eye contact with anyone for the time being. She could hear a table of female store owners and clerks yammering away about the current upgrades to the Rotary Park in between bites of pot stickers and sips of Pinot Grigio. Two men—a well-known owner of a famous B&B and a mortgage broker—nearly bowled her over in their hurry to grab more chicken-sausage-pineapple skewers. Consumed with their own conversation, they failed to notice Goldie.

Oh, how she loathed the noise of the world today. People always prattling on and on about their families, taxes, politics, sports, the price of gas. She'd been exposed to it all when Gloria was still at the studio; the novelty section of the store drew flocks of tourists, and Gloria Eagle had earned a master's degree in small talk. The technology of today did nothing to assist her need for quiet and solitude. The endless loop of horrific news blaring from the televisions about traffic jams, worrisome weather, criminal activity. But most of all, she hated the endless need for talking—the banality of the shallow and uninspired, stuffing up precious moments of silence with meaningless jibber-jabber.

Goldie realized after her second plate of food that she had not spoken to one soul other than Bruce and Abe Axelrod when she first arrived. She finally sought refuge next to Louie and Matt, two of the stock boys from Swain's who'd been assisting her for years on her many trips to the hardware store. She caught them in the middle of a casual conversation about the new shape of Cove Beach after last autumn's nor'easter and how that would affect their surfing. Not expecting much input from Goldie, the boys served as the perfect companions.

Feedback screeched from the microphone, abruptly slicing through the din of the crowd with the ease of a Ginsu knife. A sea of heads turned toward Jocelyn standing at the lectern.

"On behalf of *Hope Down the Shore*, I am grateful to you all for being here and for your most generous contributions. I joined the effort some four years ago, and the outpouring of support has been nothing short of spectacular. Thanks to each and every one of you standing here with us tonight, we have been able to remove more than twenty-three individuals, including five families, from a life on the street and find them affordable housing, jobs, and resources."

The crowd broke out in applause. Jocelyn paused to soak in the cheering.

"And we are only getting started. I expect that number will steadily increase over the course of the next year. In a place like Cape May, where we are afforded so much between small-town life and a strong sense of community, wouldn't it be grand to see all our citizens contributing and participating? We will not rest until the only people sleeping in tents in Cape May County are the summertime campers."

Jocelyn smiled through the thrum of more applause.

"We have a magnificent array of items on auction this evening from some of the most talented artisans in our community, as well as fun raffles from the tastiest restaurants and coolest shops in Cape May. Our auction is a silent one, so all you need to do to participate is jot your name down in the left-hand column on the clipboards provided at each of the tables along with the amount of your bid to the right."

Shamelessly, Goldie was tickled to see a line forming in front of the mermaid. She maintained her distance, not wishing to appear self-indulgent by glancing at the bids. From the looks of the players visiting the table, she knew it was sure to raise the most money; at least four people had already returned to the table to place a second bid.

Before she said her goodbyes for the evening, Goldie went searching through her carryall for a pottery class flyer to hand to Krystal. Suddenly, she felt the need to hold on to the chair with one hand to maintain her balance. *My electrolytes must be off,* she thought. The new meds Dr. Carroway had prescribed for her arthritis came with a warning from the precocious young internist: "You must limit your caffeine and be sure to remain sufficiently hydrated."

Goldie had remembered nodding earnestly, agreeing with more enthusiasm than she felt. Sometimes, promises were easier to make while sitting on an examination table in nothing but a tissue-thin gown separating your doctor and her stethoscope from you and your birthday suit.

Her vision started to act up. *Optometrist.* Another professional Dr. Carroway had been on her back about.

Just as Goldie gripped the piece of paper, the dank smell of scotch announced his arrival.

Simon.

He walked the length of the pool methodically, slamming

his open palms together in applause in sync with his foot strikes against the stone patio.

It appears Goldie Sparrows is coming undone, ladies and gentlemen.

She suddenly felt as though the two women at her side were standing on the other side of a glass door. Jocelyn touched her arm. She seemed to be searching Goldie's face for some sort of answer, but all Goldie could hear was Simon's voice resounding in her head.

These new friends of yours will know everything soon enough. All your secrets, my darling. Every dirty little morsel.

She wondered if her mind was playing tricks on her or if he was really there with messages from beyond, because the moment Bruce appeared at Jocelyn's back, Simon vanished from sight.

7

Jocelyn

The blinking cursor mocked her with its incessant winking. A jumble of black lettering scattered across the monitor like a soupçon of crumbs dotting a white table cloth. Jocelyn peered at the wall clock. She'd been sitting at her desk for approximately twenty-seven minutes, including the times she got up to refill her mug of iced coffee. She still got excited over the automatic ice and water dispenser on her new refrigerator, which would serve up either whole cubes or crushed ice on command. One year of living with Bruce and being the object of his affection had shown her that it really was the little things that brought the most magic to her daily life. She remembered her grandma June once said, "The tiniest of brush strokes made over time create the masterpiece of our lives." Jocelyn now knew more than ever the significance of those words.

She had spent the morning wrestling with her disjointed timeline, adding exactly seventy-six words in three sentences only to delete them within four minutes of dropping a period at the end of the last sentence. After prancing up and down the paragraph for what seemed like an hour, she grabbed a notebook and pen from the top drawer. She likened the crafting of her second novel to giving birth for the second time—it would still come with its own host of challenges, and there would be excruciating moments of agony, but this time she knew what to expect and could prepare herself. Of course, you never really knew what to expect. Her second novel was just as arduous as the first, if not worse, because she knew how heavy-handed and fastidious the editors would be.

A black fly buzzed by her head, taking a kamikaze dive into the window pane to her left. *Ouch!* She rolled her chair over and turned the crank on the screen, willing the little bugger back outside. Once the breeze kicked up, the fly seemed to sense the fresh air and darted out through the opened window. That made it seven flies Jocelyn had saved since the beginning of the spring. The words *fly whisperer* came to mind. She smiled to herself, but it faded quickly with a glance at the clock—another ten minutes slipped by effortlessly. She tapped the delete key on the incoherent fragment in front of her, having no recollection of her initial intentions for the sentence. The cursor started to remind her of that stuffed monkey from the Energizer battery commercials banging a drum. She'd picked up the stuffed dolphin in her lap from Billy's room to keep her company while she wrote. He was a sad little creature, falling apart at the seams, and in need of a suitable successor, but Jocelyn found it nearly impossible to part with the sweet, sad dolphin. It was the first companion who had kept watch over her infant son—stuffed toy or not, such items were invaluable to a mother.

In the course of her thirty-seven years, Jocelyn had seen her share of rainy days. She suffered many a broken heart from break-ups to betrayals of those she considered her closest girlfriends. She had spent countless nights alone, nearly penniless, while she roamed her studio, tipsy from too much cheap wine, deaf from the same old tired CDs, wondering what kind of future the world could possibly offer a struggling writer. She'd held her frail mother up as the caskets of Jocelyn's grandparents were lowered into a muddy ditch. She'd heard of kids she'd known since grade school dying in car crashes, of drug overdoses, from suicide. And yet, nothing in all of her life experiences had prepared her for the pain now paralyzing her. Billy had called her mobile earlier that morning. She'd been lying awake in bed, for hours, when the phone broke through the muffled sounds of Bruce's snoring. Seeing Trevor's name on the screen so early in the day released a downpour of adrenaline.

"What happened?" Jocelyn catapulted from her pillow. Bruce followed suit, placing a tender hand on her shoulder, wiping the sleep from his eyes.

"Good morning, Mommy."

"Baby, are you okay?"

"Yes. We're going on Daddy's boat today, and I wanted to say hi—" Jocelyn heard Trevor in the background prompting Billy, who was repeating his father's words in fragments "—and we will be out . . . most of the day . . . didn't want you to worry . . . can't talk later . . . *in case*, I can't talk . . . can't *call* you later . . ."

"What is it? Is it Billy?" he said.

She covered the receiver. "He's fine."

Her loving, supportive husband. Even without Billy at home, Bruce gave her enough of a reason to get out of bed in the morning.

"Your daddy told me you're going to camp," Jocelyn said.

"I love camp!" The spike in Billy's voice was sweet but jarring.

"That is so wonderful, honey. I'm so happy."

Bruce cocked his head to the side in wonderment. Suddenly, Jocelyn felt more naked beneath her cotton nightgown.

"And, Billy? Mommy loves you very much."

"I love you too."

"Hey." Trevor's curtness was like a knife through their tender-hearted exchange.

"Please be sure he wears his life vest today. And don't take him too far offshore. Where are you going, anyway?" she said.

Bruce gave her a kiss on the cheek and headed for the bathroom.

"I need to talk to you about something," Trevor said, ignoring her questions. "Hannah and I have been researching private schools for the twins. There's one only ten minutes from us. Once the twins are of age, we're going to send them."

"That's lovely." *What did this have to do with her?*

"I would like to send Billy there as well."

"What?"

"He's my son too. I don't want him to think that my other kids have it better because I love them more or that I've abandoned him or something."

"But he loves his school here," she said.

"I'm sure he does, but I want the best for him. And quite frankly, I'm the one who can afford to send him to the best. He can live with us during the school year. You can have him on holidays and for the summer."

"You must be joking. Or high. Have you lost your *mind*?"

"Listen, all I ask is that we try this out for one year. Give him a chance and see how he does. I know he'll thrive there. It's such a great school. Really."

"You can't possibly think I would say yes to this."

"No. I didn't think you would. Which is why I am fully prepared to change our custody arrangement."

Jocelyn felt as if she had been struck in the gut.

"You would do that?"

"I don't want to, but decisions about Billy's schooling are well within my rights as his father. I only want what's best for him. You know that."

"And that includes taking him away from his mother?"

"I'm going to email you the link for the school. Check it out when you can. I think you'll be impressed. Sorry, I gotta run. We'll talk about this more another time. Just think it over."

She was flabbergasted and felt physically ill. What was Trevor thinking? Where was this all coming from? What was she supposed to do now?

The morning exchange did nothing for her psyche as Jocelyn slowly became hypnotized by the mind-numbing starkness of the blank page. Inserting a brand-new scene from nothing into a work in progress was in many ways more difficult than starting from square one. She wrung her hands together, willing the comfort she felt at Bruce's side from earlier that morning to return. It was absurd to wait for the conditions to be perfect before she could muscle the effort to tackle this manuscript. Her eyes drifted to the clock. Forty-seven minutes and counting.

A schedule. That's what she needed. A set routine with time allotments and editing goals to carefully follow. With that thought, she found herself on Amazon looking for the perfect day planner, still preferring to have a hard calendar at her ready over a virtual one. There were several options. Brown or black? Cardboard or faux leather? Snap or zipper? Velcro or elastic band? The decisions were overwhelming. Her brain was going into overload. She felt herself being called toward the kitchen with an urge to create. Perhaps she could surprise Bruce that evening with a few new recipes.

Feverishly, she began scribbling a list of items needed to whip up a batch of mini-quiche mushroom-and-goat-cheese tartlets topped with caramelized shallots. She began rifling through the pantry for ingredients. Nearly every one of her recipes could be correlated to a time in her life—content, blue, excited, heartbroken—and they also served as a gauge to how far beyond a situation she had come.

The squeaky brakes of a truck called her attention—the landscapers had arrived to begin their raucous task of tending the grass and flower beds. Much as she wished she could maintain her own lawn, the time suck just wasn't feasible at the moment. As the roar of the mowers and spur of the weed whackers sprang to life, she could feel the beauty of the day. Her eyes perused the green leaves of the maple dappled in sunlight. She hadn't realized it until just then, but she was suffering from a case of "beach fever," which did not bode well for a pressing deadline. For Jocelyn, her writing productivity was commensurate with precipitation: the crappier the weather, the more work she accomplished. She now fully understood the draw for some writers to seclude themselves in a snowbound cabin with no internet access, no social media, no reality television. There's nothing else to do in those conditions other than stay inside, read, write, cook, eat, and sleep. A writer's paradise.

Jocelyn had tried to gain sympathy from her agent over the woes of living in a shore town and how the sunny weather killed her writing.

Jeannie said, "Only you can decide how badly you want this."

Thinking of the workload ahead, Jocelyn inhaled sharply. Her breaths were so shallow at times that she became lightheaded. A stream of air filtered through the screen onto her face, allowing her to close her eyes and bask in the warmth. And yet every time she tried to quiet her mind, her conversation with Trevor returned.

Her late mother-in-law, Daisy, had a safe that had been turned over to Bruce when she died. He and Jocelyn kept it down in the basement next to the washing machine and used it to store all their important papers: her passport, court documents from Bruce's divorce, the terms of Jocelyn's custody arrangement. She had to revisit the specifics of their agreement even though this was the last thing she needed to be worried about. Needing to use the next installment of her book advance to secure an attorney was not in her plans. Bruce was relying on that money to relieve the financial burden on him. As she reached in for the file folder, she pricked her finger on a piece of wire. There was a beat-up spiral-bound notebook tucked beneath the felt at the bottom of the safe. She slid the notebook out, taking great care not to rip the worn paper. Written in a black marker on the outside cover: *Property of Daisy Jane Anderson 1974 Cape May, New Jersey*

A folded piece of paper slipped from the pages, revealing a handwritten letter.

Winter 2008

To my darling son, Bruce,

I suppose all those years of baking on the beach with shiny reflectors and baby oil finally caught up to me. And we even tinted ours with iodine back then. Can you imagine? Such foolishness. Your grandfather was right: youth is wasted on the young. And that is not an easy thing for me to admit. The part about your grandfather being right, I mean.

I know children are more aware of what's going on around them than adults care to believe, and I know you had a ringside seat in your early years to the bickering between your grandparents and me. It made for a tense home life in that cramped house, and I never had a chance to properly apologize. I am sorry, Brucie. If I had to do it all over again, well, I don't quite know where to begin with that one. There is so much I would change. But we don't live our lives in retrospect. We live it on fast forward, and there is no option to rewind.

At the risk of sounding as though I am making excuses, I feel it's important to explain myself before I ask for your forgiveness—not only for the combat you had to experience at such a young age but for the decades-long cold war that followed once I was able to afford a place of our own.

While Bruce had mentioned that Daisy and her parents had had a somewhat contentious relationship, he tended to skim over details. Jocelyn wondered just how heated things had become in that house.

I'm sure I could have handled it better. Looking back, I didn't have to respond with such animosity when your grandfather pounded his chest that a "woman's place is in the home" or when your grandmother suggested I needed to marry the first available boy lest the neighbors think of me as "loose" for getting pregnant out of wedlock. I may not agree with their beliefs, but I do understand where they were coming from, and I am grateful to have made my peace with them before I lost them both.

And now, here I sit. Looking down the last stretch of highway in my own life. I have found when we reach the end of a journey, our memories take us back to the beginning. And there is much about your beginning that you never knew. As I was cleaning out the attic, I found a number of things that I hadn't even remembered, let alone looked at, in ages. This journal, the one you are holding in your hands, was started the summer after I graduated from high school. Some of the things I had forgotten all about and may be difficult for you to read. But I have always believed in doing what is right. And even if it may have taken me all this time to come clean, I believe you have a right to know the story, the whole thing—the one that started before your own story began. I cringe at some of the half-baked ideas and reading how my actions contradicted what I wanted to believe about myself, the world, and how I related to others. What can I tell you, Brucie? I was a young girl, trying to find her place in a complicated system.

This is the story of Daisy Jane Anderson and how she landed where she did as a single mother. This is part of your history, but that is all it is. One small piece. You deserve to know the truth. And you will have volumes to add to the complete story of your life when all is said and done. I don't know if you will even find this notebook. You know your mother. She has always been a firm believer that whatever is meant to be will be.

Remember, my precious boy: for every dead dandelion you pluck from the soil, I will be watching. As you send your dreams soaring through the air on the backs of the white seedlings, your adoring mama will be at the ready, waiting to fulfill your every wish.

See you on the other side.

Jocelyn felt a pang thinking of what it must have been like for Daisy to write such a letter to her only son, knowing her days were numbered. The written word had always been Jocelyn's forte, and yet the thought of having to write such a letter to Billy seemed far too emotionally excruciating a task. She marveled at Daisy's fortitude to face such a feat.

Slipping the faded green notebook from the desktop, Jocelyn brushed a tender hand across the worn cover. She opened it to the first journal entry.

~Journal of Daisy Jane Anderson~
August 9, 1974

The world has gone completely mad. Last night, I wedged myself on the couch between Mom and Dad watching the president of the United States resign from office on national television. They said it was because of that whole Watergate scandal. If the leader of the free world can quit his job, certainly I shouldn't feel guilty for wanting to take time to explore after graduating from high school. When I was younger, it was my dream to travel and see the places I'd only read about in American History class. I tried to broach the subject with Mom and Dad at the beginning of the summer, and they didn't handle it well. Mom had one of her crying fits she has mastered so well over the years. Dad becomes difficult when pushed and can easily snap and begin shouting. After seeing the concern on their faces following the president's speech, I knew last night was not the best time to mention my plans.

There is a life out there waiting for me. A world of experiences and friends and untouched places. The first three years at LCMR flew by like a blue heron gliding low across the Delaware Bay. *WHOOSH!* I spent my senior year like a child marking up an Advent calendar, counting down the days until graduation. Dad forced me to enroll in some classes at the ACC for the fall semester. Since my best friend, Laney, and I didn't have enough money saved for our excursion, I had no reason to refuse. By the spring, Laney and I are outta here. I've secured a job at Swain's Hardware for the winter months, and I'll be saving every last dime I can. Her boyfriend, Tommy Myers, is in a band and has gigs up and down the eastern seaboard. He likens himself to David Bowie. (Of course, he's nowhere near as cool or hip or outlandish, but I'd never admit that to Laney.) Tommy says there are boarding houses we can stay at, and in the warmer months, there are campgrounds where everybody pitches tents and makes bonfires and smokes and drinks and plays music into the wee hours of the morning. It sounds like a dream. I was only in middle school the summer of Woodstock, but that doesn't mean we can't try and capture some of the magic, making our own peace, love, and music.

I need out of this sleepy one-horse town—okay, okay. Maybe that's a little harsh—it's not *that* bad. But only the true locals know the loneliness of a February morn. The visitors come once, maybe twice a year, and they call it paradise. *Heaven on Earth*, some have said. All they know are the quaint little boutiques, seafood restaurants and pizzerias, ice cream and fudge shops. During the holiday season they see the town aglow in a rainbow of twinkle lights and holly. They carry their piping-hot cups of cocoa through the streets decorated like a Norman Rockwell painting to tree-lighting ceremonies and line the perimeter of the streets in folding chairs and blankets, watching the West Cape May Christmas Parade on the first Saturday in December.

They know nothing of a northeast winter experienced from an island no bigger than 2.7 square miles off the tippy end of the Garden State Parkway, where the earth drops into the Atlantic. They haven't seen the vitriol of the surf as it ravishes the landscape of the shoreline with rancor. I wonder what they would think of their lush tree-lined streets made bare by the punishing, unrelenting wrath of salty air. Or the insidious silence of a haunted city teeming with troubled souls from the Victorian era, floating in discord through the empty streets. Or the threatening sound of metal hooks and latches tapping against frozen metal poles with no flags.

My parents never understood me, and they never will. I have known that since I was a kid and Mom would spend hours sewing party dresses for me on her Singer; I'd always end up ripping the lace and fringe and making myself headbands and matching wristbands that gave me "superpowers." Dad was forty and Mom thirty-seven when I was born, which by 1956 standards made them old to be having a kid. During Halloween, they insisted I dress up as a princess. A *princess*. Me. You should have seen the look on their faces when I insisted on going as a soothsayer in the first grade.

All Mom ever wanted for me was similar to what she had: find a nice local boy with a decent job capable of providing for me and our babies. Dad has always been the one pushing for my education. And not because he expects me to be the next pioneer for women's rights like Betty Friedan, author of *The Feminine Mystique* and cofounder of NOW, or the first woman to own a seat on the New York Stock Exchange like Muriel Siebert. The women who came before me burned their bras and fought for civil rights. How exhilarating and terrifying it must have been for Shirley Chisholm to assume a seat in Congress as the first black woman in 1968, just four short years after the Civil Rights Act. What kind of a sell-out would I be if I conform now when my sisters are only getting warmed up? Dad wants me to learn how to type notes and documents for overworked, underpaid men in boring polyester suits with untrimmed ear hair and stale coffee breath. That's what the working women from their generation did. I'm a Boomer. A revolutionary. Like that silly Virginia Slim ad says: "You've come a long way, baby." Well, I for one am NOT going back.

"Teaching is a lovely, respectable profession for a young woman," Mom said.

She may have had me up until "*for a young woman*" . . . What the hell does that mean? Other vocations aren't "respectable" for women? Is there a list somewhere? Some unwritten code detailing professions that are considered acceptable or unacceptable for *young women*? And if there is, who makes the rules in the first place, and what makes them qualified, and why do we have to blindly subscribe to them? Sweet as Mom can be, she's *way* out of touch.

Dad could be a tad more reasonable but only in theory. He called me to his study one evening just before supper and asked me what it is I want to do with the rest of my life. I told him sketch, write poems, and travel.

"Those are admirable endeavors, Daisy Jane. But let's not forget: everything comes with a hefty price tag. Even our dreams," he said.

Why is he always throwing money into it? I know why. Because he lived through the Great Depression and still thinks it's necessary to ration provisions. (And why do they call it that, anyway? What was so damn "great" about it?)

I want to sit in nature before dawn in the company of the morning dew, inspired by my surroundings. I have dreams, big ones, and I'll be damned if I'm gonna let my parents suck me into their tidy little box of who they think I am or who they think I should be. As I said, they will never understand me. And that's fine. I accept it. My biggest fear—and the one that haunts me on nights when I lie in bed staring at the shadows from the lava lamp across my ceiling—is that I may never come to understand myself. I guess I still don't know who I am quite yet. Does any seventeen-year-old know? I'm working on it. And that's why I need to take this trip with Laney and Tommy.

"May God's grace be with you in all the days ahead."—President Richard Nixon

Those were his final words at the end of the speech. He stared right into the screen. Even though I knew he was addressing the American citizens, it kinda felt like he was talking right to me. Then again, I had taken a few hits just before Dad called me to join them in front of the set.

"Daisy Jane, get your butt down here! Our president is on the tube with an important message."

"On the double!" Mom chimed in as backup, nailing her role as Mrs. June Cleaver supporting her Ward.

"This is history in the making," Dad called up the stairs.

I told them I'd be right down, trying not to cough while carefully stubbing out the joint into the clay saucer I made in the second grade. I popped a Lifesaver and checked my eyes in the bathroom mirror. They were pretty damn bloodshot, but I could easily chalk that up to allergies. I'd done it dozens of times. If Dad pressed too hard, I'd make some uncomfortable reference to "that time of the month" or "female issues," which would shut him right up. Silly Mom thinks I've become more religious by burning incense in my room to cover up the smell. I guess that's one good thing about having older parents: they really have no clue what goes on, man.

To Peace on Earth, love, happiness, and escaping life in a small town.

Daisy Jane

8

Krystal

The most treasured moments in Cape May for Krystal were the mornings spent in solitude strolling the stretch of shoreline near her house known as Poverty Beach. One day, while browsing through the Cape Atlantic Book Company at the Washington Street Mall, Krystal stumbled upon Alfred Kimmel, author of two well-known books on the history of Cape May. Alfred was a vet and retired coastie, married father of four, and grandfather to twelve whose ages ranged from newborn to twenty-one. He was originally from Punxsutawney, Pennsylvania; Krystal always got a kick out of that groundhog named after the famous town.

Alfred had been visiting Cape May since his early childhood and joined the Coast Guard at eighteen. Krystal serendipitously entered the store on a day he was there for a book signing. She had always heard that Poverty Beach got its name from the locals who dubbed it that as a joke once the beach was extended and zoned out as a business venture for fancy homes. Alfred had a different take from his research and explained in great detail how the beach had never been owned by anyone, making it free to all. Its roots went all the way back to the colonial days, when this particular stretch of the shore reached as far as Ocean Street toward the center of town. Each time new developments pushed the city limits eastward, Poverty Beach shrunk a little bit more (before being relegated to its current location, tucked west of the USCG training base). Cape May was developed before Beach Drive existed, and even after the road was established, property owners maintained rights to the beach in front of their cottages, businesses, and hotels. Back then, there were no required tags or entry fees to access the beach, but it was recognized that certain sections of the beach were privately owned. Many cottage and hotel owners went so far as to put up fences in an effort to mark their turf, whereas Poverty Beach remained wide-open to all from the poorest of locals to the rich vacationers.

Krystal edged the shoreline. A jolt of frigid water sent currents up her legs, cooling her sweaty and dampened skin from the blaze of the morning sun. She'd been collecting shells and rocks and sea glass along the water's edge and surrounding the jetties since midsummer last year. Her collection seemed to expand exponentially overnight, forcing her to clear out all the shelves in one of the four closets on the first floor of their home. Naturally, Abe hadn't minded—his wardrobe could rival most women's, and he saw to it that Bruce worked closely with the architects to accommodate his need for ample storage and closet space. Abe could be a bit of a packrat himself, but their housekeeper, Pearl, did a good job of tidying after Abe, as she'd been doing for decades.

Pearl Whitaker had been with the Axelrod family since before Abe was born. Initially, she was responsible for maintaining the household chores at the family home in Westchester County, New York. From cleaning to laundry to meal preparation,

Pearl handled it all. And yet, according to Abe, she wound up spending half her paid time as a companion for Mrs. A while Mr. A traveled the world on business—whatever had initially attracted the Axelrods to one another dissipated not long after the exchange of their vows.

"Let's just say it was a short-lived honeymoon," he had said of his parents' marriage.

Between his philandering father and unsatisfied, pill-popping mother, Abe didn't reject the idea of matrimony so much as he didn't take much of an interest in it. The failure of his parents' union deterred him from seeking a commitment beyond the casual dinner-date-and-movies routine—that is, of course, until he met Krystal.

Once Abe and his sister, Rebecca, came along, Pearl's role within the family had morphed into governess of the two children. It was a charmed position that none of them knew at the time would fix her with lasting job security for all her days. Nearly a decade after Mr. Axelrod's passing, Abe's mother expressed an interest in selling the family estate and moved to a condo in Sausalito. Rebecca was distressed over losing their childhood residence, but Abe's bigger concern was what would become of Pearl. He'd just purchased a condo in Baltimore, and between his thriving law practice, financial windfalls from his investments, and a reasonably healthy social life, all he needed to complete the picture was a piece of home, and the one woman who'd served as both a loving and authoritative figure for as far back as he could remember.

The day he introduced the "two most important women" in his life to one another, Abe carried on like a schoolboy giddy over his new skateboard. It took Krystal only seconds to realize this woman, whom she'd only heard bits and pieces about, was far more important than simply a housekeeper. Pearl and Abe's interactions seemed familial, as though she were a favorite aunt who'd been there from the first time he was burped to the last of his commencement ceremonies.

"Pearl Whitaker. I'm pleased to make your acquaintance." She turned to Abe. "Will your guest be joining us for supper?" She spoke the word *guest* with the tiniest hint of disdain, detectable only to another female; it had conveniently escaped Abe's awareness.

"Of course she is!" Abe said, pulling Krystal in with one huge arm and slapping a sloppy and noisy kiss on the side of her head. The flat line of Pearl's pale, thin lips downturned as if Krystal had been the one to step from her place with an inappropriate show of affection.

Abe fussed with his phone while Pearl let her eyes run the length of Krystal's body, landing on the bare toes poking through her glitzy sandals. Krystal immediately cringed for not replacing the garish blue polish with a tasteful, ladylike pink.

"I suppose it's safe to assume you're a vegetarian of some sort," Pearl said.

"She's a carnivore and will love anything you throw her way." Abe beamed. "And she likes meat on her men." He rubbed his belly with both hands like a proud expectant mother.

Even after that awkward first exchange, Krystal always felt like an intruder when she visited Abe. Pearl was territorial and made it a point to subtly remind Krystal of her place by constantly doting on her; the "make yourself at home" policy was not one Pearl employed. Of course, Abe would say Pearl was just being polite and fulfilling her duties, but Krystal knew better. Pearl's behavior wasn't borne of sheer kindness and hospitality. It was meant to serve as a gentle reminder that Krystal was a guest—*only* a guest—and nothing more. After Abe's proposal and subsequent purchase of their new home, the game between Krystal and Pearl changed significantly. The house was designed and bought just for Krystal, and no matter how long Pearl had been in his life, Krystal was the one with the key to Abe's heart. She was no longer just a visitor but the lady of the manor. A fact that could not be denied, disputed, or ignored by anyone—including Pearl.

"I'm going to build you your dream home," Abe had said. "You have no budget, baby."

Of course, Krystal couldn't fathom the idea of not following a budget and made sure to keep her selections reasonable while working closely with the architects and Bruce. Everything in the home, from the flooring to the tiles of the backsplash in the kitchen to the fixtures in the six bathrooms to the color of the paint on each and every accent wall, was of Krystal's choosing. The space had become *hers* in the truest sense of the word. Once Abe sold his place in Baltimore, Pearl entered this new palace with a touch of humility. She was quiet and skittish, like a foster child placed with a new family. Krystal sympathized and made a peace offering to put the old woman at ease.

"You're the master chef around here. You should have your say as to how the kitchen is set up."

Pearl's astonished gaze trailed Krystal's face as if making certain her words were genuine. After a few beats, Pearl said ever so quietly, "Thank you kindly."

It was the nicest thing she had ever said to Krystal, who was perfectly happy with the response. The last thing she wanted was a miserable person dwelling in her living space, sucking up all her positive vibes. Krystal casually watched as Pearl went straight to work gingerly unpacking her glassware and placing her fancy cooking gadgets in their new homes within the cabinets and drawers of the massive kitchen. There was an unspoken agreement between the two women to coexist while not having to become best friends. Of course, ignoring one another was not an option with Abe constantly traveling back and forth between Cape May and his satellite office in Baltimore. When he was home, Pearl would automatically prepare all three meals without question. When Abe was traveling, Krystal was given a choice of being served her meals, which she had always politely declined, not wishing to put the old woman out. It didn't matter how big her house or how many digits she had in her account balance; Krystal would never get used to being catered to and waited on like royalty.

The night of Krystal's gathering had arrived. She was expecting a handful of the girls from her old neighborhood. Amber and Georgia had been at Krystal's wedding and shower. Abe was not a fan of these two. They had jagged edges and an unsophisticated manner that he didn't feel matched his wife's elegance. Amber got so drunk on punch at the bridal shower she had to be escorted to a taxi waiting out front. Remembering the sideways glances and snickering coming from the wives of some of Abe's associates still made Krystal queasy. At the wedding, Georgia made a spectacle of herself with the bedraggled guy she brought as her date. The two started dirty dancing and necking right there out in the open with no consideration for anyone, least of all Krystal, who was mortified by the display. After an unfortunate incident involving Georgia's cranberry vodka and another guest's dress, Krystal broke down in tears outside the hall, apologizing to her new husband.

"Don't feel bad. Shit happens," Abe said. "Hey . . ." He curled his finger under her chin and delicately dabbed her eyes with his handkerchief, taking great care not to wreck her professionally made-up face. "I love you. And you love me. And that is all that matters. Come on, baby. Now's not the time for crying. This is your night. Our night. Let's go back in there and show these people what real dancing is."

Abe had the uncanny ability with the snap of his fingers and the right words to flip Krystal's mood instantaneously. It wasn't until some time long after their honeymoon when he had spoken candidly about these so-called friends from her former life.

"In a word? Disrespectful. Boorish," Abe said.

"That's two words," Krystal teased. It was a retort Abe would have used.

"Funny. But really, honey, these girls are beneath you," he said, firmly. "You're nothing like them. You never were." She couldn't respond because she had nothing to say. Abe had struck a chord. They both knew it.

"And you know what? You don't owe them anything. Not anything at all. Nothing."

Sometimes, Krystal felt as though Abe could see right through to the deepest part of her soul. The part that even she wasn't aware of. The part that she never bothered to examine or question because there had never been anyone who cared enough to make her look.

Krystal kept her husband's wise words in the back of her mind as she prepared the house for the arrival of the women. Her reason for the gathering was to gain feedback on the jewelry and knickknacks she'd been making with her seashell collection. Over the course of the past year, she'd made a series of necklaces, bracelets, and earrings, on which she received a flurry of compliments wherever she went. One day while strolling through the crafts and artist's fair on the promenade, she stopped at a booth selling items made by hand with treasures from the beach. A voice she had never heard before spoke from deep inside.

I can do that.

Krystal returned home and purchased several crafting manuals to thumb through while ideas slowly trickled in. Before long, she was making candle holders, wine charms, and trivets. More recently, she had tackled bigger challenges like a full-length standing mirror and beach bags. With Abe always running between the two offices, there hadn't been a time when he'd ever seen his wife in all her glory—a scrubby T-shirt and sweats, bits of glue stuck to the ends of her hair, paint staining the beds of her fingernails—while having the most fun she had ever had in her life. She hadn't deliberately kept her passion from him, but the subject never seemed to come up. The world he was living in was so grand in stature, she felt her frivolous hobby paled in comparison and wasn't worthy of mention. The only thing he really knew was that Krystal was eagerly looking forward to hosting some friends to show off some of the crafts she'd been playing around with in her spare time.

Pearl indicated she would be retiring to her bedroom in the east wing of the house and reading quietly before bed. Krystal was only too happy to have the woman out of her hair. She spent the entire morning and afternoon setting up the finished basement, bought a crushed velvet covering at the fabric store to drape over the tables, and placed several tree stands to showcase her bracelets and earrings. The floor mirror was strategically placed in the corner of the room to reflect each display, and the lights were dimmed to create a warm, inviting atmosphere. The room looked not only fashionably entertaining but professionally done. If Krystal didn't know better, she would have believed she'd stepped into a high-end boutique. She even had price lists laminated like menus to avoid tacky price tags on her creations.

The tour of the house took longer than Krystal expected. Of course she knew six thousand square feet was a lot to cover, but she didn't anticipate that the women would linger for as long as they did in the kitchen. They seemed more interested in gabbing about the cost of everything in the home while nibbling chips and salsa.

"How much did you pay for all this? Tell us!"

"These wine goblets cost more than my first used car."

"What are the property taxes on a place like this?"

"I can't imagine the maintenance fees on all that fancy landscaping."

"What do you do all day? It must be nice to be rich, but I bet it's also boring too. Am I right?"

The last snarky remark came from Tammy Frill and had all the women dribbling into their own cocktails. She stared straight into Krystal's eyes. A challenge. She still couldn't believe she let Amber manipulate her into letting Tammy join them.

"Come downstairs and I'll show you what I've been doing for the last year," Krystal said.

As she approached the staircase and balanced the glass of wine in the crook of her arm, every one of her nerves stood at attention. She navigated the narrow stairwell against the backdrop of the tipsy women behind her, hoping they would simmer down once they reached the soothing ambiance she had created.

As the door opened, the flameless votives flickered to life. Naturally, Tammy was the first to offer an opinion, sending a direct message that she was the one in charge. She had ruined the last two years of high school for Krystal and was now on a mission to win over the crowd and do whatever was necessary to make her look and feel like a worthless piece of crap. As Krystal became more frazzled, she began to repeat herself—a trait she hadn't been able to kick since childhood. And one that she knew, especially after tonight, she'd never live down.

"What's wrong, Miss Boors?" Tammy said. "The needle got stuck on the record?"

Referring to Krystal by her maiden name was all-telling. Tammy was purposefully and openly disrespecting her home, marriage, and status in front of the other women. That was the moment she knew she had to face reality: the evening had barely taken flight and had already crashed.

)(

Krystal kicked off her pumps and rubbed the area just above her Achilles tendon, where the straps had been digging in like tightly wound rubber bands all night. She had wicked blisters on both pinky toes and a new patch of calluses surfacing on the arch of her right foot. All she wanted to do was wipe the makeup from her face, brush her teeth, and crawl under the covers. And yet she knew she could never hide the remnants of the evening from Pearl. It didn't seem possible for eight women to create such a disaster. There were two empty magnums of Pinot Grigio, seven wine coolers, smashed tortilla chips on the hallway carpet runner, and an unidentifiable brown slime dripping down one of the cabinets, which, upon closer inspection, she determined was guacamole.

"Good thing you don't need a college degree or a high IQ to make things with your hands."

Tammy Frill's callous words had been utterly derailing. Her earlier vision of how she would detail the unique crafting process for each piece disintegrated against the biting remarks. She was heartsick from the failure of the evening but hadn't the luxury of succumbing to her hurt feelings and squashed pride. Cleaning up after those disrespectful pigs who had treated her home like some kind of Steak and Brew only added insult to injury. *Never again*, she thought while delicately rubbing out the greasy, cheap lip gloss from her precious wine goblets. She wanted to cry, but she held strong thanks to the one empowering thought that became a mantra while she cleaned: *Never again*. It offered her comfort to know this would be the last night she would ever subject herself to those selfish, inconsiderate cretins.

With Abe at his satellite office for the week, the quiet of her bedroom without his heavy breathing gave the voices in Krystal's head a stage and microphone from which to torment her.

"Save your money. I know a place that makes better quality jewelry for a lot less."

Tammy had a number of wicked and backhanded remarks, which Krystal had heard from the other side of the bathroom door. Drunk women didn't know how loud their whispers could be.

"Are you crazy? Don't buy anything. Does she look like she needs the money?"

The women carried on as if they had stumbled into some fancy gift shop with time to kill before a dinner reservation. This was Krystal's *home*. These were things she had made with her own hands. Didn't any of them feel even the slightest bit obligated to acknowledge her achievement or at least her effort? Was everything about *money*? Couldn't they see her for who she was now? Couldn't they appreciate how far she had come and how much she had to offer? All Krystal wanted to do was change the image they had of her from high school. Prove to them, once and for all, that she was no longer Krystal Boors the cheerleader who was ostracized for years over those topless photos floating around the school.

She wrapped herself under the duvet, unable to read or listen to anything from her Law of Attraction gurus or lectures. She wasn't open enough to properly receive their underlying messages, having fallen too far down the rabbit hole of self-pity. Her phone lit up with a text from Abe checking in on how her "big night" had gone. A lump developed in her throat as she typed back, "Okay." Her phone rang twenty seconds later.

"Hey, baby!" Abe was always so happy to speak to her. "Just okay? What did the girls think of your newfound talent?"

Hearing his enthusiasm and compliments after such a monumental letdown was too much to bear. She became untethered and began whimpering into the phone.

"Honey, what happened? Tell me."

The sweeter and softer he became, the worse she felt. She was mortified. She had made such a fuss over getting things just right. This gathering was all she could talk about, think about for over a month. How was she supposed to tell him the women barely gave her work a glance? How could she tell him they hadn't said one nice thing about all that effort? She was devastated. No, humiliated.

"It doesn't matter," she said through tears. "They didn't care about any of it."

"What do you mean they didn't care? You've made some beautiful things. What the hell is wrong with these bitches?" Abe was not one to call women foul names. Krystal knew he was amping up his display of anger in solidarity.

"It doesn't matter. Just forget it." She wished she could erase the nightmare of the whole evening from her memory.

"Of course it matters, sweetheart. Like I've been telling you, this is not your crowd anymore. They're not worthy of Krystal Axelrod. They never were."

He went on to encourage her to find some new companions. Winners, like her, who would appreciate her generosity, creativity, and good nature.

"People love you. Just look at Bruce's wife! Jocelyn thought you were terrific."

"That was the alcohol talking," she said, but then felt sorry for the remark. She had really enjoyed her time with Jocelyn that evening.

"She was just letting loose. She really liked you."

"How would you know that?"

"Bruce told me."

Krystal dabbed her nose with a tissue. "He did? What did he say?"

"He said that Jocelyn thought you were really lovely, and she wants the four of us to have dinner when I get back."

She was too tired to question or refute his opinions and knew if she pushed it, he would only persist.

Krystal woke earlier than she had intended. Her sleep was disrupted as her mind reeled with negative thoughts. She finally gave up the struggle with tossing and turning and plopped herself at the island in the kitchen with a full mug of coffee and the latest issue of *People* magazine.

"Morning," Pearl said. She was surprised to see Krystal beat her out of bed, but she'd never admit such a thing. "How was your soirée?"

"Fine, thanks," she said, pretending to be engrossed in an article. She could feel Pearl's dubious eyes on her but refused to look up.

"I see. Very well then. Would you like some breakfast?"

"No, thanks. I'm good," Krystal said, almost daring Pearl to passive-aggressively correct her improper use of the word *good* as she had in times past. She did not.

Krystal continued to sip and flip while Pearl placed a pan on the stovetop.

"I'm preparing a spinach-and-Swiss omelet with button mushrooms," Pearl announced as if to no one.

She had a way of blurting out statements without addressing Krystal directly and with no indication of whether she was making an offer, asking a question, or just blowing hot air into space.

"Thanks anyway," Krystal muttered.

As she looked up, she could see Pearl was perturbed, unable to remove her eyes from Krystal, who was unusually dispirited.

A few beats later, Pearl was standing at the opened refrigerator. "What in the heavens . . ." Slowly, she removed a half-drunk wine cooler from the top shelf. She held it at arm's length with a scowl and *tsk-tsk*'d as she brought it over to the sink. The trashy red lipstick markings around the mouth of the bottle appeared hideously offensive in the light of the morning.

Tammy Frill. That miserable cow. Stirring the pot without even being present.

Pearl placed the bottle in the sink and, in an exaggerated show of disgust, retrieved two yellow gloves from beneath the cabinet and began emptying the contents of the refrigerator as if everything inside had been contaminated. Krystal refused to ask her what she was doing or offer assistance or apologize because that was exactly what Pearl was expecting from her, and she was not in the mood to play this game or feed the old woman's ego. Not now.

Dump the stupid thing in the recycle bin and keep your nasty glares to yourself, you old bat!

She needed to get out of the house and away from Pearl before she snapped and said something Abe would certainly make her grovel for later. She closed the magazine, placed her mug in the sink, and left the room. Her purse was sitting on the bench near the rear entrance. She headed for the garage, secured her bag into the basket of her bicycle, and hopped on.

Krystal tried to drown out the noise in her head, allowing the briny sea air to tickle her lips as the sunshine enveloped her. She marveled at the flower beds, the wind chimes, the perfectly manicured yards of her neighbors. A grandfather showed his grandson how to properly trowel the soil surrounding their sailboat mailbox. These were the sights and sounds and people of her neighborhood. All intricate parts of the greater whole, creating the charm, ambiance, and small-town appeal for which the seaside town was famous.

Without notice, ten minutes had passed. She arrived at one of the many bike racks on the perimeter of the Washington Street Mall. She dismounted and locked up, heading straight for Coffee Tyme to treat herself to a cappuccino and watch the horse-and-carriages as they passed by. As she dug for her wallet, she retrieved a crumpled piece of paper. It was the flyer for Little Birdie Studio that had fallen from Goldie's hand the evening of the charity event. She wondered how Goldie was doing. That evening, after her unsightly episode, Goldie jabbered on about some new medication she'd been taking for arthritis or something. It was difficult to follow her train of thought. The poor woman seemed downright ashamed and took her leave as soon as Bruce and Abe joined the women on the patio. Bruce seemed the most taken aback by her abrupt departure. Jocelyn tried to explain what had happened, but Bruce either wasn't buying it or didn't want to believe something could be wrong with his friend.

Krystal grabbed her coffee and sat at one of the café tables under the awning. She unfolded the paper, smoothing it over with a tired hand.

The first class began in exactly one hour.

9　

Goldie

G oldie scanned the large studio, trying to picture how to
arrange the desks and tables. The price of the new com-
mercial-grade, front-loading kiln was alarmingly high and out
of her range, but it was necessary and worth it. At her age, she
simply couldn't and wouldn't contend with the bending associ-
ated with top loaders. She stepped out behind the building to
the parking area. There were newspapers covering the entire
space behind the studio. Three weeks earlier, she'd gone on a
scavenger hunt for yard sales in the area. Instead of spending
cash on brand-new desks and tables and chairs, she hand-
selected a few odds and ends and jazzed them up with a fresh
coat of spray paint, assigning a theme for each workstation: deep
purple with little white rabbits for Alice in Wonderland; black
and white staffs, treble clefs, and musical notes; rainbow polka
dots with sour balls, bubble gum, and peppermints; grass-green
with herbs, trowels, and watering cans. Her tastes were eclectic,
and she wanted both her home and place of business to be an

extension of her personality: eccentric yet approachable, unusual yet comforting, disorganized yet clean.

"You two better behave yourselves. The folks you'll be meeting today are paying customers." She looked down adoringly at her two Himalayans. "Laverne, if you jump on anyone's lap, I may be forced to relegate you to the back office. Are we clear?"

With eyes wide enough to swallow the whole of Goldie's heart, Laverne sprang from the floor straight into her arms.

"All right, little one. Get it out of your system now." She stroked the purring cat, which began the nesting ritual of digging her claws into her mother's arms.

Both her babies were a bit rattled from having been tossed in their carriers, which for years represented one thing and one thing alone: the veterinarian. *Ahhhhhhh!* She could only imagine how Gloria Eagle would have reacted if she knew the "house pets" were free to roam the store.

For seventeen years, she'd been forced to leave them at home due to Gloria's alleged allergies. Goldie was convinced these issues were borne from an inherent dislike of felines (or any animals, for that matter). Looking back, she found it surprising that she was able to achieve such success with a tenant who didn't share her love of animals. She'd never forget how Gloria's face had twisted into a tight knot the day she visited Goldie's home. Malcolm had been especially cheeky that day and started pelting seeds through his cage. Brutus kept his distance, not bothering to ask for a pat on the head, while Shirley glowered at her with a raised back from her stealthy hideout beneath the buffet table at the far end of the room. Her babies always knew where to find the love and could easily decipher whether they were in the company of allies or foes.

Distracting herself with the business of the cats helped take Goldie's mind off her stage fright. One-on-one interaction was one thing, but standing at the front of a room with all eyes and ears aimed in her direction wreaked havoc on her self-confidence. She reviewed the list of the five women who had signed up—not many, but it was a start. One of the two neighbors joining them was Gloria's youngest daughter, Tara, who used to pop in several times a day to visit her mother. Tara always came bearing gifts, from a mocha latte to a midafternoon dark chocolate break. Gloria loved to make a great show of Tara's doting and drop-ins, smooching her full-grown daughter hard on the face with noisy kisses as one would a toddler.

"There's nothing more precious in life than a daughter. You simply haven't lived until you've experienced the sheer joy of being a mother."

Gloria could be remarkably inconsiderate of others' feelings, especially when it came to Goldie, who had grown accustomed to such flippant remarks over the years.

Twenty minutes to blast off. Her nerves were a jumbled mess. She knew the art of throwing a piece better than anyone, but smoothing the lumpy parts of her insecurity had always been the most challenging task of all. Of course, she'd lived long enough to know the mere thought of an event was oftentimes more daunting than the actual experience. In the weeks leading up to her first attempt at the mermaid, her belly had flip-flopped like a sketchy presidential candidate on the campaign trail.

She trusted the three women down here on vacation would be the most enthusiastic of the lot. Gloria used to have an unflattering term for the summer people: *shoobies*. It was derived from the days when the Philadelphians would take the train to the coast for the day. The lunches they would order on the railway were delivered in a shoe box. They'd spend the day on the beach and browse through shops before returning to the city. Truth was, these summer people fueled her business, and she relished their arrival. Once upon a time, she was also a mere visitor to the town. Life circumstances had led her to the tip of New Jersey, and she'd been instantly swept away by the charm of the quaint town; she was proud to call Cape May her home for the last near thirty years.

Tara Eagle was the first to arrive, ten minutes early. She entered with the same singsong voice she inherited from her mother. Her phone was lodged in her hand—Goldie was convinced the device was a permanent extension of young people's arms. Surely Tara had been sent by Gloria to document every little detail like a sleazy reporter. Goldie would be damned to make a fool of herself in front of this little snitch. Somehow, she knew Gloria would take a morbid satisfaction in learning that Little Birdie Studio might fail without her. She trusted that the first thing Tara would tell her mother was the matter of Laverne and Shirley being in the store during business hours.

By the time Goldie had completed setting up, all five women had arrived.

"Welcome, everyone. I'd like to give you a little background on myself before we begin. My name is Goldie Sparrows. My lifelong romance with clay began when I was a small child at the side of my grandmother, Margaret Elizabeth Sparrows. I never was one to be coy about my age, and I'm fairly certain you can all tell by my witchy grey hair and sunspots that we are talking about well over six decades."

She received the flurry of chuckles she was aiming for, which encouraged her to press on.

"Growing up, I took several pottery classes and eventually had the luxury of studying with a studio potter. I opened the Little Birdie Studio here in Cape May back in 1983. It would be impossible for me to estimate how many pieces I've thrown in my lifetime—"

The woman sitting at the garden-themed desk raised her hand and in a sweet voice asked, *"Thrown?"*

Goldie smiled. "Throwing is a term we use in the creation of pottery. It can be an extremely cathartic and rewarding experience. As with anything new, it comes with a fair amount of frustration without proper guidance. Clay is truly one of the most fascinating gifts given to us by the earth and isn't all that unlike a cat: moody and temperamental, but with enough love it can be quite responsive and forgiving.

"In the next eight classes, I will walk you through each stage of the process so you have a full understanding of the techniques. At the very least, I hope you'll all leave here with a few new creations and an appreciation for the craft. Together, we'll discover the magic of *fire*, which will bring your projects to life."

Tara raised her hand. "Hi, everyone. My mother, Gloria, used to be a business partner in this shop."

Goldie nearly gasped. Gloria had been a tenant. She rented a few measly tables. How dare she?

"I took a few pottery classes when I was at UVM, and I learned a lot from observing over the years. Mind if I give you a for instance?"

Goldie was fully put on the spot and conjured a vague smile to be polite.

"When joining clay parts together, they should be equally wet, meaning have the same moisture content. As the clay dries, it shrinks because the water between the clay particles evaporates, and the clay particles draw nearer to each other. If a wet clay piece is joined to a drier clay piece, the wet clay piece has more shrinking left to do than the drier piece, so as it shrinks more and creates stress, it will want to crack away from the drier piece. For beginners, you still may be able to join a wet piece of clay to a near bone-dry piece, but in the end, no matter what you do, the wet clay will shrink more than the drier clay, and all that effort is wasted. The simple solution is to spend a little effort before attaching things to re-wet the drier piece, and/or dry out the wetter piece, until the parts are evenly wet, then join them back together."

Tara sat back down. A long and stringy self-satisfied smile stretched across her lips. Rattled by the young girl's brazenness to commandeer the floor so unexpectedly, Goldie studied the expressions of the other participants, who seemed both enthralled and perplexed with the barrage of details coming at them. Suddenly, she remembered a day last season when Tara went stomping out of the store after a rift with Mommy Dearest. Things had not always been so peachy keen between mother and daughter, who were so much alike they often locked horns. After Tara's unsolicited soliloquy, she was convinced more than ever that something had clearly gone awry in the DNA of the Eagle women.

"Thank you, Tara. It certainly is a pleasure to have you all—"

Without warning, Laverne took a flying leap from the desk and landed right on her bull's eye: Goldie's chest.

"What the devil . . ."

The ladies giggled and aww'd. She stroked Laverne while catching her breath. The segue was perfectly timed—no one knew her better than her animals, and no one ever could. Stirred by all the cooing, Shirley began to weave through Goldie's legs at the makeshift lectern.

"As I was saying, it is a pleasure to have you all here. On behalf of myself and Laverne and Shirley, we welcome you and hope you enjoy your time with us."

Luckily, the ladies seemed to love animals and had no issues with their feline company. As she gently returned Laverne to the floor, she asked the women to take a moment to thumb through the booklets she had made for them. A moment later, she started seeing double—a pesky phenomenon that had been occurring with more regularity. She figured it was the hubbub of her thoughts and twisted nest of nerves. She quietly excused herself to the back.

Unable to get a crisp focus on her own reflection in the bathroom mirror, she was unable to discern her eyes from her nostrils. She rubbed her closed lids and shook her head, trying to keep the panic at bay. She must follow through with Dr. Carroway's orders and find an optometrist. She simply must. Just as she added that item to her growing list of concerns, she inhaled a whiff of scotch.

Please not now, she thought. But it was already too late. She could feel Simon at her back. She squeezed her eyes shut, wishing to banish his presence.

Just another aging artist. Teaching pottery to a pack of amateurs. You shouldn't have been so generous with your inheritance.

She slowly opened her eyes. In the reflection of the window at her back, there was a figure pacing on the sidewalk right in front of the shop. She turned around for a better look. As her focus slowly returned, she could see it was that blonde she'd met the other night at Bruce's. The one married to the heavy-set, rich fellow. What the heck was his name? And what on God's green earth was she wearing? Goldie squinted her eyes for a closer look at the scantily dressed woman.

Now, there's a girl who looks like she knows how to have a good time.

Simon's voice was garbled, as if he stood on the other side of a closed door, which meant he was drifting back to where he had come from. She closed her eyes once more, as if her hearing could be controlled through her sight. How wicked for her mind to be playing such tricks.

She wondered what impression she must have given this girl; one minute they were standing poolside enjoying a pleasant conversation, and the next, Goldie was having one of her episodes. She'd been mortified by the whole ordeal. She could only imagine what Jocelyn had told Bruce once Goldie fled the scene. She wished she could erase the entire night from her memory.

I could have had a ball with that one.

It can't be you. You're not really here. I'm imagining it all, Goldie thought. *You have no business being here.*

It struck her that she wasn't certain if she was addressing Simon or the blonde, who had ceased all movement and was now staring straight through the window directly at her.

10

Jocelyn

A fly buzzed past her head, smashing into the screen at her back. These hopeless creatures were becoming haphazard. Jocelyn raised the pane, willing it outdoors, which entirely defeated the purpose as another two darted inside. She'd wait and wait, hoping they'd feel their way to the opening and stop crashing into the top part of the window. Suddenly, she felt a pang of empathy for the little buggers, who didn't seem to know how to stop getting in their own way—Jocelyn knew what that felt like.

Her phone buzzed with an incoming text message, and her heart took a flying leap, thinking it might be Trevor, which meant Billy was standing by and waiting to speak to his mommy.

Read your email, slacker!—Jeannie

SHIT.

Her stomach took two umbrella twirls and a spin up the runway. Such a message from her agent was about as nerve-racking as being sent home with a letter of detention from the principal. She wasn't in the right frame of mind for a lecture on how she had missed the editor's deadline for revisions. She resolved to check her email that afternoon and prepare an excuse for why she'd been away from her computer. Thankfully, she had rectified the snafu in her timeline. It ended up being an easier fix than she'd expected, requiring only a minor tweak in making one of her main characters five years older. Done. Problem solved.

A black fly landed on the edge of her desk.

"Well, hello there. Might there be something I can help you with?"

Talking to flies. What was next? Taking them for walks on leashes of waxed dental floss? She desperately wanted out of the house, but there was no way she could leave. Her hand covered the mouse, which should have been headed straight for her inbox but seemed to slide across the pad and click on the Facebook icon—what an endless waste of time that racket was.

With its horoscopes, selfies, clickbait articles, advertisements, political debates, and inspirational memes, Jocelyn couldn't believe how fast one hour (or three!) could be devoured, leaving her with nothing to show for it. When she first opened her account—as with any new friendship or relationship—she was struck by the wonder of it all, finding almost everything irresistibly engaging. These days, she did more snickering than "liking" or commenting. There were those friends who announced daily greetings at the onset of each day as if hosting their own private morning shows, and the lot who had nothing thought-provoking or stimulating to add and so just put up premade cartoon memes in rapid-fire succession throughout the day; the one she saw last week with Snoopy and Woodstock dancing for joy in front of a *TGIF* banner was about as irritatingly banal as it got.

Then there were the useless calls to action: *Please post this on your wall for one hour in support of all those suffering from Restless*

Leg Syndrome. When not tied to a specific disease in its idiopathic form, there is no known cause. More people suffer in silence from this harrowing condition. They shouldn't have to suffer alone. Or the more random, vaguely religious, guilt-inducing prompts: *All prayers needed right now. May I ask my family and friends, wherever you may be, to kindly copy and paste this status for one hour to whisper a prayer for all of those who have family problems, health struggles, job issues, sprained wrists, splinters, or worries of any kind and just need to know that someone cares? NO SHARING. Praying for several families in need! If I don't see your name, I'll understand.*

She would think to herself, *Is that so? Good. Because I would rather take a video clip of myself in a bra, singing into my hairbrush with eye snot, than post that message to my wall.*

Of course, Jocelyn was all for the greater good; she welcomed the Facebook posts petitioning for animal rights or the GoFundMe projects for those legitimately in dire need of assistance—like that young couple unable to cover their daughter's medical bills who'd spent the last year of her life in critical care at the oncology unit of St. Jude's, or the mother of four who stood one mortgage payment away from losing her home after her husband of the FDNY lost his life battling a three-alarm blaze in a Queens apartment building. One of the biggest problems was even hours after logging off, her thoughts were often coated in a sticky film, as her awareness became mired in the anguish and turmoil spinning through this graceless age of humanity. She thought of several taglines that summed up her feelings on the social media outlet: *Facebook—The Most Dizzying Time Suck Since the Rubik's Cube; Facebook—Raising Your Stardom and Popularity One Like at a Time; Facebook—Where You Can Cry, Laugh, and Argue with a Perfect Stranger All Within a 10-Minute Session; Facebook—A Necessary Evil for Networking and Promotion.*

That last one was closest to the truth. Much of the literary world resided in cyberspace. She had met throngs of writer friends online and been a little late to the game, as she was still trying to drum up fans for her author page. Other writers were much more skilled at maintaining a daily presence by interacting with their followers and readers, who seemed to be waiting like giddy fans at a concert hall. Jocelyn kept her occasional, quippy posts relegated to her personal page. She found herself turning to Facebook when she was stumped on a scene. Even though once the post was up she'd inevitably get sucked into an exchange with friends and pulled from her work, she had come to rely on such frivolous breaks throughout the day. Unlike writing a novel, which took countless lonely hours, social media provided a sense of immediate gratification and a brief connection to the outside world. Sadly, once the flurry of exchanges died down, she returned to the quiet of her own solitude feeling lonelier and more empty than before.

Still avoiding her email, Jocelyn resisted the sudden temptation to read on-line book reviews for some of the new releases. There were several new (and much younger) up-and-coming sensations who had already hit the bestsellers' list. She had read one or two of their novels out of curiosity and was impressed by only some; she wished she could learn what it was that made readers react one way over another. Some of her friends had written fabulous literary novels that went virtually unnoticed. It was a grueling and frustrating business, to say the least.

Closing her laptop, she pondered if she had the proper ingredients for a fresh salad. And then she thought of Billy and wondered what he would be eating for lunch today. The thought saddened her. In their last conversation, he seemed distracted. This separation was pulling him even further from her. What if he forgot about her? What if he discovered he didn't need his mommy anymore because he had his dad and Hannah? Maybe Trevor was having an effect on him. Maybe he was trying to show their son how fun and exciting life could be over at Dad's.

She immediately moved Trevor's email about the private school to her trash folder. There was no way she was going to permit anyone to take her son from her—father or not. She had a call in to that lawyer she used to draft the custody agreement and was waiting to hear back.

Then, she checked the clock. *3:48.* Still kind of early. What was that old saying? It's five-o'clock somewhere?

She headed for the kitchen to see how much wine was left over from last night's dinner. There was a bottle of Chardonnay with about a quarter of the bottle left. She'd just pour a little. Just to take the edge off. As she went down to the basement, she was flooded with comfort knowing she was about to step back into Daisy's world. It was the perfect escape from her own life.

~Journal of Daisy Jane Anderson~
October 1975

First time I saw him, he was checking out at the register. On the counter, there was a copy of the *Wall Street Journal*, Juicy Fruit gum, a package of Hostess cupcakes, and some Binaca breath spray. His fancy dress shoes, with tassels dangled like church bells on the front, gave off a high sheen. In his black suit and overcoat, he stood out like a sparkly Rolls Royce in a used car lot. I never thought such a well-to-do, polished man would turn my head, but I couldn't seem to draw my eyes from him. As I approached the counter, the wafting scent of his musky cologne pinched my nose as my body became flooded with tingles in all the right spots. The last thing I was expecting was for a hippie like me to capture the notice of such a gentleman, but I did. Just as soon as I stepped into the parking lot, he was standing there wearing a spicy grin. His eyes worked slowly and methodically, trailing the length of my body as if drawing a sip from every inch to quench an untamed thirst.

"Frank Cooper." He extended his hand. I gave him mine

and he kissed it! Up close, he was younger than the way he was dressed. The getup made him look like an older man, but when he turned around and flashed that toothy white grin framed by a deep pair of dimples, I could see his youth. (Among the other bodily reactions I experienced in that moment, my knees nearly buckled.)

Frank slipped me his business card. The next time we went to town, I used the last of my change to call him at his office. He asked if I would mind waiting at the minimart until he was able to break away from his meeting. "No more than thirty minutes," he said. Laney wanted to head back to the campground. I told her I would walk back.

"That's seven miles!"

"And?" I smiled my biggest and brightest so she would catch on.

"I see your point. Just be careful, please." Before Laney drove away, she added, "Hey, Daise, maybe this one's a keeper."

I was in the middle of taking a sip from my Mountain Dew, so I just nodded, which forced the fizzy liquid to go down the wrong pipe, and I started hacking. All I could think as she drove away was *SHIT!* She just cursed me. As usual, I was right. I ended up sitting there watching people come and go for almost two hours. When I first plopped myself onto the curb in front of the store, the sun was peeking out over my left shoulder. By the time I stood up, it had moved well past the middle of my chest and was hidden behind a huge weeping willow. These are the little things you notice when you have nothing else to occupy your thoughts. Under different circumstances I wouldn't have minded. I love being in nature and having a chance to observe its subtle nuances, but I didn't even have my journal or a book to read. I'd already spent my budgeted money for the day on supplies, so I couldn't scrounge for a stupid comic book, which was the only sort of reading material the minimart had to offer.

Without being able to read or write or sketch, I was just taking up space and wasting time, which I really hate. If I'm not creating or learning, what's the point of existing?

After two hours and twenty minutes, I began walking back to the campground, silently cursing myself for being one of those girls who was willing to sacrifice my time and peace of mind on the promise of some random guy. Of course, Frank is actually a man, but when I'm mad at him he becomes just a guy again. Men are solid, trustworthy, forthright. Guys are just assholes.

It wasn't dark yet, but it was getting later, and fast. The sun began its slow descent toward the edge of the earth, which made me pick up my pace some. I thought I heard my name being called through the passing cars but chalked it up to my own hallucinations. Then like a mirage Frank was walking toward me with that same enticing grin. He was carrying a dozen red roses. Was this real? I wasn't certain until he was right in front of me and I got a whiff of that delicious, manly scent.

"Would you do me the honor . . ."

I was too shocked to speak. I waited for more.

". . . of accepting my apology?"

Ever the charmer, my Frank. Even now something inside me comes undone when I look into his hazel eyes. I have never felt anything like it before. He leaves me feeling all gooey inside. We've been together ever since that moment and the long passionate kiss following his apology.

I thought I'd spend a couple of nights at a local motel until I figured out what I was going to do. Frank took one look at the dump and put me up at the Holiday Inn around the bend from his office. I told him I couldn't afford it, but he footed the bill.

So that's where I've been for the last ten weeks.

I stay at the Holiday Inn and Frank comes after work every weekday. He says his commute is too far to bring me to his house and he wouldn't want to take me there. I don't know why, but

I try not to press him. I suppose I learned that from observing Mom. Once, she made me hide out in the kitchen with her as we spoke in hushed tones in order to let Dad decompress in his study after a particularly upsetting day at work.

She told me, "Men don't like to be prodded when they are under pressure. He'll tell you what he's thinking when he feels the need to share. Just go about your business until then. He'll poke his head out of the turtle shell when he's ready."

Frank said he hasn't found the right woman. Last time he said that, he pinched the tip of my nose between two knuckles and kissed me hard on the lips. I know some men have a difficult time expressing themselves. Maybe he is trying to say I'm the right woman? I hope so. But I won't press him for an answer before he's ready.

He can never seem to have enough of me. It's hard to believe a thirty-four-year-old man is so full of desire and passion. He's shown me things I didn't even know were things until I met him. He must love me. I mean, I have never had a boyfriend so obsessed with my body, always telling me how soft my skin, how perky my breasts, how firm my ass. I've heard women's bodies change once they hit their thirties. I'm lucky I still have two whole months before I turn twenty. I've only been with one guy, in that way, and the only thing he concerned himself with was how high he could get to satisfy himself. Frank takes his time with me.

Every time I scrounge enough change to call home, Mom whisper-cries into the phone as if she just cannot bear to hear the sound of my voice. I forgot all about the whisper-cries, which would happen at the beginning and ending of every school year and whenever she watches *Miracle on 34th Street*. Dad just hounds me about my plans. All I want to do is tell them all about Frank, but I know better than to mention a man to my parents, who expect me to hold on to my virginity until my wedding night. Even though I know my parents would love Frank once they got to know him. He would fit the bill of being a "wonderful provider." I'd even be willing to have a baby for him if he wanted. Or three. I would make sure he had dinner on the table every night waiting for him. (Maybe I was too rough to pick on Mom for wanting those same things. The only difference is that I would have my own voice in our marriage. Frank hasn't seen just how strong-willed I can be. Well, not yet, anyway. But he will.)

Afterward, I would lead him up the long wraparound staircase of our magnificent home and serve him dessert in bed. We would make love and kiss each other's bodies all night with abandon. Then in the morning he would wake, and I would serve him breakfast and send him on his way with a long, deep kiss. He would pat my ass and tell me how he couldn't wait to escape all those boring people and stifling meetings and return home to my warm, wet body.

Sometimes when my parents invite the neighbors over for bridge and cocktails on Friday nights, I've heard them make quips about how things change when "the honeymoon is over." Frank and I have such incredible passion I know that won't happen to us. I'm going to make sure that never happens to us.

To Peace on Earth, love, happiness, kisses from the fairies of the forest, rock & roll, and true love!

Daisy Jane

11

Krystal

"Did you bring a smock, dear? I'd hate for you to ruin that pretty blouse." Goldie's words were soft and gentle, but the temperature in the air-conditioned room suddenly jumped several degrees. Krystal could already feel the judgment emanating from the watchful eyes of the other women like a hissing steam.

"I'm sorry. I . . . I didn't know I needed one."

"No matter. I have plenty in the back." Goldie wore the same easy smile she had the night they met at Jocelyn's. The one that made Krystal feel as though they were old friends. She imagined most people probably felt the same way upon meeting her.

"I don't suppose you have a craft knife or sponge in that pretty purse of yours." Goldie dropped her voice. The skin surrounding her eyes crinkled like gift wrap.

"There was a list of items to bring for class." A young, over-caffeinated girl waved a flyer in Krystal's direction. It was then that she noticed an odd array of unidentifiable tools in front of each of the women. The girl's smug smile was revelatory, and Krystal knew this was her abrupt introduction to the class know-it-all.

"I have plenty of everything. Don't you worry, honey." Goldie passed by, placing a flat palm on Krystal's right shoulder, delicately trailing it across the tender space just below her neck until reaching the other side. It was a comforting gesture that magically erased the embarrassment of turning up ill-prepared.

The women immediately resumed their own personal chit-chat. Krystal casually grazed their shoes and realized she was in a mixed crowd with both locals and tourists. You could tell a lot about a woman from her shoes. The visitors were easy to spot with their fancy sandals, so fresh and new, as though the cardboard inserts and tags had just been removed. One middle-aged woman (a local) was wearing designer knock-offs, which appeared to be about eight years old from the frayed edges around the toes and the scuffed heels. The know-it-all had on pretty lace-ups to show she was wise enough not to come overdressed yet stylish enough to still look cute. Krystal always preferred high heels because they were slimming and accentuated her calves and curves, but since she'd ridden her bicycle, she was wearing bedazzled platform flip-flops.

The three out-of-towners spoke to one another in hushed tones like giddy girls on the first day of school. The two other locals examined some of the merchandise displays, while the loudmouth took furtive glances at Krystal like a censorious old lady planted in the first pew. Suddenly, her loose-fitting summer tank top began to feel like a negligee.

"Where have I seen you before?" She pointedly addressed Krystal and introduced herself as Tara.

"I don't know. Been here my whole life." Her stomach did a somersault. This girl was too young to have been in her graduating class, but that didn't mean she didn't have older siblings or cousins, and everyone knew one another in this area. This is exactly why she was still fretful about being around strangers and learned never to reveal too much about her past or present life.

"You look *very* familiar. It's driving me crazy. I know I've seen you before."

Tara was unrelenting.

The Axelrods had been in the paper a few times over the past couple of years, once for a sizable donation Abe had made to the children's charity for education and then again while their home was being built in a two-page advertorial featuring Bruce's construction company. Krystal didn't think it was anyone's business that she was a real-life Cinderella.

"I know! You're married to that rich lawyer dude from Maryland. Right?" Tara said.

Her words, steeped in soupy gossip, perked the attention of all the other ears in the room. Abe was originally from New York, but Krystal wasn't about to correct this busybody.

"My husband's name is Abe."

"That is some house you got there!" Tara was now standing and turned to the other local, a slightly older woman. "Mary, this is the woman who just built that castle on the harbor."

Mary looked as if she was accustomed to exerting as much energy as a river toad; she jutted her bottom lip with complete disinterest. Her eyes drifted back to her own desk as she began picking at a caked-on piece of clay that looked as if it had been there since the Y2K debacle.

"What's your last name again?" Tara was at it again.

Now, even the three vacationers had ceased their conversation and were tuning in and sizing Krystal up. Scrutinizing. Even the fluffy white cat perched on the desk at the front of the room was gawking at her. Why did she come? Why did she think she would be able to fit in? Classroom settings had never been her thing.

As a child, her nemesis was the stale smell of cigarette smoke permeating her clothing and hair. She couldn't do much to hide it. Between her two parents, four packs were burned up daily, and her mother would often fall asleep on the couch with a lit cigarette, filling the small living space with a poisonous cloud of smoke. Krystal would carefully retrieve the burning stick from her mother's mouth and lightly stub it out while she snored away the afternoon. She did this for years, undetected, until the one time her mother caught her.

"How . . . *dare* . . . you."

The rage in her mother's voice was frightening as she dragged out each of the words. With expert precision, she wound an extended arm behind her head like a pinch hitter stepping up to the plate. The opened palm cocked well behind the other side of her mother's head left her with only one thought: *This is gonna hurt.* Not a moment later that open palm sailed through the air like a cannonball, landing on its target with precision: the entire left side of Krystal's face.

The cigarette odor became imbued into the cells of the tiny home—the walls, the area rugs, the curtains—much like the stench of unhappiness permeating her parents' dissatisfied marriage and unfulfilled lives. She had grown so accustomed to the putrid smell she wasn't able to detect it on herself. It actually disrupted the other kids in her class, who complained to the teacher. After several unanswered letters home, the principal finally got involved, asking Mrs. Boors to join him for a private conference in his office.

"You gonna tell me I cannot smoke in my own home? Just who in the hell do you people think you are?" Her mother's voice bounced against the heavy wooden door like angry knocking.

Krystal was sitting in the waiting area, listening to every hateful word slowly filling her with hot shame. The secretary smiled gently and motioned her toward the desk. Even at the tender age of eight, she knew the woman felt sorry for her having such a horrid and embarrassing mother. She offered her a hard candy, which Krystal gratefully accepted with both hands. The tangy burst of cherry distracted her for a few moments of bliss as she tried to drown out the sound of her mother spitting a torrent of vicious words. She could picture her scowling at the principal. At this stage of the rant, she would be on her feet.

Later that afternoon, Krystal was banished to her room without supper. Her mother had a way of punishing her for no good reason. She crawled on top of her comforter and cried herself to sleep. It wasn't the first time she'd gone to bed with an empty belly and an aching heart—and it wouldn't be the last.

Thankfully, Goldie returned, breaking up Tara's Spanish Inquisition.

"All righty, gang. Let's get started." She wheeled in a flatbed cart. "I went ahead and prepared a dough for each of you for time's sake. If anyone is interested, there are dittos up at the front with step-by-step instructions on how to make the clay. Feel free to grab one on your way out." She placed a large mound swaddled in a damp washcloth at each workstation.

"There are two principles when joining clay that will be useful to you if you keep them in mind as you work. The first is: the wetter the better." She made air quotes with her fingers with a wry smile, as if she were imparting sage wisdom. "The wetter the clay, the easier it will be to join. And the second is: join like to like." She used another set of air quotes. "The pieces being joined should be the same dampness." Krystal caught a flash of the little girl behind the long silver tresses cascading over Goldie's shoulders.

The women were instructed to peel back the damp cloth and acquaint themselves with the "hidden masterpiece," as Goldie put it. Krystal was daunted by the slimy lump of clay because of the huge wedding ring jutting out from her finger. She felt someone standing at her side.

"You may want to remove those." She indicated Krystal's rings and bracelets. "You want to protect your jewelry when you're throwing pottery."

Tara was like a television that someone left on in the other room. She never shut her trap, and all the women seemed inclined to flock to their new den mother for assistance. Krystal refused to pay homage to her. It was Goldie's class, after all. She tried desperately to follow her instructions and make sure she was doing it right. It was bad enough that she hadn't come prepared with the right materials or attire, and the last thing she wanted was to stick out even more by making a mistake. Every so often, she tried to think of an intelligent question, but when she would look up, she caught Goldie already peering at her, along with the white cat at her feet. She had no idea what could be going through this woman's mind, but she suspected that wasn't a good sign; surely, she wasn't wanted there.

As the others packed up their belongings, she tried to seize the opportunity to pay for the class, but Goldie was scurrying around the studio, popping in and out of the back room. At this rate, it seemed nearly impossible to catch the woman for a moment alone. She assumed cash would be preferred, knowing full well merchants took a hit on credit card payments, and decided to wait for the others to filter out first.

A second later, the fluffy white cat that had been inspecting Krystal leapt from the floor straight onto her lap. To stall for time, she pet the purring kitty for a while and then reached into her purse to apply a light coat of lip gloss. As she flipped open the compact, the reflection of Goldie standing at her back sent her heart into her throat.

"Do you have a few minutes to spare after class? I'd like to speak with you."

"Yes. Sure . . ." She was about to add "and I want to pay you," but Goldie was yet again sucked in by Tara, who ushered her toward the back of the room in what appeared to be some sort of deep and secretive conversation.

Every so often, the young girl's eyes would wander over to Krystal's direction. She felt queasy. Tara was the type of girl who would have laughed in her face right along with the other girls on the squad. She couldn't imagine what Goldie could possibly want to speak with her about. Maybe she was going to be lectured on proper attire or chastised for not coming prepared or asked not to return or questioned as to what she was doing there in the first place. Maybe Tara was telling her not to have her back to the class. Well, that was fine. She had no plans to return. Now all she had to do was figure out where to go next. Home was just a reminder of her failed night with that awful group of women posing as friends. And she could only imagine the foul glares she'd get from Pearl after the wine cooler incident. There was nowhere to go. The only person who wanted her around and cared enough (or at all, for that matter) spent half of his time in Maryland. She just needed to stop trying so hard and accept her situation for what it was—there was no place she belonged. Spending time alone was safer than opening herself up for ridicule and rejection. She had learned that lesson years ago. Being so loved by Abe had distracted her temporarily, but her reality would always be the same: the world was just one big, uninviting place.

"How about a cup of tea?" Goldie interrupted her exercise in self-loathing.

Tara whizzed past, heading for the front entrance. "See ya! Have a good day, ladies!" she called in an exaggerated pitch and volume more appropriate for a stage performance.

Goldie forced an exhale through the side of her mouth in a quick puff of air, causing her bangs to jump like a white curtain against an open window before slowly settling on her forehead strand by strand.

"That one sure is a handful, I tell you. She's more like her mother than I realized."

"Her mother?" Krystal asked.

"Gloria. She was my former tenant."

Krystal was more confused than ever. It must have shown on her face. "Tara is Gloria Eagle's daughter. That whole apple-tree theory holds true in this case."

"Oh. I see."

"I had no idea she was planning on taking the class. But I should have suspected as much. Of course that Gloria would wonder what I'm up to and just couldn't resist the urge to send her little spy."

Krystal felt herself relax a bit as she realized Tara's presence hadn't been welcomed to begin with.

"I can't seem to take my eyes from this necklace of yours. May I ask where you purchased it?"

"This?" Krystal fingered the long strand of shells and sea glass hanging around her neck. "I made it."

"You made it. Yourself?"

"Yeah." She could see Goldie was still incredulous and aiming for a closer look, as she swept back a tumble of hair behind her shoulder. "Your attention to detail is impeccable. I'm impressed."

Growing even more comfortable, Krystal told her about some of the other pieces she had created. As she spoke, Goldie's eyes waltzed to and fro.

"Would you like to join me at my home sometime this week for lunch?"

Krystal couldn't believe what she was hearing. "I'd love to. What can I bring?"

"Just yourself. And a bag of your creations. I'd love to see some of your treasures. I mean, if that's okay by you, of course."

The smooth timbre of her voice was as hearty as a crock of French onion soup.

"I can't wait."

Goldie faltered a bit, taking hold of the desk to maintain her balance, and blinked as if needing to adjust her focus. Krystal offered a helping hand but was rebuffed. She looked at Krystal, trying to place her, which was terrifying. It was the same behavior from the first night they met—as if she were disappearing.

"Sorry, dear. I'm fine. Just fine." She sounded as if she were trying to convince herself as well.

The only thing pervading Krystal's thoughts was: *Something is haunting this peculiar and extraordinary woman. What is it? Or who?*

12

Goldie

Goldie was beginning to wonder just how much of her temporary memory loss and vision problems were becoming apparent to others. More than once during the class she caught herself losing track of thoughts midsentence and had to continually repeat herself.

It's getting worse. Isn't it, my darling?

She felt her legs give way and grabbed hold of the chair in front of her. The room became topsy-turvy as her vision blurred. When she was in this place it was almost impossible to return, as if forcing herself awake from a nightmare. The only sound to be heard was Shirley's distressed mewing in the corner.

Over the last year, her vision and balance issues had become more prominent, Simon's voice ever louder. She wasn't able to tell reality from imagination. All she knew was that her body and mind were failing her.

A whiff of scotch.

Not now. Not here. Please disappear. She tried to quell his presence, letting her eyelids fall.

She was back in the past. Seated at her vanity in North Carolina. It was 1971. The morning of Patrick's funeral.

"What is that around your neck?" Simon had that admonishing edge to his tone, which made her blood pressure soar.

He stood at her back. She held his reflection in the mirror.

"This?" She touched the silver hummingbird and large pearl, her birthstone, at the end of the long, ropy chain.

"That belonged to my mother."

She swallowed. Saliva caught in her throat like a wedding ring on a knitted sweater.

His top lip curled as his face tightened. He began wringing his hands. His mother's chain was around Goldie's neck, and he was not happy about it.

"Patrick, I mean, your father gave it to me," she stammered.

"Well, it wasn't his to give."

His words and abrupt departure from the room flooded her with hurt. The sweet memory of the afternoon Patrick first surprised her with the timeless piece was dampened by her husband's distress. He had hand-selected the necklace from his wife's vast collection and watched with a smile as she fastened it around her neck, admiring the shiny daggerlike beak centered at her collar bone.

Simon hadn't asked for her to return the necklace, and he didn't have to. She could see how bothered he was by his father's gesture. Of course, it wasn't reasonable that he should hold her accountable for innocently receiving a gift—whether it belonged to his late mother or not—but she wasn't in any position to argue the point. He was steeped in resentment for his father.

Things had shifted with the three of them living under the same roof over the course of those few years. Patrick never curtailed his praise for Goldie, lauding her talents and projects freely at the dinner table in front of Simon. She remembered feeling uncomfortable seeing Simon's taut skin, his eyes averted when Patrick held up a vase that she had finished that afternoon.

"Would you just look at what your wife is able to do? Have you ever seen such skill?" The more Patrick pushed for a reaction, the quieter Simon became. She felt as though she'd been thrust to the epicenter of an awkward and strained dynamic between father and son. She started to see that Simon placed the blame on her for their issues. Their differences. He became closed off. When she would ask him about his work day or why he was so quiet at dinner, she was met with curt and cold responses. And he stopped inquiring about anything having to do with her and showering her with kisses upon his return home. She could see from his aloofness toward Patrick that he no longer wanted his father to live with them. And yet Simon couldn't provide the lifestyle his father was able to afford. Patrick was the one with the money. Once he waved a house at his son, there was no way he could turn it down. And he was in no position to ask his father to leave. Instead, he had to swallow the situation like a bitter pill while the acridity over his father and his wife's connection coalesced into a poisonous brew.

Something shifted in their marriage the day of Patrick's funeral. An invisible albeit icy wall had solidified between them. He knew how deeply Goldie cared for Patrick, but his better judgment was shrouded in jealousy. He could not and would not acknowledge his wife's bond with his father, which served as a reminder that the men had never shared such a connection.

At first, she wondered if things would change for the better in her marriage after Patrick's passing. Maybe Simon needed time to heal from his father's death. Maybe he would return to her as the guy she first met and fell in love with. Months passed. Then a year. The old Simon—the one who would sometimes surprise her by drawing a warm bath and offering her a glass of wine—never did return to her. No matter how many pieces her heart had splintered into, she knew she was never going to find solace or comfort in him, who had intimated that she was never a *real* daughter, and it was he who reserved the right to grieve as Patrick's only son.

"I just want to rule some things out. These balance and vision issues are of growing concern," Dr. Carroway said.

"Can't I just go see an eye specialist or something?"

She didn't mean to challenge the young woman, but sometimes she felt as though these spring chickens of the medical profession had something to prove. Goldie came from an era where the doctors were old men with hair sprouting from their ears and nose and an abundant supply of sage advice to dole out. They were not petite, attractive, vibrant, or female.

"A vision exam will only cover your eyes. I'd like to address some of my larger concerns." Goldie waited for the doctor to elaborate—she did not. "There's nothing to worry about."

Gee whiz. Thanks a whole bunch, Doc. Basically, there's nothing to worry about, until there is, she thought.

Sitting in that hideously drafty dressing gown, she lay on the table as the technician placed electrodes onto her scalp. If that weren't enough of a torment, the technician reassured her they were testing her brain's electrical activity. She was no scaredy-cat, but she wasn't comforted by the fact that the doctor was looking into anything having to do with the sanctity of her brain. She had to undergo an MRI. The last time she had the pleasure of experiencing one of those was right after Simon died; her life had become consumed by a series of wicked migraines, crippling her from accomplishing anything. Even walking to the bathroom was agonizing, as a stampede of wild boars felt as if it were crushing her skull. She tended to live by the "No news is good news" principle. Thankfully, the headaches had begun to wane after the test.

As she lay still on the cold metal surface, a chill ran up her backside. She hadn't remembered the test being quite this daunting, but then, she had been in so much throbbing pain the first go around it made sense that she wouldn't remember the details of the experience.

Goldie closed her eyes and tried to remain as still as possible. As she practiced her deep-breathing meditation, she became enveloped by fear mingled with a faint trace of scotch.

13

Jocelyn

Daisy had entered her dreams. Every night, as Jocelyn slipped into unconsciousness, she would find the mother-in-law she never met waiting for her in a vast field surrounded by flowers. As she approached, Daisy offered her hand to hold, and the two would begin their journey. Once she crossed the threshold from sleep to her waking state, she wasn't able to recall their conversations. But she awoke feeling uplifted, centered, whole. Throughout her day, Jocelyn found Daisy on the edge of her consciousness, dangling her feet like a child observing in wonderment. She could feel the tug on her awareness as Daisy called to her, ready for play. Of course, she could also feel the draw of real life pulling her out of her fantasies, forcing her to face reality.

Her stomach roiled as she kissed Bruce goodbye that morning. In Jeannie's email she had scheduled a mandatory Skype session with her editor, Nina, to review her progress (or lack thereof) and to discuss the ramifications of missing the last deadline. She'd been remiss and knew she'd have to work double time to make up for all the lost time.

Running her brush under the water, Jocelyn tried to slick her untamed hair to eliminate the windswept, carefree impression. Not much could be done about her bronzed skin and ruddy cheeks at this point. She held off on refilling her iced coffee, as the caffeine had already taken hold of her unsteady hand, and her heartbeat was as staccato as microwave popcorn.

Jeannie's face was the first to show up on Jocelyn's screen when she logged on to Skype. She looked professional and businesslike in an ivory silk shell underneath a navy-blue suit jacket. Her pale skin indicated her status as an overworked, undersunned city slicker holed up at the office like a prisoner in the middle of the summer.

"Well, hello, stranger. Look who it is. My long-lost Exit Zero novelist," Jeannie said. "You look like you just got back from a cruise in St. Tropez."

"Hi, Jeannie. I can assure you I did not."

Nina was next to join the session. "Sorry. My previous call ran late."

"That's okay, Nina. I need to keep this short and sweet as I have another appointment to get to, but this was too important not to squeeze in."

Jocelyn sat wide-eyed, knowing it was better to keep quiet until asked.

"Let's regroup, shall we? Nina, what is it you need and by when so we can get ourselves back on track here?" There was no love in Jeannie's voice.

"I'll need at least four weeks to review those last twenty chapters I've been waiting on. So . . ." Nina flipped her calendar. "I need them no later than August first."

"Jocelyn? Got that?"

"Got it. No problem. I'll get it done."

"Good. Because we will be in breach of contract if this is not turned in on time."

With that, Jeannie's face disappeared from the screen as she logged off the call. Jocelyn had never heard such hostility coming from her. It was unsettling, at best. She tried to drown out the scream in her head that was bemoaning the several all-nighters it would take to pull this off. But this situation belonged to her and her alone. She had had months to finish and next to nothing to show. This mess was of her own design.

The group session was, in fact, *short*, as Jeannie indicated, but there had been nothing *sweet* about it. She lowered the cover of her laptop in time with the lids of her eyes as the weight of the task chained her in place. A fly buzzed past her ear, landing on her sleeve. She flung it away in disgust. A wave of guilt washed over her for showing cruelty to her innocent friend. She was the one who deserved to be flicked away.

She thought of some of her author friends who were bestselling novelists and all seemed to have their shit pulled together. Some were parents of special needs children or had elderly family members to look after. A few had even been diagnosed with cancer and sustained major surgeries. Others had buried spouses, lost siblings, braved nasty custody battles, and prayed fervently for family members fighting in wars overseas. Yet despite their hardships, all had managed to meet their deadlines with no risk to their professional reputations (and no breach of their contracts).

She established a new rule: when she was in front of her laptop, she would be working. Right now, she needed to clear her head. She'd drunk the last of the wine the day before and needed to replenish inventory. She would give herself this one last day. Tomorrow, it was back to the grind. No more bullshit.

On her way into town, she passed two men digging out a driveway on a new construction project, which made her think of Bruce. She often wondered how he spent his workdays. When they first started dating, he'd taken her to a bunch of job sites.

What an honor it was to be on the arm of the youngest, most reputable contractor in town. Awash in the glow of newfound love, she would observe her boyfriend while remaining desperately smitten as he paraded around his crew.

Jocelyn yearned for the beginning stages of love when everything was fresh and new as in the waking days of spring. Those rare moments of magic when fingers touch ever so slightly, igniting an untamable fire within. When a lingering glance, a tender kiss sent a flood of thrilling sensations you'd forgotten existed until you were pulled in by the all-consuming hunger of love's tide.

Of course, there was much to be said for reaching new plateaus along the journey. She relished the comfort borne of matrimony. It was only since the start of summer, in Billy's absence, that she felt herself longing for the old days when Bruce would insist she join him on the road. She was saddened to learn that men seemed more eager to share the intricacies of their lives with their new girlfriends than with their new wives; she was starting to see that there were drawbacks to be had with every new achievement in life—including marital status.

She waited before crossing Ocean Street as the trolley rolled by, packed with tourists. Navigating the side streets in the summertime could be tricky; the traffic was one thing, but the biggest threat posed to bicyclists was getting clotheslined by the opening door of a parked car. Visitors weren't always aware that the narrow streets were designed to be shared and vehicles were expected to yield to bicyclists and pedestrians.

Upon reaching Little Birdie Studio, Jocelyn spotted a gawky teenage boy with an underbite stationed in front of an advertisement offering ten-percent-discount coupons for a two-day sale. That was a first. Goldie seemed keen on drumming up business, which was understandable given the circumstances. She wondered if the poor woman was going to make it now that Gloria Eagle had taken off.

As she meandered over to the opened door, some vacationer barked orders at her husband with an armful of shopping bags. Embarrassed by the charade, she felt a set of eyes peering at her from inside the studio.

"Why, hello there." Goldie had that same warm, welcoming smile she'd always worn.

"Nice to see the place in full swing," Jocelyn said, watching another three customers enter the store.

"Sure makes me happy."

Goldie was distracted. She kept looking down to address the cat nibbling on her shoelaces. She wondered what Bruce would think of his friend allowing her pets to roam freely in a place of business. When she thought of his reaction the night Goldie wigged out at their home, she remembered being unable to get through to Bruce as she and Krystal tried to explain what they'd witnessed; he wasn't really tuning in. Even in her tipsy state, Jocelyn knew she and Bruce had both done more than their share that night and the subject was best dropped.

"Pardon me, just one moment, dear." Goldie turned her attention to a customer looking at a set of mugs on the shelf. "May I help you?"

To keep herself occupied, Jocelyn awkwardly pretended to browse. She picked up a wizard dressed in a purple cape, wearing a large hat painted with bright yellow stars and moons. Some heavily perfumed visitor with a thick Philly accent bumped into her, sending the wizard soaring into the air. It landed hard against the concrete floor and fractured into several pieces. Jocelyn stared down at the long pointy hat and wand now separated from the man. She trembled.

Goldie and the customer she'd been tending to were beside her in an instant.

"Oh, *shit*," the woman said.

Jocelyn was about to lose it, but she stopped herself—freaking out on one of Goldie's paying customers would be like punishing a sick child.

"I . . . I am so sorry." Jocelyn's voice was limp, weak, pathetic.

"That's all right. These things happen." Goldie grabbed the dustpan.

The woman who had bumped into Jocelyn left the store without saying a word or making a purchase, which made her want to crawl into a pile of dirt.

"It's not all right. I must pay you for that. I'm terribly sorry."

"No need. Really." She swept the broken limbs and body into the pan. "See? All gone."

"Goldie, please let me pay you. I know your pieces are irreplaceable. I won't be able to live with myself if you don't let me try and make this up to you."

She seemed to be listening without a budge to her deflated smile. Jocelyn didn't know what to make of these expressions. Whether it was lack of interest or distrust, it was as if Goldie deemed her to be disingenuous, and she could think of nothing worse. She may have her anxieties and neurotic tendencies, but one thing she was not was a damn phony.

"You pulled off a lovely evening." Goldie changed the subject. "Simply lovely. I don't know if Bruce told you, but I enjoyed myself immensely."

"Oh, thank you. I'm glad you did. I love planning events."

"Bruce tells me you're quite the cook as well."

"I do love to cook. And bake. If I wasn't a writer, who knows . . . I probably would have been a chef or baker or event planner or something. They say the average adult changes careers about three times in her lifetime. Of course, I love being a mom too. But I guess you can be anything you want and still be a mom. I mean . . . within reason, I suppose." Jocelyn knew she was rambling and hated herself for coming undone. Why did this woman make her so self-conscious, as if she had something to prove?

"You have a lovely home. Perfectly constructed. And the new kitchen is divine."

"Yes. Bruce is good."

"They don't come better, m'dear. Of that, I can assure you," she said, wearing that enigmatic smile once again. Jocelyn wasn't sure if she was referring to Bruce the contractor or Bruce the man, but she found herself wanting to get off the subject.

"How are your new classes working out?"

"So far so good." Goldie turned on her heel and swept a lock of her long silver hair over one shoulder.

After a few minutes, Jocelyn called to the back to say good-bye, but she received no response. She had a pretty good handle on the many layers to a character; her instincts told her Goldie Sparrows was about as complex as they came.

Returning home, she entered the kitchen and realized that with all the hoopla she hadn't properly thanked Goldie for the sensational olive dish she'd made. How absentminded could she be? Not only did she bust a piece of merchandise, she forgot to thank her for the gift.

Jocelyn plopped into the chair at her desk with a full glass of wine. Her computer glowered at her while she sipped. For a lifeless piece of equipment, it could be as disapproving as a toddler amidst a tantrum. She could fool her husband and friends about the tally of her daily word count or the hours spent on editing, but the laptop was all-knowing. There was no hiding behind cleverly sculpted lumps of horseshit on her progress.

By her third trip into the kitchen for a refill, she had an impulse to call Trevor.

"I want to speak to my son."

"He's not here. Hannah took the kids to the arts and crafts fair, and then they're stopping off at the museum."

"Boy oh boy. She sure likes to keep busy."

"It's important for us to expose the kids to all sorts of new experiences. And since Billy is here, what better way than to see new things with his siblings?"

All Jocelyn heard was "us" and "siblings," an equation that did not include her. She was being squeezed out of his life.

"Did you check out the link I sent you on the school?" Trevor asked.

"Of course not. He's not going to a private school in another state away from his mother. That is out of the question."

She forced an exhale and topped off her wine.

"I tell you what. I think it's best if we talk about this in person. It's only a few weeks before I drop Billy off at the ferry station. We can talk then," he said.

"There's nothing to discuss."

"You always insist on doing things the hard way, don't you? Okay. Have it your way."

"Is that a threat? Just what are you saying?" She did the two-step over the words as she tried to articulate.

"Are you okay? You don't sound right."

"Of course I'm not okay! The father of my son is threatening to steal him from me!"

"Okay. I can see you are incapable of carrying on a dignified conversation. You know what, maybe changing this custody arrangement is the smartest idea I've ever had. Maybe I don't want my son living with a lunatic who can't seem to get through one simple conversation without flying off the rails!"

Her heart slammed against her ribcage. She lowered her voice to keep from crying. "Trevor. *Please*."

"This conversation is over."

Her life was spiraling out of control. She had no power over anything.

She headed for the basement to be with the one person who could console her. She and Daisy were kindred spirits. Both mothers with one son. And both had become pregnant out of wedlock. Such journeys bonded women in ways men could never understand.

~Journal of Daisy Jane Anderson~
Winter 1976

Things are good again, but last week was the worst week of my whole life. I cried so much my eyes burned. The last time my face was that swollen, I was three sangrias in before realizing there was cantaloupe mixed in with the medley of fruit. (Cantaloupe, or any melon for that matter, has always been my kryptonite.) And, as I found out, so are married men.

Last week Frank and I were in our place—Room #101. We had just finished our second round of sex. Every time after he finishes, he jumps from the bed and runs off to the shower even though we usually end up doing it a couple more times. He says he doesn't like feeling sticky and dirty and not fresh. I can't really understand that. I thought girls cared more about that kind of stuff. Anyway, he was in the shower, and I spotted something by his pile of change on the nightstand, peeking out from his wallet. It was a ring. A gold band. When I asked him about it, he got very quiet. I knew right away. "I'm a married man, Daisy."

When I asked him why he'd told me that he never found the right woman, he said, "Well, that's true. My wife isn't the right woman for me."

He seemed surprised and defensive that this would upset me as much as it did. And he didn't know how to console me. It was as if he was afraid to come near me once I learned the truth and started hyperventilating. (Either that or he just didn't give a crap.) I got dressed and ran from the room. He didn't even call after me. Didn't even bother trying to follow me or explain the situation. Hours passed, which turned into days. There was no way for me to contact him. I knew where he worked, but he made it clear from the beginning that calling him at the office was not a "wise idea." Plus, I needed to save my change for calling home. I was starting to hate him. I mean, really, really hate him. And then, he made everything better again.

I received a bill under the door indicating that it was time for me to check out. I was panicked. I tried the front desk for more information, but it was late at night and some kid named Jed was covering the phones, and he didn't know me or Frank and had no idea how to assist. I was confused. And hurt. But mostly furious. And then the front desk called, interrupting my tear-filled eruption. The room was being covered for another two weeks. And! There was a letter waiting for me, which they delivered to my room.

In his note, Frank explained how sorry he was that he'd hurt me. While he never blatantly lied to me about the situation, he admitted to "lying through omission." He said his wife was sick. Not physically, but mentally. "She's not right in the head," as he put it. "She needs me. I can't just leave her. We have no life together, but there's no one else. No one to look after her. I can't just leave, baby. Please understand. She's likely to do something crazy." He continued, but my mind was a blur from all the information. He did make it perfectly clear that he felt "immeasurable remorse" about the whole thing.

It made me love him even more. To see this beautiful man so devoted to a woman he had virtually no marriage with and to watch him so torn between caring for her and his love for me. I was overwhelmed. I realized how immature and selfish I was being. I couldn't do that to him. I had to consider Frank's positions and be supportive. The next day, I saw him at the minimart. He was waiting there for me at noon just as he promised he would in his letter. We made love all afternoon and into the early evening. We took a bubble bath together and ordered room service.

I asked him about his sick wife, but he reassured me she was covered so we could have this time together. I was tempted to know her name, but I knew I'd only obsess about it, so it was better not to know the details. I also knew it would make her seem all the more real to me, and I didn't need the guilt.

Frank explained that even though he cannot commit himself to me through marriage at the moment, he wanted me to know how much he loves me. Everything seems to be falling right into place. I am so happy I could cry. I never pictured myself falling in love with a married man, but some things are just meant to be. Who knows what will become of his wife? Frank makes it sound like she is on her last leg and doesn't have much time left. I would never wish anyone dead. And I don't. I just hate not having him all to myself.

Last night, after a few glasses of whiskey, Frank admitted something to me. He said his wife was unable to have children due to her poor health, but becoming a dad was always a part of his lifelong dream. It was then that I realized why we'd met—I am supposed to be the one to provide him with a child. Even if he doesn't know it yet. Men take a while to come around to things like this. My mom always said females were more mature. Maybe he would even consider leaving his wife if I became pregnant with his child. Who knows? I'm not saying I'm hoping for that—well, maybe I am. But I'd never tell anyone such a thing.

To Peace on Earth, love, happiness, kisses from the fairies of the forest, rock & roll, true love, and babies!

Daisy Jane

14

Krystal

As Krystal rummaged through the old boxes from her child-hood and younger years, she had a vision of the closets from her past. While she was growing up, the linen closet in her parents' small house didn't have a door. The shelves were disorganized, and crap was always spilling out onto the floor, forcing anyone passing through the hallway to step over the pile of junk. Eventually, her mom was sick of looking at the messy shelves, but not enough to purge its contents. When Krystal returned from school one day, she found an old bedsheet rid-dled with moth holes and unidentifiable stains tacked with pins above the door frame. She was forced to walk past the ratty sheet dozens of times a day. After her parents died, she'd spent weeks cleaning out the contents of the space in an effort to make it presentable for showing. She'd never forget the feeling she had as she approached the unsightly closet for the last time. She stretched her arms up and balled her hands into tight fists as she twisted the fabric. The laughter of some of the neighborhood kids echoed down the hallways of her memory. *Why does your mom staple bedsheets to the wall?* With all the fury and strength she could muster, she shut her eyes, ripping the fabric clear off the wall. Decades-old particles of paint and sheetrock rained down upon her head, catching in her hair. The tacks clicking against the floor all around her was a victorious sound, one she had only fantasized about when struck with the urge to lash out in defiance against her mean and punishing mother. It was an exhilarating moment, which left her feeling empowered, vindicated, and emotionally depleted.

Krystal vowed her future closets would be pristine and orderly. The one from her first apartment was organized, but the door hadn't closed properly because the track was all rusted out. One of the first things she did, before she even painted the place, was spend a chunk of her paycheck to replace the track for a proper door.

When she was working on the layout of the new house with Bruce, she made sure to include several closets to organize by theme: bath and hand towels, beach items, soap and toothpaste, bedding and pillows. It wasn't until marrying Abe Axelrod that she discovered one large closet would be dedicated solely to storing suitcases. He loved to travel and surprised her with a full Louis Vuitton luggage set before their honeymoon so she could travel "in style."

Krystal used the massive bag to bring some of her more delicate creations to Goldie's, which was the safest way to transport them without risk of breakage. Delicately, she wrapped napkin rings, plant holders, and wind chimes in tissue paper and placed each item inside the bag. Next, she needed to get dressed and find any pair of shoes with less than a four-inch heel. There was a box tucked in the back of her walk-in containing a pair of Tory Burch flats that were given to her by the wife of Abe's business partner for Krystal's last birthday. They were expensive and lovely and far too fancy, costing more than she'd ever deem appropriate for footwear—especially *flats*, of all things. Krystal slipped a cotton sundress over her head and found a passable pair of black flip-flops she wore on her beach walks. She coated her lips with a light shade of gloss, taking great care not to apply too much mascara or foundation, considering it was daytime.

As she emerged from the elevator near the kitchen, rolling the massive suitcase in tow, Pearl was standing at the sink scrubbing a pot. She shut the faucet, wiped her hands on her apron, and faced Krystal.

"I didn't hear anything about a trip," she said sternly.

Krystal resented that she was made to feel like a little child around this woman, small even.

"I have a lunch date with the owner of Little Birdie Studio at her home. She asked to see some of the things I made over the last year."

"Pardon me? Oh, never mind. Enjoy." Pearl turned her back, flipped on the faucet, and resumed her washing.

She hated not being taken seriously by Pearl and wished Abe would set the old woman straight, but she needed her energy, and now was not the time for such thoughts.

Goldie Sparrows's yard was the epitome of organized chaos. There were several large water fountains positioned inside the wrought-iron gate. Two cherubs and a Buddha in the lotus position seemed to be the keepers of this grand garden, as if awaiting the arrival of the Dalai Lama himself. Brimming with colors and various plants, the yard was about twenty by twenty feet and overrun by greenery and lawn ornaments. The most eye-catching section was the vibrant array of flowers, over which at least a dozen butterflies floated as if under some sort of spell.

"That's one heckuva bag," Goldie called down from the porch. "You're not moving in, are you?"

Krystal looked up at her, squinting in the sunlight.

"This was the safest way for me to transport my pieces," she said apologetically.

"Oh, honey. You're gonna have to get used to my looney bird humor. I'm way more silly than I am serious, if you haven't guessed that by now. Come on up. May I help you with that?"

Krystal politely declined and began her ascent up the staircase. The two fluffy cats from the studio were buzzing up and down the lemonade porch. One jumped from the perch on the banister and began brushing up against Krystal's bare arms, clearly looking for a head scratch. She recognized it as the same cat who jumped on her lap at the end of class.

"I believe you two have met," Goldie said. "This is Laverne. Something tells me you'll be seeing a lot of each other." Addressing the cat, she said, "You have taken quite a liking to Mrs. Axelrod, haven't you, little one?"

The other cat seemed more discerning as she weaved in and out of Krystal's legs.

"Shirley's just trying to place you. Pay her no mind. If she gets on your nerves, feel free to tell her to scat." Now, addressing the other cat, she said, "You haven't been feeling like yourself lately, my sweet girl, have you now?"

Goldie slowly opened the creaky screen door, and Krystal followed. It took her a split second to realize she was entering some sort of living area. There were so many knickknacks all over the place she didn't know where to look first. The home was filled with sparrows. Not live ones, but birds made of clay in every shape, color, and size imaginable. An army of sparrows standing two feet tall lined the hallway, holding swords like the Knights Templar. Each of the eleven was adorned with armored shields engraved with a different word: *Powerful, Productive, Friendly, Persistent, Integrity, Simplicity, Caring, Creativity, Vigilant, Communal, Empowerment.*

In the living room, stacks of magazines and how-to booklets

were centered on the hearth, surrounded by little clay sparrows riding unicycles.

"Did you make all these?" Krystal asked.

"I most certainly did. The symbol of the sparrow reflects the self-worth we should feel for ourselves regardless of external factors. This energy and passion are embedded deep within our hearts, waiting to be awakened."

Krystal looked on in awe. It would have taken her the better part of a day to appreciate the level of detail in each one. Across the mantel, a choir of sparrows was perched in front of pedestals with opened sheets of music.

"These little songbirds want us to sing our soul's own song just as they do. They inspire us to love ourselves. The sparrow spirit guide also symbolizes other joyful and caring qualities, such as creativity, community, friendliness, and the importance of simplicity."

As Krystal's eyes darted from bird to bird, the wet snoot of a huge boxer sniffed the back of her knees before proceeding to lap the lotion from her bare legs with long strokes of his enormously wet tongue.

"Knock that off, Brutus. Our guest is freshly showered. She certainly doesn't need your slobber, silly boy."

Goldie had a way of speaking to her animals as if they could understand her soft demands, and yet somehow, they seemed to do just that; Brutus promptly put his tongue back where it belonged.

"Come along. We'll set up in my studio. I've cleared the table for us."

Krystal followed as instructed. Just as she was trying to gain her bearings, she was startled by a piercing avian screech coming from the other end of the hallway.

"Now, now, Malcolm. Behave yourself, Mister," Goldie chanted.

They entered an alcove with an impressive cage holding a large grey parrot of some sort. He was preening himself as the ladies approached and stopped at the sight of Goldie.

"Would you like to introduce yourself, Malcolm?"

"Pretty boy, Malcolm. Pretty boy. Hello. Goldie's home."

Krystal was stunned. "He recognizes you?"

"Sure does." Goldie beamed. "Malcolm, this is Krystal Axelrod. Can you say *hello*?"

The bird bobbed his head and stuck to the script he knew well. "Pretty boy, pretty boy. Goldie's home."

"Wow. I can't believe that," Krystal said.

Goldie reached into the large produce bag dangling from her arm, pulled out a handful of fresh greens, and tossed them into the cage.

"Is that *kale*?" Krystal asked.

"Sure is. My handsome young man needs his calcium. All greys do." As the bird started chomping on the leafy greens, Goldie whispered, "Be back soon, Malcolm." She ushered Krystal out of the alcove.

Once they were out of Malcolm's view, Goldie said in a hushed tone, "I didn't want him to hear. He can be awfully sensitive and a bit on the proud side when it comes to his vocabulary. Malcolm has the ability to recognize my face by matching it to my voice. His bird brain is making the association and regurgitating the words he has heard me say over the years." She paused, waiting for Krystal's acknowledgment. Krystal nodded and Goldie continued. "But, please, he considers himself to be highly intelligent. This is never to be discussed in his presence."

In a flash, Goldie's mood shifted from solemn back to sunny, and she continued her effervescent saunter down the hallway. However endearing the treatment of her pets, Krystal was beginning to question Dr. Dolittle's sanity.

The in-house studio looked as if the animals had been left

in charge of the straightening. There were bolts of fabric, boxes of glaze, and paintbrushes everywhere. The oblong white table in the center of the room was bare, save for a plastic covering. Krystal took her time removing each item from the suitcase, placing each one with great care. Goldie listened wide-eyed as Krystal explained in detail how she came up with the ideas and the processes she learned on her own through research and by trial and error.

The first step in bleaching the seashells involved covering them in a pot of cold water. She added two tablespoons of chlorine bleach to one cup of water. Once it reached a roiling boil, the heat was dropped to a simmer for five minutes.

"Not only is chlorine a powerful bleach, but it also serves to loosen the lime substances and other discolorations that stick to the surface of the shell," Krystal explained. "Since their color is built into the structure, it is not affected by the bleach."

Goldie was fascinated by the loose shells, examining each one carefully.

"The second step is to coat each shell lightly with baby oil using a soft watercolor brush. You can also use mineral oil, if you want. I let the oil soak in overnight and then wipe off any excess with a cotton cloth or crumpled up paper towel." Krystal picked up one of the shells. "This wasn't as brightly colored when I found it on the beach. I try and stay away from the ones that are too sun-bleached. They can be somewhat improved but won't come out perfect."

"How do you get them to stick together so well?" Goldie asked.

"Epoxy cement. It binds nonporous materials together permanently, like shells to glass, metal, plastic, wood, or shell to shell. Oh! And you have to be really careful with this stuff. I always wear gloves. I saw a few You Tube videos, and someone actually glued her fingers together and had to have them surgically separated. Can you imagine?"

"I cannot. And the jewelry is exquisite. How on earth did you manage to insert these tiny clasps into the sea glass like that?"

"With this little gadget." Krystal retrieved an electric drill from her canvas bag. It was the shape of a gun with a pistol grip and trigger release. "The bits are removable and come in several thicknesses. The best surface to work on is a half-inch-thick cork tile. It absorbs vibrations and minimizes the danger of shattering the shell. Unfortunately, I learned that the hard way.

"I start off by marking the shell where I want the hole to be. A fine drill bit will pierce the shell's surface faster and cleaner than a thicker one. I start off on slow speed and apply light pressure, increasing both depending on the quality and composition of the shell. Once a good indentation has been made, I lift up the bit, put a drop of water into the depressions, then drill away until the hole is made all the way through. For larger holes, I'll either rock the drill bit around the edges or just replace the bit with a larger one."

Goldie rubbed her finger over the surface of a seashell.

"For these guys, I drill from the inside out so there's less chance of cracking. The one time I drilled from the convex side, the drill slipped and cracked the shell in half."

Krystal raised the drill in her hand.

"This thing has been a godsend. I'd never be able to create half of these pieces without it."

"You are extraordinarily talented, my dear," Goldie said. "I am overwhelmingly impressed. You have certainly done your homework."

It was one thing to have someone relish Krystal's work and creativity, but Goldie was validating her as a creator, an inventor, a professional. It was the merit she so desperately craved when she'd had the women over for the gathering, and yet this was altogether several steps above. Goldie led Krystal onto the lemonade porch for raspberry tea, crudités with hummus, and cucumber finger sandwiches.

"You must be wondering why I brought you all the way over here today when you could have been enjoying this beautiful day at the beach," Goldie said.

"I get plenty of sun as is. I was excited to come here."

"I mentioned my tenant has vacated her post. Gloria Eagle. Well, I'd like to offer her section of the store to you."

"What?"

"Those items you create are one of a kind. These are just the type of treasures tourists look for on their beach vacations. Think of the crowds we could draw with your handcrafted gems. You can keep all your earnings. I'll just need to charge some rent for the floor space."

Krystal was stunned. She tried not to cry from joy. As she dabbed at the corners of her mouth and tried to speak, she thought she just might. Goldie jumped up from the wicker rocker, causing Brutus to jump up, stand at attention, and wag his tail.

"Then it's settled. Come to the store first thing tomorrow morning and we'll clear some shelf space."

"Sounds great. I'll bring the coffee," Krystal said, still stunned and fumbling for words.

"No need, dear. We have a coffeemaker in the back. But so long as you're stopping, an everything bagel with a thin layer of vegetable cream cheese wouldn't be the worst thing in the world." Goldie winked. "And we'll need a spot for you in the back. . . ." Her eyes drifted across the yard. She tucked an index finger under her nose in deep contemplation.

"In the back?"

"The back of the studio. . . ." Goldie turned to face her. "You'll need your own workspace, at once."

Krystal couldn't believe what she was hearing. Even with

all the visualizing she had been practicing through her Law of Attraction studies, she never imagined things could turn out this promising.

"Okay then. We'll seal the deal." Goldie stood and opened her arms.

For a kid who had never been hugged, Krystal wasn't used to such open displays of affection. The sentiment caught in her throat as she allowed herself to be swept into an embrace.

"I knew there was something special about you." Goldie's pool-blue eyes twinkled as she spoke.

"Me?"

"You. I have an eye for these things."

Goldie held onto Krystal's arm, as they took careful and deliberate steps down the staircase and headed into the butterfly garden at the helm of the yard. A patch of grape-violet flowers stood out against the backdrop of the gold-and-yellow black-eyed Susan.

"What's this one called?"

"*Buddleja davidii*. That's my Black Knight. Beautiful, isn't he?"

"Very."

"Would you look at that!" Goldie pointed to an orange-and-black butterfly sitting on the tip of a flower petal.

"Which one is that?"

"That is a monarch. It's a little early in the season, but I always have at least one standing watch over my garden."

It was easy to see Goldie's preoccupation with her plants. The butterfly garden was hypnotic. Krystal could have sat there all day. Just behind the Black Knight, she noticed a patch of dark purple berries encased in a tight wired netting. The glossy sheen made them appear juicy, tempting her to pluck one and eat it straight from the vine.

"Wow. Those look scrumptious. Are they sweet?"

"Heavens, no!" Goldie said, startling both Krystal and Laverne, who ran for cover in the shade of a juniper bush. "Apologies, dear. I didn't mean to frighten you. This is my belladonna, or as the Italians would call her, *beautiful woman*. One must not be fooled: tempting as she is, she will strike a man dead in one swallow."

"Oh my God," Krystal said, puzzled as to why Goldie would keep such a lethal plant around.

"That's why I keep her secure, away from animals and humans."

As they approached the belladonna for a closer look, Krystal noticed the padlock secured in the front of the small cage.

"Let's just say, this beauty keeps the Black Knight in line."

Goldie's expression was indescribable. Almost . . . wicked. Not like Goldie at all. Her eyes flickered as if communicating with the plant. Krystal was flooded with chills and so immersed she hadn't noticed the barking. Brutus was at their backs and sprang to life in a bluster of noisy exuberance.

Jocelyn Anderson stood silently, holding a small gift package, a splash of bright and cheery ribbons streaming from the top, belying the deflated look on her face.

Goldie's arms fell. Her lips parted. She straightened her posture. Krystal suddenly felt as if she'd been caught in flagrante delicto.

"Hi, ladies," Jocelyn said.

The air between them was suddenly stale and musty, like that ratty old sheet that hung from the hallway of Krystal's youth.

"I felt awful about the other day and what happened in the store," Jocelyn said. Her chin fell a few inches as she looked up at Goldie with remorse. "I baked a few dozen batches of my zucchini bread. I hope you like walnuts." She placed the bread into Goldie's arms.

"How kind. . . ." Something about Goldie's mood had turned as damp as a wet swimsuit.

"I didn't realize it until later: I never properly thanked you for the stunning olive dish. I use it constantly. I cannot get over how beautiful it is. That must have taken you forever to make."

"Well, it certainly didn't take forever, I can assure you." Goldie scoffed.

"I'm only too sorry about the wizard. I wish you'd let me pay you for him," Jocelyn said.

"Accidents happen," Goldie said dismissively.

Krystal didn't know where to look, so she fixed her eyes on the free performance of the dancing butterflies. Brutus had given up on Jocelyn once she paid him no mind, but he was now back licking the rest of the lotion from Krystal's other leg. Laverne plopped herself onto her feet and began digging her nails into the top of Krystal's sandals. Goldie treated her animals well, perhaps even too well. They were sweet and lovable and spoiled beyond redemption.

"I accidentally broke one of Goldie's masterpieces in her shop yesterday," Jocelyn said, addressing Krystal.

"Oh. I'm—"

"He certainly wasn't a masterpiece," Goldie said, cutting Krystal off. "A lump of clay and oil glaze does not a man make. If there was a pulse, a heartbeat, then there'd be cause for remorse."

The women locked eyes. Krystal removed her hand from the top of Brutus's head, not knowing where to rest her eyes.

15

Goldie

Goldie had a hard enough time these days staying focused on any one topic and was beginning to feel dizzy. This unexpected visit from Jocelyn was not only ill-timed but an intrusion. Wishing for an escape, she walked the perimeter of the yard, allowing the girls a chance to blather on without her participation.

Three days earlier, Goldie had met with Bruce at the Salt Water Café.

"I don't want to say anything yet, but I am about to close a deal on an excavator," he told her.

She loved watching Bruce's excitement.

"I pay those guys one thousand per day: five hundred to rent the equipment and another five for the operator. My next three projects will require excavation. I'm already making out on the deal. It's gonna cost, but if I can throw enough cash down, I can easily manage the financing over the next ten years."

"You've worked hard. You've earned this. You should be darn proud of yourself. I know I certainly am."

Bruce smiled wide. "Mom helped big time."

Goldie sat quietly, careful not to interrupt.

"I'm going to share something with you that only my wife knows," he said.

Goldie pressed the tips of her index finger and thumb into one corner of her mouth and slid across her lip crease in a zipper action. Bruce giggled—that ever-present little boy who was never far from the surface.

"Mom had this old music-jewelry box thingy. It was in pretty decent shape, but the gears were busted. It hadn't played music in years. She loved the damn thing. I never understood why she kept it. She used to say, 'You don't throw away things that were once close to your heart just because they're no longer beautiful or they no longer work, Brucie.'

"Anyway, the week after her funeral I was clearing out her bedroom and I found the old music box tucked into her pajama drawer. It caught me by surprise. I hadn't seen it work in years, and there it was. Something inside me broke open."

Bruce's voice got snagged on the last word. He coughed and took a sip of black coffee.

"I couldn't throw it out. I just couldn't. I decided right then and there I would take it to a repair shop and have the gears replaced. Good thing I checked inside before I dropped that stupid thing off. I found a tiny envelope with my name on it tucked inside."

A cluster of patrons entered the café, diverting his attention for a moment. Goldie leaned in so Bruce could keep his voice low.

"Inside there was a piece of paper with the code for a combination lock. I had no idea what it was for. I mean, it's not like she left instructions or clues of any sort." Bruce shook his head. "That was Mom for ya. Everything was a damn mystery. A scavenger hunt. A couple of days later, I found the safe tucked into the back of her closet. So I plugged in the code, and it popped right open."

He paused. Looked around once again.

"It was filled with cash."

You did right by him, Goldie thought. *You did the right thing.* She could feel her heart smiling.

"Your mother sounds like she loved you very much and wanted to be sure you would always be cared for," Goldie said.

"It wasn't like winning the lottery or anything, but it definitely doesn't hurt having that money. I'll need more to make this purchase, but I have Jocelyn now. Once she gets her advance, we'll be able to afford this with no problem."

"This is wonderful news."

"I just don't know how the hell Mom did it. I never really thought of how she made it all work. It's not like she made that much with her measly part-time jobs. But it meant the world to me. I just wish I had a chance to say thank you. You know?"

"Bruce." Goldie laced her hand over his sinewy forearm. "You just did."

He smiled. "Mom always believed in guardian angels. 'Fairies of the light,' she called them. She said if I were ever in need, all I had to do was believe. 'Whatever you do, baby, never ever stop believing,' she would say."

"You were raised by a wise woman."

"She was. But I never gave her credit for that. When you're a kid, you try so hard to fit in and all. The last thing you want is to stick out or be different in any way. And it's one hundred times more embarrassing if your parent is the one who comes across like some sort of a kook. Having a silly parent only draws more attention to you, which can be terrifying when you're a skinny kid with a gaping hole between your two front teeth and your face looks like a slice of pizza with the cheese ripped off."

Bruce's good looks came naturally to him. He was so strikingly handsome Goldie had a hard time picturing this awkward teen he was describing. She had never remembered him looking like that. She hung on his every word, waiting for any information he might choose to share.

"Then you grow up and you realize the opinion of others and a quarter will buy you a stick of chewing gum. I didn't fully appreciate her until it was already too late. I can't help but think of all those years wasted. All those times she kept smiling even as I rolled my eyes at the crazy things she said or the thousands of kisses I wiped off my cheek when we were in front of my friends. Makes me feel like shit when I really think about it."

"It's not fair for you to burden yourself with this guilt. You don't deserve it, and it isn't something your mom would want you to be focusing on. Little boys aren't supposed to know such profound things about anything, especially their mothers. Such wisdom is what makes a man, and that requires time and a heap of life experience."

Bruce insisted on picking up the check, which she graciously accepted, knowing the gesture meant more to him than her in that moment.

As she spun the digits on her bicycle lock, she heard the brakes of Bruce's truck squeak behind her.

"Hey, Gold, can I ask you something?"

She turned to face him and straightened. "Anything."

"You think she can hear it?"

"Hear it?"

"The music. I mean, Mom. You think she can hear the music box? Now that I fixed it?"

Goldie couldn't feel the wind, and yet she knew it was there from the rocking of the charter boats anchored at the dock, just as she could detect Simon's presence from the chill now trailing each side of her bare neck. Some ghosts lingered at the threshold between realms, demanding to be remembered.

"I believe she dances with life every time you raise the lid."

Bruce's dark shades may have hidden the sadness tucked

deep inside those baby blues, but they weren't able to conceal the emotion revealed by the tensing of his pronounced jaw.

"You are going to make some lucky child very happy one day, Little Birdie."

She could have been a mother. But her body had other plans. Goldie's visits with Bruce, while wonderful and awe-inspiring, gnawed at her. And she knew part of making her peace with it was to forgive herself for not giving Patrick a grandchild. She'd have given him the world if she could, and deep down she had to believe, wherever he was, he knew that.

A shower of rain pulled Goldie from her reverie. Krystal and Jocelyn ran from the fenced-in yard as the automatic sprinklers kicked on. Goldie's running days were long over, but she managed to amble across the slick blades of grass just a few paces behind them without slipping. The women roared with laughter once they reached the patch of concrete at the foot of the stairs.

"Whoopsie," Goldie said. "I guess I didn't realize how late it was getting. The sprinklers are set to kick in post-lunch, pre-suppertime. Here, let me get you two some towels."

"Oh, no. We're fine. It actually feels good," Jocelyn said, wiping water down her arms. "It was getting pretty hot out there."

"You kidding? I was sort of hoping that would happen," Krystal said, shaking off her glitzy sunglasses.

They all laughed. Goldie liked being in the company of those who didn't take themselves too seriously. A blunder like this would have sent Gloria Eagle into a tizzy. Goldie could only imagine how she would have shrieked at her coiffed hair getting wet on such a humid day. Picturing Gloria's mangled tresses, dripping mascara, and stained silk blouse sent Goldie into a fit of giggles, and she was soon joined by the other two in stereo.

"People are going to think we are a bunch of nutjobs if they see us out here like this," Goldie said, wiping her brow.

"But we are, aren't we?" Jocelyn said.

Goldie smiled. Perhaps she and Jocelyn had started out on the wrong foot and just needed to become better acquainted.

"We sure are," Krystal said.

Goldie politely thanked her guests—Krystal for coming by, Jocelyn for the zucchini bread—and sent each on their way with a hug.

"I'm really very happy. Thank you so much for this opportunity," Krystal said quietly before turning to leave.

As am I, new friend, Goldie thought. *As am I.*

Brutus's snout nudged her hand for a pet, and Laverne leapt from one of the steps into her arms. The three of them looked on as the cars pulled from the driveway, heading down Madison.

There was a time when Goldie had always been the baby of the group. Not just her male suitors but even her close girl-friends had a significant number of years on her. She had discovered a decade or two earlier that eventually the pendulum starts to swing in the other direction. New friends enter your life, younger friends, and before long you assume the position of the wise old owl—or grumpy old crow, depending on the day. Instead of feeling splintery around talented and beautiful young women like Krystal and Jocelyn, Goldie felt herself become absorbed by their vibrancy. It was a marvel for her to discover the different chapters and characters at every bend in the road.

As she ascended the staircase, she thought back to how nimbly Krystal had flown up them earlier, while she was having more and more trouble these days. No one warns a single middle-aged woman just how fast those twilight years will creep. That just because you've reached a point where you can finally afford the crowning achievement of a Painted Lady Victorian with its impressive peaks and many floors doesn't mean you should. That the most advantageous thing to do is secure yourself in a reliable and practical ranch house without any stairs and within walking distance of the market. While the girls may have conjured her youthful spirit, Goldie's body was busy making other arrangements.

Just before reaching the porch, the smell of scotch filtered through the first floor of the house as the sheers billowed to and fro against the opened windows.

Keep a close watch on the brunette. Fiction writers are not unlike actors, capable of masterfully concealing the darkness behind sunny facades.

Goldie stopped moving.

"*It's in the eyes, Little Birdie. The eyes will reveal all. But first, you must be willing to see.*"

The voice Goldie heard belonged to a man. A Knight. But for the first time ever, that man wasn't Simon—it was Patrick.

16

Jocelyn

Jocelyn crumpled up the piece of paper, aimed for the waste-basket at her feet, and missed it once again. It was the third transfer funds slip she'd scrapped since entering the bank. By the time she filled out all the information properly, she was a jumble of nerves. Transferring money from one account to another was an everyday occurrence. Doing so on the sly behind your husband's back—in your joint account—was not.

Jocelyn couldn't believe how much these lawyers were asking for a simple inquiry. A $600 flat fee for the initial consultation and then $250 per hour thereafter. There was no way she would be able to afford the $5,000 retainer many of these firms required.

She had to be armed for whatever Trevor was scheming. Their last few conversations were less than amicable, and she had somehow managed to turn him into an enemy. (Making an antagonist out of your child's father who is threatening a custody battle was just about as foolish as it got. She would never have written one of her protagonists this way.) She sucked it up and spent the $600, deciding to just keep a careful watch on her clock time.

Jocelyn really hated lying to Bruce. The other day he came home from work excited to hear how things were going with the book.

"Is my baby working hard?" he said. "How's it coming along?" She froze. She hadn't been able to write in weeks. She was completely stuck.

"When do you think they'll send the book advance?" he asked.

"Honey, I don't know. I have to concentrate." She felt awful for being snippy, but the guilt was raising walls all around her.

Trevor's words kept playing in her mind. That bit about how he and Hannah exposed the kids to new experiences. It wasn't easy competing with Mary Poppins when, more often than not, Jocelyn felt like Oscar the Grouch. She vowed to do more cool things with Billy when he returned. Instead of reading on her beach blanket or scribbling notes on her yellow pad, she would join him for boogie boarding. On rainy afternoons, they could work on a puzzle together or she could color with him instead of sticking him in front of the television and hollering at him to keep the volume down so she could concentrate at her desk. She was willing to make mud pies, sleep in a tent out back, and go digging for earthworms like she did as a kid. There was nothing she wouldn't do for her Billy goat.

"I miss you, baby," she said to him during their last phone call, trying desperately not to display the emotions that would only upset him.

"Me too," Billy said.

"You too? You miss yourself?"

Billy erupted into laughter. "No, silly. I miss youuuuu."

"That's more like it."

Naturally, Billy had handed the phone back to Trevor even though he and Jocelyn weren't exactly on speaking terms.

"Well, I better run. And for what it's worth, you should feel good about letting him come. He's really having a blast over here."

Oh, how she hated him. Putting her in the position of not being able to react with Billy and Hannah sitting right next to him. What kind of a mother gets angry to hear her child is having fun?

"Have him call me tomorrow, please."

"Yeah. I will. Uh, hang on for a second. Hannah wants to ask you something."

This was unexpected. "Sure."

"Hello, Jocelyn? How are you? How's your book coming?"

"My book is coming along. Thanks. How are you, Hannah? Is everything okay?"

"I just wanted to double-check something with you. Billy's been having some nightmares. Don't worry! I always get to him right away. And once he falls asleep, he's fine for the rest of the night. I just wanted to know if this was something that happened a lot."

"He's had them here and there. But not recently," Jocelyn said.

"Oh, I see. Okay. I suspect he's missing home. He's been away from you for a long while. It's not easy for kids at that age. It's a big adjustment."

Jocelyn heard Trevor grumbling in the background.

"Well, I don't want to keep you. If it happens again, I'll be sure to let you know," Hannah said sweetly.

More grumbling from Trevor.

"Hannah? Thanks for checking in with me. I really appreciate it."

"Of course, of course. You're his mother. I've got two of my own. I know what it's like."

Jocelyn was tempted to ask her what she thought of Trevor's plans for Billy, but they were already exchanging goodbyes.

She immediately jumped on her computer to draft a series of questions for the lawyer as warm tears spilled from her eyes without warning, like a sun shower.

After the awkward interaction at Goldie's, Krystal phoned the next day, inviting her over for lunch. The temptation was too great to turn down. Jocelyn agreed to a quick visit, promising herself she would spend the remainder of the afternoon writing, even if that meant picking up takeout for dinner.

The Axelrods' home was by far Bruce's most elaborate and lucrative project to date. The figurative feather in his cap. Jocelyn was taken by the stone encasing of the oversized mailbox with the family name engraved on the brass plaque. Walking along the brick pavers on the extended driveway, she remembered learning of the significant upkeep on the delicate and costly natural stone, which scratched easily, making it unsuitable for snowplowing.

Baby pines lined the perimeter of the property, adding to the privacy. An exquisite Japanese maple and pink dogwood welcomed her as she stepped onto the path leading toward the mahogany double doors. The only time she'd ever seen such a remarkable entrance was on the Real Housewives TV shows.

Jocelyn had visited the property in the beginning stages of construction, but with its dirt floors, it was nearly impossible to picture what the house might look like in its finished state. She had seen the initial drawings for the master suite, and Bruce had helped her climb the ladder while she held his arm tightly and balanced along the beams. He proudly pointed out the location of the bathroom, Jacuzzi tub, and walk-in closet, but to Jocelyn, it all appeared like one big warehouse with wood beams sticking out of the floor. Her envisioning capabilities extended to storytelling only.

Between the wedding and honeymoon, there never seemed

to be enough time in her schedule to join Bruce for a visit to the site. For months, maybe longer, he had been urging her to join him on a walk-through before the Axelrods moved in. And she wanted to. She remembered wanting to. Looking back, the only thing she could recall occupying her time and attention was negotiating the terms of Billy's stay with Trevor and the business of preparing for his departure. Not to mention settling into her new life as a married woman in a new home. All that and, of course, the matter of her deadline. The list seemed endless, and yet it didn't seem to amount to all that much in the scheme of things.

Now, standing on the front stoop of the mansion that her husband had built with his own hands, Jocelyn felt sad. More than sad, she felt downright awful. Guilty. A more loving wife, a better wife, would have insisted on seeing the finished product of her husband's most prized achievement. And yet, somehow, she'd always been too distracted and consumed with the minutiae of her own craziness. She could almost hear him now on the few occasions he said to her, "I know, I know, you writers have a busy inner world. I get that. But it's okay for you to include me, baby. I'm safe. There's no coup d'état or anything like that on your horizon." Bruce's casual style had always been unassuming; he was far more intelligent than one might suspect. Jocelyn knew the wattage of the bulb she had married.

She pressed the doorbell, setting off a series of chimes throughout the open foyer like the regal sound of old English church bells. She wished she could be swept away by the gentle melody. Her only escape, at the moment, was a silent promise to be more present, more involved in her husband's work and interests. As the humidity continued its endless assault on her skin, her mind and spirit were held hostage by the tight cords of regret. She was grateful for the patter of hard soles crossing the marble floor to the entryway and yearned in quiet desperation for the presence of another to save her from the episode running on an endless loop in her mind.

A stately older woman opened the door.

"Hello. My name is Jocelyn Anderson. I'm a friend of Krystal's." She flipped her sunglasses to the top of her head and squinted in the afternoon sun.

What the woman didn't say with words, she was able to communicate through her body language. Her eyes examined the length of Jocelyn's body, which made her feel as if she were dripping wet on a bathmat and waiting for a towel. She wasn't able to see very well, but she could have sworn she detected the slightest hint of a scowl.

"Krystal is expecting me."

"I got it, Pearl!" Krystal came bounding down the curved staircase. "That's for me!"

Pearl held the door open and stepped aside—a meager, if not rude, invitation for Jocelyn to enter the house.

When Krystal reached the landing, she was winded. "Hi . . . sorry . . . I was in the bathroom." Her breathing was heavy, as if she'd just finished a session on the elliptical. Turning to the older woman, she said, "This is Bruce Anderson's wife."

This detail didn't seem to impress Pearl, who pressed her lips together ever tighter. "Will your friend be joining us for lunch?" she asked, looking pointedly at Krystal.

"Yes. I got it covered. You don't have to worry about a thing," Krystal said almost too sweetly.

She led Jocelyn down the hallway to a closed door. They crept down a long flight of carpeted stairs leading to what appeared to be a finished basement.

"I know you're dying to see the house. Do you mind if we take our tour after lunch?" she said once the door was closed behind them. "I just want Pearl to settle into her wing so she won't eavesdrop on our conversation."

"Who *was* that woman?" Jocelyn said, immediately regretting the censure in her tone. "She's not a relative of Abe's or anything, is she?"

"No. Not really. Sorry. It's not you. She's our live-in housekeeper and hates my guts, so she makes it a point to embarrass me in any way she can," Krystal said as breezily as if it were an old, tired story that held no interest.

"That's awful. Abe allows her to treat you this way?"

"You know men. He never sees it. And even when he's there, he never really *sees* it. You know?"

"Ha! I'm quite familiar with the Mars-Venus disparity. Where did he find her?"

"He didn't. His parents hired her before he and his sister were born. She sort of raised Abe. He never had much of a relationship with his own mother, who was cold and had . . . *issues*." Krystal spun her index finger at the side of her temple and made her eyes all wonky.

"Ah. So he's attached."

"Sort of. Pearl was his primary caregiver. She's all he's ever known. I can't take that away from him."

"I get it. He's got mommy syndrome. There's a codependency thing here."

Krystal's eyes widened and began to dart back and forth like those lazy black flies at Jocelyn's workstation. She was either confused or offended.

"I just mean he's attached to her. Can't let go. And now that you've described his relationship with his own mother, I sense his need to hang on to Pearl is even deeper than we realize."

"You're probably right," Krystal agreed. "You hungry?"

"I am. . . ." Jocelyn was lost in thought. "You're Abe's first wife, right?"

"Yup. He's been a bachelor for years. I mean, he had girlfriends and whatnot, but never anything serious." Krystal filled their bowls with arugula, cubed watermelon, and chunks of feta.

"That explains Pearl's animosity. Before you came into the picture, she was the only woman in his life."

Krystal's eyes sparked with recognition. She paused, staring at Jocelyn, waiting for more.

"Whose idea was this house?"

"Abe's. It was a present for me. Some present, huh?" Krystal giggled.

"So. Pearl resents not only you but also this house. And that's why her jaw tightened when you mentioned Bruce. She resents the whole situation: you, your home, and anyone who had any part of it."

"Wow. I'm glad someone is finally explaining it to me. I've never been anything but nice to the woman. She's never warmed to me."

"I can imagine. And I know it's difficult not to take her jealousy personally, but you can't own it. It's her shit. She sounds like she's always been a lonely woman. It's kind of sad, actually."

The deeper Jocelyn came to know Krystal, the more she saw hidden beneath the flashy surface. Delving into the psyche of a person to discover what made them tick went with the territory of being a writer, painting characters into existence from thin air. She wondered about this bubbly and sweet-natured blonde-haired beauty from scant beginnings who ended up with the handsome king. What was all that hair and makeup about? Why the need to amp up the cleavage? It was as if Krystal were suiting up to distract onlookers from getting to know the woman behind the shimmery veneer because she herself didn't know who that woman was yet.

After a lovely lunch and a tour of the magnificent home, Jocelyn offered to drop Krystal in town so she could deliver some of her pieces to the studio. She kept the subject on safe topics like the husbands and Billy, knowing she needed to be careful not to pry. Yet she couldn't deny her own curiosity about how much Krystal knew of Goldie Sparrows. Men didn't understand the art of sharing juicy details, so trying to get information from Bruce was useless. She vaguely remembered him mentioning a late husband; Jocelyn pursued the topic.

"I know this is out of left field, but I'm just wondering: Has Goldie ever mentioned a spouse to you?"

Krystal grew quiet. The sudden shift in gears was jarring, and Jocelyn knew it, but she simply couldn't resist.

"Uh. No. Not really. I mean, I think she was married once and he died . . . or something . . . but that was a long time ago."

By the way she was fumbling, Jocelyn could tell she didn't know much and wasn't comfortable discussing Goldie's personal life.

"She's never mentioned a name or anything," Jocelyn said. It was a question posing as a statement, and they both knew it.

"Never. I just know that he died."

"I guess they never had any kids." Jocelyn hated herself for how nosy she sounded but couldn't control her impulses.

"I don't think so." Krystal's attention seemed to wane—an indication she was looking to change the subject. "I try not to ask too many personal questions. I feel like it's none of my business."

She respected Krystal's polite, inadvertent way of telling her that she should, in fact, mind her own business as well. And she knew it would be inappropriate to bring up the night of the charity event. Jocelyn was enjoying her new friend and didn't want to give the wrong impression. Not to mention, Krystal would now be working with Goldie, which automatically made Jocelyn an outsider.

By four thirty, Jocelyn was back at her desk, giving her three hours before Bruce would be home. With the final deadline the next morning, she didn't have much choice but to turn in the material she had. It was far from her best, but she could fix whatever was needed. The main thing was not to miss the deadline. Aside from her professional reputation in the literary community, there was the matter of her advance—and she needed to replace the money she'd borrowed from her joint savings account with Bruce to retain a lawyer.

A squeak of brakes on an old truck came from the front of the house. Jocelyn looked at the clock. She may have hoped, but of course it wasn't Bruce. Her handsome husband whom she had done such an impressive job of ignoring. She knew once things settled down, she would find a way to make it up to him. Just as soon as he walked through the door, she would ask him every detail of all the jobs he was working on. She would take an interest as she had when they were first dating. And maybe, just maybe, he would want to take her around to job sites again. She had failed their situation, in more ways than one. Not just with her lack of focus on him but from not sharing her deepest fears over Trevor and the custody and taking money behind his back. This was not the image she had in her mind of how the first year of marriage would go for them—a tangled web of disconnection and secrets.

Instead of preparing dinner, she retreated to the basement to be with Daisy, who had become Jocelyn's safe place. Her refuge. Somehow, she felt closer to Bruce through her own inexplicable and wondrous connection to his mother.

~Journal of Daisy Jane Anderson~
July 4th Weekend 1976

Last month, I missed my period. And I'm like clockwork. I've always been one of those girls who can set her watch to the day and hour of when it will strike. It's been over one week. I'm scared. Especially considering all the sex Frank and I have been having. I make him wear a rubber and all, but there have been a couple of instances when we got carried away and I haven't wanted to kill the mood by nagging him about contraception.

The last time Frank and I were cuddling up, I tried feeling him out about how he would take the possibility of a pregnancy.

"You said you want to be a father someday . . . right?"

"Uh, sure. Yes. One day."

"Why can't your wife have any again?"

"I told you. She isn't well. Anyway, why are you bringing this up?"

He abruptly propped a pillow up against the headboard, letting my head slide off his chest.

"Just asking," I told him.

I was panicked. The last thing I wanted to do was upset him. WHY did I bring up his sick wife? That was a dumb thing to do. Frank clams right up if I ask any questions about her. Now there was no way I could mention my missed period. SHIT. While I know how unhappy he is at home, he has never indicated that he'd ever leave his wife or how long she has to live. And that's not a question I am comfortable asking him. Especially not now.

I'm going to buy one of those home pregnancy tests just to be sure. My friend Laney promised she wouldn't say anything, not even to her boyfriend, Tommy. I think Tommy has always had a little thing for me. He's kind of obvious about it. But what can I do? It's not like I've ever flirted with the guy or anything. Plus, there is a good possibility I am carrying another man's baby, so Tommy just needs to get over it and get on with his own life. Carrying a *baby*? I can't believe I just wrote that.

To Peace on Earth, love, happiness, rock & roll, true love, babies, and new beginnings!

Daisy Jane

17

Krystal

Krystal became mesmerized by the white reverse lights of the Jeep Cherokee approaching from the driveway and was left to wonder why the universe was showering her with so much goodness. Everywhere she turned, there seemed to be a new friend waiting to make her acquaintance. Obviously, she was doing something right. New friends, new conversations, lifting her to higher ground. Whatever ride she was on, she hoped it would never end.

"There we go. All set," Jocelyn said, whisking a sprinkle of bangs from her long eyelashes.

She was one of those woman who always seemed to have it all together no matter what life threw her way. Krystal was overcome with curiosity, wishing to know what her secret was, but felt like an idiot asking such a thing.

"You sure about this?" She watched Jocelyn load the bags of carefully wrapped items.

"More than sure. Why mess up those buttery leather seats on that hot number?" she said, indicating the two-seater convertible parked in the driveway.

Krystal's BMW was a Christmas present from Abe a few years earlier. After finishing a batch of Pearl's famous blueberry pancakes (Abe's favorite), they'd plopped back onto the couch to open stockings. Krystal secretly slipped a shot of Bailey's into Abe's coffee as an extra-special holiday treat. He started to behave goofy, which was customary during their nightly cocktail hour before dinner, but baffling to Pearl who was not the least bit humored by his unusual display of silliness. He was a bit more juiced up than Krystal anticipated and insisted on presenting his fiancée with her gift before Pearl's Christmas goose was served. That day was a defining moment, as both women realized Krystal had gained prominence.

As they drove to the studio, she thought of Pearl. After Jocelyn's assessment, she had a new understanding of the old woman and felt a little sorry for her. Maybe she would think things through and discuss it with Abe next time he was home.

"Once I knew I was pregnant with Billy, I said to myself, 'No matter what happens from here, you better not become one of those soccer mom minivan drivers,'" Jocelyn said. "Then I realized when it comes to having kids, there's a fine line between idealism and practicality. So, I opted for a jeep. It's not as sexy as the two-seater Acura I used to drive, but certain things become unimportant once you're a parent. I don't mind the dirt from Billy's muddy cleats ruining my floor mats or if the car ends up stinking like french fries on the *very* rare occasion I treat him to Mickey D's."

Krystal couldn't relate but tried to think of something to add to the conversation.

"He sure is handsome."

"Isn't he, though? Thank you. My Billy goat. God, I miss him so much. You'll have to meet him when he gets home. Oh, he is going to fall in love with you. Billy has an eye for pretty women. And he *loves* blondes."

That made Krystal giggle.

"He also has this weird obsession with breasts."

Krystal's left hand immediately flew to the right strap of her bra, which suddenly felt as though it was sneaking down her shoulder.

"You have to hear this. I'll never forget the first time I had my agent, Jeannie, and her new boyfriend over for dinner. Billy had just turned two, and I was weaning him off the boob, if you know what I mean, and onto formula. . . . Anyway, toddlers can become part of the flooring, and Billy was no exception. He kept crawling around Jeannie's feet, playing with her ankle bracelet, pinching her toes. It was distracting her from the conversation, so finally I just scooped him up and placed him on her lap. Next thing I know, Jeannie gasped and nearly spat her Chardonnay clear across the dining room table. He had wormed his grubby little fingers into her bra!"

Jocelyn howled remembering the story. "Half his arm disappeared into her shirt!" She was laughing so hard she almost missed the turn onto Carpenters. "Can you imagine? I was mortified. Naturally, the men got a huge kick out of it."

"But of course." Krystal laughed, imagining the kick Abe would get seeing a toddler getting handsy with her. "How's your new book coming along?"

Jocelyn blinked as her smile faded.

"I'm sorry. That's probably too personal a question."

"No, no. You're fine. It's a question writers get about ten times a day. The book is coming along, shall we say. I'm on the verge of clearing a big deadline. Then, I wait for feedback. This writing business is a whole lot of hurry up and wait."

Krystal decided to change the subject.

"Abe loves your husband," she said. "It's not like him to take to new people right off the bat like that."

"They are having a bit of a bromance, aren't they?" Jocelyn

said. "Bruce *adores* Abe. It's cute. And kind of odd when you think about it."

"What do you mean?"

"They're from entirely different worlds, and yet they carry on like long-lost cousins or brothers or something."

Krystal thought about Jocelyn's words and knew she was right—there was some sort of inexplicable familial bond between the two men. It was undeniable.

"Bruce would probably kill me if he knew I was telling you this, but . . . do you know what he told me once? About Abe? He said that he wished we had all met sooner so that he could have chosen Abe to be his best man."

"He said that? Abe would cry if he heard that."

"Cry? Abe? No way."

"He would. I'm telling you. He's quite the Gushy Gus when the mood strikes him."

Jocelyn was beautiful when she laughed. Her eyes danced. "When does he return from Maryland?"

"Sunday afternoon. He's already made dinner reservations at PSI. He has this thing about treating me to a date night after he's been away."

"What a sweetheart. We love Peter Shields Inn. We always go there for all our special occasions. If you two are around the following weekend, pencil us in. I'd love for the four of us to go out."

"It's a date!"

Parking spaces were like buried gems during tourist season. Jocelyn looped Jackson, Lafayette, and Ocean Street twice before she finally caught a break and spotted someone stuffing shopping bags into her trunk. She helped Krystal load up the rolling cart. Goldie had two stock boys lined up waiting to assist them at the door.

"You've helped enough. I know you have to get back to your

writing," she said, sensing Jocelyn wasn't altogether comfortable with seeing Goldie.

Krystal wanted no part of the tension she had witnessed the day before. Both women had favorable characteristics and charm, and each had their special place in her life. She certainly was not about to pick sides or get caught in the middle of whatever invisible storm might be brewing between them.

"Thank you so much for having me today. Your home is absolutely exquisite," Jocelyn said.

"And we have your talented husband to thank for that," Krystal said, returning Jocelyn's warm hug.

They promised to secure dinner plans for their double date with the guys for the following weekend. It felt good to have a new girlfriend. Jocelyn was talented and smart, witty and sassy. It had only been one week, but Krystal felt worlds away from that night at her house with those hideous women. She felt as though she had graduated to a higher level of being. It was true what she learned about the Law of Attraction: once she changed her thoughts and raised her vibration, she began to attract circumstances and people who resonated on the same wavelength.

Goldie gave Krystal the warmest welcome she'd ever received.

"There she is!"

She wrapped her arms around Krystal with the second heartfelt embrace in the last five minutes. It was as if Krystal were making up for all those hugs she'd never received as a child. Goldie pulled back while keeping a firm grip on Krystal's forearms, if only to get a closer look, much like a grandparent might.

"My better half," Goldie said.

Krystal was by no means a business partner, but this made her feel as relevant and vital as one. As promised, Goldie had cleared several shelves and a closet for Krystal's work materials.

She approached the new workstation designated just for her and felt a wave of gratitude. In the center stood a handmade mug with Krystal's name painted in cursive on the side.

"I hope you like cobalt. I thought it would bring out the color in your eyes," Goldie said, handing the mug to Krystal, who took it with both hands. "It's always been one of my favorite colors. May it fill you with inspiration to dream and create."

Krystal could feel the weight of the mug in her hands: solid, sturdy, important. Once she peeled her eyes from this precious gift, she fumbled over the right words that would give justice to her feelings.

"I love it . . . so so much. . . ." It was all she could squeeze out.

Goldie had introduced Krystal to metal clay. It was a special craft Goldie had been wanting to delve further into, but she hadn't had the time. Krystal acquainted herself with the many tools in the kit: ceramic tiles, plastic wrap, roller and rolling guides, ruler, craft knife, slicer blade, paintbrushes, water pot, simple modeling tools, needles, drying equipment, needle file, sanding pads, sandpaper, stainless-steel brush, firing equipment, burnisher, polish, polishing cloths, tweezers, needle-nosed pliers, and wire cutters.

Goldie guided her through the process of mastering how to work with soft clay, which was the most widely used type of metal clay and the most versatile.

"Foundation is key with any new artistic endeavor, which can be bewildering for the uninitiated. The basics will serve as your springboard and launch you as far as your mind will allow."

Krystal had spent some time in the evenings on Pinterest and similar websites, and she was filled with creative energy and ideas.

"I shall leave you to your work. You know where to find me if you need me," Goldie said, gently closing the door behind her.

Krystal decided to tackle a basic medallion to go on the

end of a long chain. She opened the packet and removed the clay, scraping the bits stuck to the inner wrapper, and began kneading it briefly to ensure any moisture was well distributed throughout the clay. Goldie had shown her how to use the rolling sheets evenly to refine her work, which would lend itself to the inherent professionalism of the piece.

Once the soft clay had been shaped and dried, she reached the pre-finishing stage and was able to apply some detailing before firing. She'd read that shrinkage of about eight to thirty percent was possible and wondered how the finished product would come out.

A short while later, Goldie asked, "How you making out back here?"

"I've got four pieces firing as we speak and five more ready to go." Krystal waved her head in the direction of the kiln.

"Wonderful! I can't wait to see. I'll be locking the front door shortly. I'm fairly certain the bulk of the shoppers have receded for the day. Tomorrow, a new sun will rise. "

Krystal looked at her watch. Hours had passed since she'd arrived. Utterly enthralled with her work, she didn't notice the afternoon and early evening had completely slipped away.

"You didn't realize it was so late, did you?" Goldie smiled wryly.

"No. I can't believe it."

"Losing oneself in one's work with no concern for the time is one of the greatest life treasures to be had."

Once the front door was locked, she joined Krystal in the back to demonstrate the ins and outs of properly sanding a fired piece.

"The medallions should be held in your hand or placed on a flat surface. If you need to work on the edge, you must take great care to support it well on both sides with a finger and thumb of the other hand."

Goldie seemed almost misty-eyed as she picked up the butterfly Krystal had made. She rubbed the sanding pad gently back and forth over the wings. A small shower of powder rained down gently onto the table.

"We don't want to ruin the lovely detailing you created in her thorax and abdomen. The textured surfaces require more care, since the sanding pad may remove too much clay." Goldie's hands trembled. She released a quiet sigh, gently returning the butterfly to the work area.

"I suppose it's just years and thousands of projects, but these hands seem to lack coordination. Whatever you do, my beauty, do not get old. It's no picnic."

Krystal smiled but felt sad. Despite the twenty-two years between them, she understood all too well how the body changes with each passing year and wished she could make it better for her friend.

"I'm sorry you're having a hard time."

"Such is life. Such is life. . . ."

Krystal felt a stirring at her feet. She looked down at the uninhibited Himalayan, which then leapt into her lap.

"Honest to goodness, Laverne. We are trying to work here. You really love your Krystal, don't you?"

"The feeling is mutual." Krystal stroked the cat's fluffy mane.

Goldie sauntered over to the kiln for a peek. Krystal's eyes remained on her friend, and she hoped "getting old" was the only thing plaguing her. She couldn't bear to think there might be something more serious at play.

"After the clay has been fired, it can be polished, filed, soldered, and worked using normal metalworking techniques by hand or with simple electric tools. This should be easy for you since you're already an expert with the drill."

Goldie jumped right back into work mode, clearly wanting to change the subject.

"For silver clay, you can brush firmly over the piece to lay down the white crystalline surface, which creates a pleasing satin finish. For bronze and copper clays, you want to be sure to remove any traces of oxidation."

She explained how important it was for her to get the mermaid right for Jocelyn's auction.

"Did you notice the jewelry she wore? This is the process I used."

"I remember thinking I wished I had the medallion and wrist cuffs." Krystal had taken pictures of the stunning mermaid and visited them often when she was browsing through her photos and books. One of the things that stood out for her was Goldie's attention to detail.

"Pickling removes the black layer caused by the oxidation on the surface of the metal during firing or soldering. I bought you a bottle of acidic solution to remove the fire stain. Should you ever run out, you can make it yourself using a tablespoon of salt, one half cup of vinegar, two tablespoons of citric acid, and one half cup of water."

She marveled at Goldie's knowledge.

"They were all expecting me to fail," she said quietly. "Perhaps they still are. Some of the people in the town, I mean."

"You think that's true? That they were expecting you to fail?"

"I had to show them that Goldie Sparrows will not be closing her doors for some financial trouble." Her own candor seemed to embarrass her, so she changed the subject once again. "Oh heck, I'm just a kooky and lonely old hippie who keeps to herself and dresses like a gypsy. They don't know what to make of me."

Krystal didn't know if she should agree or disagree, so she remained quiet, knowing her friend needed to relieve her mind of the extra pounds she'd been carrying.

"In their eyes Gloria Eagle was the straitlaced one who kept me and the business tethered to any sense of normalcy. Without Gloria and that darn pole that was sufficiently lodged in her rear, they were expecting me to fall to pieces. But I'm tougher than they know. They don't know what I've lived through or what I've seen. You can't keep this old bat down. I have more of a backbone and far more fun than that stick in the mud ever did."

Krystal could feel Goldie's anger and pain simultaneously. There was so much more to discover about this peculiar and fierce little woman. She was tough on herself. More so than she deserved. But Krystal supposed that staunch resolve was what kept her afloat, in more ways than one, throughout her lifetime.

By the time she returned home, the house was dark and quiet. With Abe out of town, Pearl had long since retired to her end of the house. Revved up from her first day at the studio and intimate chat with Goldie, she was unable to sleep. She grabbed a large ice water with a wedge of lemon and headed for her office on the second floor.

The room faced the harbor with a generous balcony. What should have been designated as the prime guest room, Abe insisted she utilize for her own space.

"How much overnight company are we expecting? This is your home, angel. It's crazy for these views to go to waste in between visits, collecting dust."

It was one of the prettiest rooms in the house, and she enjoyed filling the cherrywood shelves along the perimeter with her collection of new books, from self-help to coastal crafts and jewelry-making. She picked up a fresh yellow legal pad and began jotting notes, securing stickies to pages of interest. With Goldie's guidance, she knew that there was no project, however complicated, too great for her to tackle. She was filled with a sense of confidence that had never been there before, and she owed it all to her mentor.

Assuming a cross-legged position on the area rug, she centered herself in the middle of the room, surrounded with books like a moat. A squeak on one of the floorboards in the hallway snapped like a twig in the brush. She jerked her head up to find Pearl observing in silence like an apparition.

"Hey. . . ." Krystal said, poking her head through a fog of deep concentration.

"Good evening. Is there anything you need?" Pearl asked quietly.

"Oh. . . ." Krystal looked around as if she'd find the answer among the mess. "I don't think so. I'm okay. Thanks."

"Very well then. . . ." Pearl dropped her hand from the doorframe and tented her fingers at her navel.

"Do you need anything?" Krystal said.

Pearl narrowed her eyes, not in reproach but inquiry—she seemed to be contemplating her response. "I am fine. Have a good night, dear."

Dear? That was a first.

"Goodnight, Pearl!" Krystal called as she disappeared down the hallway.

Since her lunch with Jocelyn, the dynamics of the situation kept creeping into her mind: *mommy syndrome . . . codependency. . . .* She wondered what it must be like for Pearl having to deal with so much change in such a short period. For many decades, Abe relied on Pearl to look after him. Once Krystal entered his life, he was so focused on making her happy he sloughed off Pearl's attention. It wasn't until now that she realized everything in life, however special, came at a cost, and in this case, Pearl was the one to pay it. Her role as caregiver gave her purpose, an identity. Krystal had inadvertently taken Abe away. And she was resented for doing so. Jocelyn was right: this wasn't personal. Any other woman who had swept Abe from Pearl's grasp would have been met with the same chilly reception.

Krystal stood up. She couldn't believe how her lower back and knees had tightened up sitting on the floor for more than an hour. She reached up toward the ceiling and bent her torso to the right, as she'd done for so many years, mirroring Jane Fonda on the old VHS tapes from her youth. Considering what Goldie had shared about aging, she realized that even just five years earlier, she wouldn't have felt this stiff simply from sitting on the ground.

Heading downstairs to refill her water pitcher for bed, she saw the container of plastic wrap sitting on the counter. It was unlike Pearl not to tidy up. She opened the refrigerator to dig out another lemon. Instead, she stumbled upon a small plate with a wrapped sandwich sitting on the top shelf next to her oat milk with a Post-it Note affixed to the side. She read in Pearl's dainty script: *If you don't properly refuel after a long day's work, you'll have no steam left in the tank for the next day. Pleasant dreams. P.*

Krystal couldn't believe what she was reading. Slowly, she retrieved the sandwich and almost felt guilty for looking at it as though it had been left by an extraterrestrial. Without Abe around to dote on, Pearl's affections were somehow spilling over onto the only other person in the house. Krystal took it as a peace offering. It was a huge breakthrough and the first nice thing Pearl had done for her without being required to do so.

Normally, she would never eat at such a late hour, but she couldn't risk injuring Pearl's feelings by not accepting the sweet gesture. If she didn't follow through, such an offer might never come her way again. She propped herself at the island and carefully peeled off the wrapping. In between lightly toasted multigrain bread were layers of fresh turkey, a piece of low-fat Swiss cheese, sliced avocado, arugula, and a dollop of honey mustard—her favorite sandwich. Pearl had obviously been paying better attention than Krystal knew. She was beginning to see what Abe saw in the caring, attentive woman. She grabbed one of her seashell magnets and painted *Pearl's Kitchen* across the back. She stuck it up on the refrigerator with a little thank-you note.

As it turned out, a full belly was the perfect recipe for a restful night's sleep. Krystal closed her eyes and drifted off on a cloud, feeling sated, peaceful. Those precious things missing from her childhood became glaringly clear. For the first time in her life, she was respected, supported, and honored by the women in her life—and above all, nurtured.

So why did it feel as if something was about to go horribly wrong?

18

Goldie

He was the very last person she ever expected to see. What on earth could he possibly want with Goldie? She stepped down from her work stool and invited him into the back room.

"Nice to see you. How may I help you?" She took great care to smooth any jagged edges from her tone.

"I come in peace." He raised both hands, like a bank teller surrendering to a masked gunman.

In that instance, she thought the term "smiling from ear to ear" might have been invented for folks just like Abe Axelrod.

"I hear my wife is going to be renting a few tables from you."

"Yes, indeed. Such talent should not be kept hidden in the shadows but shared for all the world to see."

Somehow his sugary grin stretched ever wider, like a piece of caramel. Laverne was perched, staring up at the man. She was twitching and shifting on her paws in preparation for one of her flying leaps into his arms. *What was it about the Axelrods?* Goldie wondered. Her mind drifted to poor Shirley left at home; she hadn't eaten a meal in two full days. Goldie had a call in to the vet, who was in the middle of a three-week excursion to Barbados.

"You see her," he said.

"Pardon?" Goldie said, confused as ever. She had too much on her mind and found this visit to be off-putting, to say the least.

"My wife. Krystal. You see her for who she truly is. Most people don't. It can be intimidating for some people to have such a beautiful and younger woman around. I'm only too glad to know you are capable of seeing beyond that. You recognize her for her talents."

"Indeed I do. She has a lot to offer. I'll do anything I can to foster those creative juices. She has quite a sharp eye, an unassuming imagination, and an innate sense of creativity. She also happens to be a natural with her hands."

"It's important for me that she stays happy. She deserves that. More than anyone I've ever known."

It was as if the lighting shifted, recasting him at a new angle. Abe wasn't some rich bully trying to pound his chest over his money or power. He was simply a man—as pure and forthright as they come—who loved his wife and wanted only the best for her.

"The last thing I would ever do is insult or offend you, Ms. Sparrows."

"In that case, you can start by calling me Goldie." She smiled.

"Yes, of course. Goldie. I hope this isn't too presumptuous of me, but I'd like to offer you a safety net. A type of insurance, if you will. Free of charge, of course."

He held both palms wide open once again, as if having to prove his own innocence came second nature.

"I'm not sure I follow you."

"You're in the center of town. A prime location. I know the

rents are anything but cheap. I want you to know that I am here to help out should you ever find yourself in any sort of trouble, shall we say. I will not stand by and see something happen to your business. It's too important to Krystal. I will do everything in my power to keep this place afloat. No matter the cost. No matter what you need. All you ever have to do is call."

A shiny business card appeared between two massive fingers. While she may not have been able to fully understand the implications of his offer, Goldie was old and smart enough to remember everything came with a price. She had to wonder what was behind this unbidden, selfless display of generosity.

"I don't want anything from you, Goldie," he said, as if reading her mind. "And I'm certainly not trying to imply you aren't capable of managing your own business. The only thing I wanted to impress upon you is that I'm here to lean on should the need ever arise. Truth is, all I care about is Krystal's personal fulfillment. I once thought marrying me and having me give her everything she ever dreamed of would be enough." He chuckled in spite of himself. "I realize now my love, devotion, and yes, even my money can only go so far. Everyone needs to feel productive. Accomplished. Now, thanks to you, she has uncovered this passion. And I don't want anything to jeopardize that. I've seen a side to her I never knew was there. A side that maybe she didn't know was there. I love watching her eyes dance with life when she talks about her friendship with you and this new venture. I've been around enough to know this kind of satisfaction is something I would never be able to provide. The only thing I can do is everything in my power to be sure it's never taken from her."

Large as he was, Abe Axelrod diminished in stature as he humbled himself before her, and she recognized with striking clarity the reason for Krystal's attraction to him.

"Is any of this making sense? Or do I sound totally crazy?"

She could feel the smile reach her eyes. More than his kind and loving generosity, Abe didn't take himself too seriously, which may have been his most endearing quality.

"It makes perfect sense," she said, working diligently to sift through the information she'd been given. "I understand. And I admire your concern for your wife's well-being."

"What can I say? I'm a lucky man."

"You are indeed. I'd venture to say, you aren't the only lucky one in this scenario."

Goldie extended her hand, bracing for a formidable shake, but was met with a tender kiss placed delicately on her cheek. After their brief but warm embrace, she watched Abe Axelrod vanish from her storefront just as quickly as he had appeared. It was easy to see his heart was pure, and he cherished his wife for reasons extending well beyond her outer beauty.

Goldie's return home was filled with tasks. Brutus, the leader of the pack, was always first in line. After a sufficient stroll around the neighborhood, she filled the cats' bowls before heading straight to check on Malcolm. She was fresh out of kale and made a mental note to add it to her grocery list. And she needed to do so before she forgot, which would likely happen within the next ten seconds. If she could only will the strength to search for a pen. As she slid the junk drawer open and faced the paper clips, rubber bands, match sticks, toothpicks, pennies, receipts, and stapler, she tinkered with an old flashlight. The batteries were dead. She popped them out and began looking for new ones. While rifling through the odds and ends, it struck her that she had completely forgotten why she had opened the drawer in the first place.

Once settled in with Laverne in her arms and Shirley at her feet, Goldie flipped off the outside lights, and the crew followed her up to the bedroom for a long night's slumber. Just some rest and she'd be right as rain.

And then she could smell it. The scotch. What was happening to her mind? How could she be conjuring scents and voices that weren't there? Her marriage to Simon had continued to disintegrate after Patrick died, as his disdain for Goldie's vocation increased.

One night had left an indelible mark on her memory. She had been patiently listening to Simon's bellyaching from a long day at the office. She sat at the table, staring into the amber of the scotch decanter. A veil of disgust draped Simon's face. He stopped speaking midsentence. With the next breath, he'd snatched her wrist with his claw to closely inspect her fingernails. Goldie had spent the better part of an hour trying to scrape the residue of clay and earth trapped beneath her nail beds, to no avail. Simon was meticulous about cleanliness and hygiene. This did not bode well for her. She remembered that night and the admonishing look upon his face as he glowered at her for several beats before releasing her hand. Paralyzed by the sadness of losing Patrick, she'd been too stunned to leave, too fragile and weak to contemplate divorce. Part of her continued to wish her Simon would come back to her. She waited for the day he returned from work and instead of aloofness, she'd be met with that wide smile and quirky disposition he had when they first met, and everything would be okay again. Unfortunately, his indignation over her connection to his father and her artistic passion plagued their marriage until his very last breath. Even now, there were times she felt his unrelenting grip over her hand—and her life.

The next morning, Goldie sat across from the doctor, resenting the confusion that had somehow become her new normal. In desperation, she was forced to ask Dr. Carroway to repeat herself four times.

"I'm sorry. I don't follow."

"Sporadic Creutzfeldt-Jakob disease. It's a rare degenerative brain disorder. It affects about one in every one million people each year worldwide. Here in the US, there are about three hundred cases yearly. It's just one of those things."

Goldie couldn't feel her legs. Or her hands. Or her face. Or her brain.

"I suppose you're telling me I'm the lucky one in a million." Her insides twisted like a garden hose.

"I take my vitamins every morning and right before bed. I walk to the studio every day. I ride my bicycle all around town. I never stop moving. I'm more active and sprightly than Mary Lou Retton ever was." She paused to emit a flurry of nervous laughter. "Heck, I have to remember to turn my car on every so often just so the engine doesn't give out. Have you ever heard of such a thing? Well, *have* you?"

"This isn't anything that you could have prevented. It's one of those awful things that strikes without warning and without cause."

Goldie's befuddled thoughts were trudging through the murky ponds of self-pity, turmoil, and panic.

"Now we have an explanation as to your coordination issues and visual disturbances, not to mention your memory concerns."

"Those are signs of aging," Goldie snapped.

She was defensive and helpless, but she couldn't stop herself. Slowly, she was losing her grip. What did she think? That she could make a good case for why this shouldn't be happening in the hope that it would change the outcome?

"And the prog . . . prognosis . . ." She never thought the day would come when she'd have to use that word in reference to herself. "What does that look like?" Her heart was now skipping beats—she wondered if a heart attack would take her before Creutzfeldt what-ever-it-was did.

"Approximately one in nine will survive the first year." Dr. Carroway's voice was low but steady.

Like a black image clouding an MRI scan, the scent of scotch from his breath filled the small room. It was so powerful Goldie searched the doctor's face to see if she could smell it too. He wasn't real. He couldn't be. It was the disease wreaking havoc on her mind.

In the end we all get what's coming to us.

Simon's voice was hollow. A thick layer of ice shrouded each one of his words.

But you already knew that, my darling.

19

Jocelyn

The next morning, Jocelyn didn't hear Bruce leave for work. Sunlight filtered through the double-paned windows, creating a greenhouse effect in the cozy room. She pulled off the cotton blanket and sat up. Her hair stuck to the back of her sweaty neck as if she'd broken a fever sometime during the night, and she saw that the morning was as good as gone by the time her feet hit the floor. Woozy, with an inexplicable dull throb in her temples, she headed for the bathroom to wash, brush, and shower her way back to consciousness.

Now that the manuscript was turned in, she had to play the waiting game. At any given moment, Jeannie would be calling about how the work was received. She remembered holding her debut in her hands for the first time. It was an indescribable feeling to see all those hours, all those days, all that work metamorphosed into a finished product. A book. An accomplishment many imagined they could achieve with only the desire to create one but not knowing the discipline and fortitude needed to cross the finish line on such a feat. She had heard other writers refer to books as their babies and liken the art of fashioning a novel from scratch to pregnancy and childbirth. And she could see why. Just like after her labor, Jocelyn was too exhausted and overcome with joy to put her elation into words. With that first book, all she had to do was pause for a moment and take in the fruits of her efforts while gloating in silent admiration. Now the only thing she could do was try to keep her food down until she heard from Jeannie.

In need of some fresh air and a decent workout, Jocelyn jumped on her bike and headed for the lighthouse on Cape May Point. Once there, she'd stop in between the ten-mile-round-trip ride for a stroll through the state park. She preferred the longer route to avoid the high-speed traffic on Sunset Boulevard. She crossed over South Bayshore Road to Stevens Street, passing Rea's Farm, Willow Creek Winery, and Beach Plum Farm. After a few more twists and turns down the back roads, she found herself in front of the Red Store, one of her favorite stops for brunch. She could almost taste the avocado toast with melted cheddar, cherry tomatoes, arugula, and smooth cream cheese, layered upon toasted multigrain bread.

On her first visit to Cape May, Jocelyn became enamored with the small town. Her college roommate was from a suburb just outside of Philly and convinced her this was the place they should celebrate the end of junior year. While on a tour of the lighthouse, the girls learned how the Mid-Atlantic Center for the Arts worked tirelessly to raise funds to restore the nearly 150-year-old structure—known as the Sentinel—and thanks to their concerted efforts, the historic beauty reopened for public tours in 1988. If Jocelyn hadn't acquiesced and had insisted they stick with their original plan to visit Myrtle Beach, she might not have had another opportunity to visit Cape May—and she never would have met Bruce.

Now, as she began her ascension up the cast-iron spiral

staircase, it struck her that she hadn't outgrown her habit of counting every one of the 199 steps in her head. She reached the first vestibule, taking in the clear view of the Delaware Bay imbued with rich hues of russet and crimson as the sun inched closer to the horizon. On the second landing, she could see Cape May Point. Every evening from May through September, just before sundown, a flag ceremony was held at Sunset Beach to honor fallen soldiers. The families of the deceased brought the American flag laid on the casket during the funeral, which was then raised on the flagpole in memory. When they were first dating, Bruce had taken her there to honor his best friend Craig's younger brother, Timothy Green—a member of the United States Coast Guard—who had perished a few years earlier during a harrowing civilian rescue out at sea. It was the first time she saw Bruce's vulnerability as he wrapped Craig in his arms. Against the backdrop of a cool and steady ocean breeze and fading daylight, no one in attendance was left unmoved. "Taps" echoed over the sound of muffled sobs, as if threading an indelible sorrow through the crowd looking on in reverence as Old Glory was lowered.

Upon reaching the third vestibule, she took in a clear shot of the mighty Atlantic. Peering out the small window, she wondered how many aerial shots, sketches, paintings, and postcards had been crafted over the years of the Sentinel's full frontal. She continued to ascend the round staircase, pausing to admire a view of the Cape May Bird Observatory from the fourth landing. Finally, she reached the top, gaining a panoramic view of the entire vicinity: the most southern location in the state of New Jersey.

A jovial father stood by with three small children, who were skirting around the red railing, squeezing in close to Jocelyn. They were snapping disposable cameras while listening to Dad's enthusiastic commentary on what he had learned from the museum shop down below, which—as she overheard—once served as the brick oil house. He reminded her of Chevy Chase as Clark Griswold from the National Lampoon movies.

"Kids, this is the third lighthouse built in this location back in 1859. It took two years to build and stands at 145 feet high," he said.

"Holy moly!" said the little boy, wedged in between his two big sisters.

"It shines the way home for ships out at sea. The light flashes every fifteen seconds and stretches for nineteen miles in all directions."

Jocelyn saw he was now reading from the open brochure in his hands. She wanted to laugh, knowing he would soon lose the little ones' attention, if he hadn't already.

"This lighthouse has two separate walls. The outside wall is cone-shaped and is approximately three feet and ten inches thick at the bottom and one foot six inches thick at the top. The inside wall is a cylinder with eight-and-a-half-inch walls that support the spiral staircase. The walls were designed to withstand winds several times above hurricane force."

"Cool, Dad," said the elder daughter of the brood. "It sure is pretty here."

Jocelyn knew she was doing right by Billy by raising him in such a special place. She watched as the father unzipped the fanny pack secured around his waist to remove a wet nap and wipe his son's hands, who looked as if he'd lost a wrestling match with a chocolate ice cream cone. She was tempted to tease the father about the perils of any food capable of melting and the need to inspect little boys from head to toe after eating most anything.

Instead, she headed for the stairwell and raced for the bottom—she needed to hear her boy's voice. She crossed the parking lot and headed for the natural trails, hoping there wouldn't be too many people around this time of day so she could have some privacy. She saw a pair of mallards sleeping on the water beneath one of the walking bridges. As she pulled out her phone, she spotted a young mother and her two young girls. The mother was wearing a standard cape and Colonial-looking dress and the girls were in prairie skirts. All three were wearing bonnets. They were crouched along the side of the path, making friends with a rainbow turtle. The mother looked up at Jocelyn and raised her hand gently in greeting. The group frequented Cape May and were pleasantly friendly, offering a certain sense of peace and well-being to the area. Jocelyn wished she could ingest that calmness to still the turbulence within her.

Just over two weeks remained until Billy's return. She wanted to be fully prepared and had made only two calls to her lawyer, Harrison Buck, in weak moments when she needed him to reassure her that Trevor was going to have a more difficult time than he anticipated trying to "upset the applecart," as Harrison put it. Both times, she was sure to keep the calls brief; if they went past the fifteen-minute mark, she would be charged for the full thirty. She started the timer on her stopwatch as soon as she heard the receptionist's perky greeting. Jocelyn was able to circumvent phone calls through e-mails. Anytime she had a question or concern—which was about once every ninety minutes—she would shoot off a message. Harrison was good enough to respond readily within the hour and provided her with a plethora of documents and articles and research to assuage her anxiety.

Without wasting another minute, she dialed Trevor. Hannah carted the kids off to the beach on a daily basis, but surely by now they'd be home. The woman loved the sand and surf so much you'd think she was a professional surfer or a lifeguard from that ridiculous nineties show *Baywatch*. Picturing Hannah trading her loose-fitting cotton and hemp for one of those skintight, red, one-piece swimsuits while running along the waterline with her perky breasts bouncing made Jocelyn guffaw.

"What's so funny?" Trevor's voice faded the image.

"Oh, nothing. I'm just being a goofball. Can I talk to Billy?"

She could hear the distinct wail of a child in the background. Her child. A mother knows.

"Is that Billy? Why is he crying? What's wrong?"

"The dog kept throwing up. Hannah had to rush him to the vet."

"That doesn't explain why my child is crying."

"Billy's just sore because he thought Hannah would be home to watch *Cars 2* with him tonight. And they were supposed to make forts in the backyard for a campout."

"Let me talk to him. I'll calm him down."

It sounded as though Trevor covered the phone, as she heard some garbled talking but was unable to make out what he was saying to Billy.

"He doesn't want to come to the phone," Trevor said.

Jocelyn felt as if someone had sprayed a water gun in her face.

"What? What are you talking about? What is he saying?"

"Saying? He's not saying anything. Can't you hear him?" And the wailing grew louder as Trevor raised the phone.

"I'll try again." Trevor released a long sigh, sounding listless, as if he was already bored with the whole routine and just going through the motions to appease her.

This time, he didn't cover the phone. And Jocelyn was able to hear everything.

"Billy, Mommy is on the phone. She doesn't want you to cry. You're making her cry too."

"Don't tell him he's making me cry!" She was livid.

"Come talk to your mother, Billy. She misses you and wants to hear about your day at the wave pool and the water park."

Wave pool? Water park?

"No!" Billy screamed through tears.

"Come on, now. Knock that off," Trevor said.

"I want Hannah! Why did she leave?! She said we could make a fort! She promised! She promised!"

Jocelyn thought she was having an out-of-body experience. She stopped walking. The trees on either side of the trail began to sway and bow, and yet there was no breeze. The air seemed to thicken like overcooked pea soup. Her instincts kicked in, and she began practicing her Lamaze breathing. She found herself having to hold on to each tree she passed so as not to lose her footing. She'd forgotten she wasn't alone until the docile young woman looked up from her crouched position, her long black skirt covering her like a blanket.

"I'm sorry. He's been acting weird all day. I don't know what's gotten into him," Trevor said. She knew him well enough to know his words were sincere.

Jocelyn made an about-face, knowing she needed to get back to the parking lot and away from people. Her lungs were shrinking. She couldn't breathe, let alone compute or respond to what Trevor was saying.

"You're panting. Are you working out or something?" he asked.

"I . . . I can't . . . talk. . . . I gotta go. . . ." Her voice cracked, revealing her emotion. She hated it. She hated him. She hated Hannah. She hated everyone. And everything.

"Wait . . . hold up . . . what's going on—"

She was trembling yet somehow held the phone in one hand and pushed End Call with the other. As if being woken from a dream, she heard an unfamiliar voice. A female's. It was tender and sweet. Comforting.

"Miss, are you okay?"

It was the young woman. She'd followed Jocelyn through

the trail back to the parking lot. Every inch of the woman's skin was covered in fabric except her cheeks and hands. Her two little girls were at her side like doting penguins.

"Is there something you need?" The woman drew nearer. Jocelyn tried to focus on her face. Up close she appeared even younger, with trustful eyes. Her long blonde eyelashes fanned up and down like fronds.

Jocelyn shook her head, unable to speak. Her eyes drifted to the children gathered around their mother's skirt.

I'm a mother. Just like you. I only need my son. My baby. He's been taken from me.

"Are you in any pain?" The young mother's melodious voice drew her attention once again.

Jocelyn knew nothing about this girl, not where she came from or what her home life might be like. But as she looked into her honest eyes, she could see her soul. She could see the countless evenings she'd read to her babies nestled in their beds. She could hear the mellifluous lullabies she sang to woo her offspring to the realm of dreams. This girl was the type of mother the world needed most, but there weren't enough to go around. Only a fortunate few had the luxury of knowing such unconditional bliss.

In the months and years to come, when Jocelyn looked back on that day, she would have no recollection of how she managed to make the five-mile trek home on her bicycle in the fading daylight. She'd only remember her sheer determination to remain focused in order to arrive safely. The rhythmic sound of the tires swooshing against the road lulled her into a hypnotic state. Every few rotations, Trevor's words filtered back into her mind like a fight she'd had days earlier, returning to taunt her. She shook her head and felt the first batch of tears beginning to sprout.

Not yet. Get home. You must keep it together. Just a little longer. Not now.

She turned the corner onto a desolate side street in the residential area of West Cape May and spotted a tribe of goats behind a wooden fence. They were one of her favorite sights along her bike ride to the point. As she approached, a doe was happily munching away on a trough of oats. Her ears flicked to and fro beneath her stubby horns while being licked by the slight breeze. Jocelyn spotted a couple of kids curled in the corner like lazy kittens and wondered what it must be like to have no cares in the world. How lucky these goats must be. She caught herself feeling envious of goats. *Billy goat.* It may have taken a beat for the words to hit her awareness, but once they did, there was no turning back.

"I want Hannah."

And that was the moment when she let it all out. All the pain she'd been carrying that summer from not having her son. All the guilt she burdened herself with for not doing what she knew to be right. All the feelings of inadequacy she felt as a wife, a mother, a novelist. Unable to maintain proper steering, her bicycle weaved all over the road like a flatbed truck packed with drunken yahoos on a windy country road. She squeezed the handbrakes and jumped off. Not bothering to use the kickstand, she tossed the bike up against the fence in order to catch her breath and regroup. The phone had tumbled out of the basket affixed to the rear of the bike. She grabbed it, squeezing it tight until her first two fingernails snapped against the plastic. She watched herself raise an arm and hurl the phone clear across the street. Within seconds, it slammed hard against a maple. The phone ricocheted off the bark, landing back at her feet. She looked down at the screen, which now bore a splintered crack like a spider's web. She didn't give a shit. Not about the phone. Not about the goats or anyone who might be able to hear what was coming next. Her vocal cords vibrated. Her scream was hideously obtrusive in the serene landscape, like a red pen mark on a white wedding gown. The doe ceased her chewing and darted to the little barn to protect the two sleeping kids. Jocelyn wished she could apologize, but her lungs were working at full capacity as she heaved with sobs.

By the time she finally made it to her driveway, she had earned herself two new blisters and a roaring headache. Once she entered the house, she was reminded that hitting ground didn't necessarily mean there wasn't further to go. One thing she had learned from Bruce stuck out in her mind: "Doesn't matter how sturdy the construction or how beautiful you decorate—a structure is only as secure as the foundation on which it stands."

She thudded into the chair at her workstation and faced the laptop perched on the desk day after day. *What is it all for?* she wondered. *What is the point of anything?* On the windowsill just behind her chair sat a black fly in a supine position. Its needle-like legs wiggled in slow motion. Choking for air. Begging for mercy. Her first casualty of the season. The one fly she hadn't been able to save. It was too late.

Taking slow steps, Jocelyn descended the wooden stairs, wishing to vanish, once again, from her own life and into Daisy's.

~Journal of Daisy Jane Anderson~
August 1976

I'm two months pregnant. (I can't believe I just wrote those words.) No one knows except for Laney, and I asked her not to tell anyone, but I'm not dumb—of course she told Tommy. And that's fine. I'm more concerned that she keep it quiet once we get back to Cape May—my parents CANNOT find out about this. Not yet, anyway. Laney and Tommy are coming back for me and will be ready to head back north within the next two weeks. I do not want to leave, but I can't let them return home without me.

I told Frank about the baby one rainy afternoon after sex. He always jumps out of bed right after we do it to wash up, but I thought maybe he would hold me a little longer just this one time. I called his name, begging for more of a reaction, but by then the water was already running. I stayed under the covers, trying not to cry, and waited for him to come back into the room. He attempted to make me feel better about the situation. "It's okay. . . . I was just surprised. . . . I have a lot to think about. . . ."

After a few days, Frank told me he thinks it would be best if I return home with my friends. He promises to send money and make sure the baby and I are okay, and will find a way to be there for the delivery. This did not make me happy, but I know he needs to figure out what is going on with his wife and marriage before he can make any drastic moves. Unfortunately, I have no idea when that will be.

For weeks, Frank was loving and sweet and made a special effort to make me feel safe and protected. It wasn't until last month when I started to feel neglected. Unwanted. Like a burden. Another item on his to-do list that needed to be handled and checked off. The hormones are making me a bit emotional. Sometimes I feel like screaming, but mostly I just want to cry. The only thing that's keeping me going is the baby growing inside me. I can't wait to be a mommy. I only wish I could be Frank's wife, but that's "not in the cards right now," as he said. He claims his wife has taken a turn for the worse, so he is needed at home. He has been coming by less and less. It's unnerving. I never thought I'd be camped out in a hotel room, unmarried, and pregnant. I have never felt so alone in all my life.

Last night, he promised to come by after work so we could talk. When he didn't show, I went out by myself to grab some dinner at the Hardee's around the corner. When I returned, there was a message waiting for me at the front desk.

"Mr. Cooper sends his regrets. He had a family emergency requiring his attention."

I became so panicked and choked up the desk clerk pulled me over to one of the chairs in the lobby.

"You're going to be okay. Don't worry," she said, handing me a little plastic cup of water and sliding a box of tissues across the table. "Is there someone I can call for you?"

I shook my head and wiped my nose. I can only imagine how I must appear to her: the pregnant girlfriend to a married man, holed up in a hotel like some prostitute. How did I let this happen? I'm starting to see how easy it is to fly off the rails in one's life. I used to sit in judgment of people who managed to screw up their lives so drastically, but when it's happening to you, it's easy to see just how fast things can spiral out of control.

Frank has asked me never to call him at work, but I was desperate this morning. I needed to speak to him and find out what was happening with his wife. The receptionist who answered the phone had no idea what I was talking about.

"Frank Cooper? I'm sorry, Miss. There is no one here by that name." I could hardly understand the woman's thick drawl and thought perhaps she wasn't understanding me.

"What? What do you mean? Is this Stratford Accounting?"

"Yes. You have the right firm, but there is no Frank Cooper working here."

I'm more confused than ever. And weepy. Very, very weepy. I cannot stop crying. This can't be healthy for the baby to hear me sobbing all the time. I'm hoping Frank has a reasonable explanation for all this. I only hope he calls me before Laney and Tommy come to pick me up.

To peace of mind, which is all I want and need right now.
Daisy Jane

20

Krystal

Thinking back to the start of the summer and the night of the charity event, Krystal couldn't believe how her life had shifted. In just one season, she'd orbited the galaxy, attributing new circumstances to positive thought and action. Amber contacted her a handful of times after that awful night. Krystal wouldn't be swayed; she would not put herself anywhere near that pack of selfish women. *Never again.* To outsiders, not much would appear all that different, but inside she felt like a completely different person, one with endless possibilities. This summer would go down in her personal history as a life-altering year.

Over the course of the past month, they had settled into a routine of sorts. Goldie would open shop—as she had for the last thirty years—and Krystal would arrive midday with fresh salads they would enjoy in the back while gabbing like long-lost friends. They covered a fair amount of ground in these conversations. Never before had she felt safe discussing her parents and the disconnection she experienced at the hands of two wildly unhappy people. She learned of the husband Goldie buried at the young age of forty-two. She hadn't gone into any detail, and on the few occasions he came up, there was no mention of a name, and as her posture stiffened, Krystal knew better than to inquire beyond.

Things between them were going well until the previous week, when Krystal noticed a change in Goldie's personality. She became contemplative, bordering on distant and cold. Instead of catching up while they ate, Goldie squirreled about in the back room, busying herself with mundane tasks. And she was spending less time in the studio.

One afternoon Krystal was manning the store and speaking to a customer about one of Goldie's more impressive works—an array of animals from the African savanna made from red clay, including an elephant, zebra, lion, giraffe, and meerkat. Each one was finely detailed and painted with high quality glazes.

"These are simply divine." A woman admired the pieces. "We're taking an extended family vacation to Ghana for my parents' sixty-fifth wedding anniversary next year. I'd love to have this collection."

"They are pretty, aren't they?" Krystal cradled the lion with both hands to look for a price tag. "I don't believe they come as a collection."

"I see. Well, if I was willing to purchase all of them and pay in cash, do you think you could swipe the tax and offer me a better deal?"

The woman's skin was flawless; her makeup seemed to be of professional application.

"I'd have to check with the owner of the store. These are her creations. She's wonderful. Not sure about the tax, but I'm positive she'll be willing to work with you on the price."

Krystal knew this would be a major sale for Goldie, and she did not want this customer to get discouraged and possibly take her business elsewhere. She could see the woman's attention was starting to wane as she pulled out her mobile to tap out a text message.

"How long will you be staying in Cape May?" Krystal asked, trying to keep her engaged.

"Until the end of the week."

"I'd be happy to keep this on reserve for you. Once I speak to my boss, I'll call you right away with an offer. Would that be okay?"

The woman looked up from over her glasses, which had slipped to the end of her nose.

"On reserve?"

"Yes. I'd be happy to." Krystal reached for a pen and pad.

The woman jotted down her contact information and breezed out of the store. Krystal hand-scribbled "Reserved for Purchase" on a stack of sticky notes, pinning them in front of each piece.

The next afternoon, she knew something was off as soon as she entered the store. The skittish teenager hired for the summer to man the register wouldn't meet her eyes. Once she reached the back room, she spotted the handful of sticky notes crumpled and sitting at the top of the pile in the waste bin.

"I really wish you had asked me first." Goldie was flustered. "What gave you the impression I employed such a policy? We never put items on reserve."

Krystal's mind went blank from nervousness. She tried to recall and relay her conversation with the woman, how she feared they might lose the sale, and she knew she was fumbling over the words.

"And what did we receive in exchange for holding up merchandise? The good word of some . . . some . . . *stranger*? What if three more people come in this week wanting to purchase those items. I mean, I wouldn't even know what to tell them now that you've promised them to someone who . . . who . . . we don't even *know*. There's a darn good chance we may never see this person again. Then what?"

Krystal had never seen this side of Goldie. She was stammering and flustered and skirting the edge of hysteria. She and Goldie both knew the chances of anyone, let alone three customers, showing interest in the exorbitantly priced items was highly unlikely. But she, of course, was not going to point that out. Goldie then vanished from the studio for the remainder of the day.

Later that evening, Krystal broached the subject with Abe over supper.

"She has been acting so strange lately. Even before this happened. I don't know. She's definitely mad at me. I wish I knew what I did."

"One of the biggest mistakes people make in life is taking things personally when it could have nothing to do with them. How much do you know about her personal life? Maybe she had a fight with her boyfriend or something," Abe said as he shoveled a third helping of Pearl's spanakopita onto his plate.

He never could get enough of the Greek delicacy of layered filo dough stuffed with feta cheese and spinach. Not only was Krystal too distracted to remind him about portion control, she had completely lost her own appetite.

"I guess I royally screwed up today." She was starting to feel sorry for herself—a state she knew was just about the worst place to be.

In between bites, Abe tried to assure her how certain he was that Goldie was "beyond ecstatic" about the new arrangement. "Trust me." She felt herself becoming irritated at his inclination to always be so sure of himself. He didn't even know Goldie. Or the dynamics of their relationship. What made him such an expert?

Suddenly, she made a decision. Instead of wrestling with a sour belly for the rest of the night, she bucked up her courage and grabbed her phone.

"What's going on?" Abe said.

"I'm calling her. I'll fix this."

Abe paused his chewing and looked at her carefully, seeming equally surprised as she was by her own determination. It was out of character for her to address something head-on as opposed to stewing over it, allowing it to poison her. But she had too much invested in the situation, not just professionally but emotionally. She really cared for Goldie and relied on her companionship. If she had offended or overstepped her bounds, she needed this squashed as quickly as possible.

She headed for her study, knowing great care was needed in order not to repeat herself as she did when her nerves were frazzled. She closed the door and scrolled through her contact list. A moment later, Goldie answered.

"I wanted to apologize about what happened today. I really was only trying to help. I never meant—"

"Pardon me. What happened today, dear?" Goldie's voice was weak, almost sheepish.

Krystal began pacing the room. Had she imagined their uncomfortable conversation—or had Goldie just forgotten all about it?

"I know that customer will return. She was only looking for a fair deal, not a bargain. I was afraid to lose the sale, and I didn't want that happening on my watch. I would never have negotiated a price on your behalf and—"

"Oh, dear. You're quite upset over this, aren't you? Much more than you need be."

The delicate lilt to Goldie's tender and good-natured voice was back. It was like feeling the sunshine again after days of grey sky.

"It's just that I value our friendship. And I take my role at the studio very seriously," Krystal said, careful not to add more, knowing the tether on her emotions was precarious and not to be tested.

"Oh, honey. I know that. Of course you do. I, too, value our friendship. Very much so. Goodness me. I must have had you in quite a state. I apologize for coming down so heavy-handed today."

"That's okay. I wasn't sure if something else might be wrong. I thought maybe you had changed your mind." Krystal's voice was trailing off.

"Changed my mind?"

"About me and the store and all."

"Heavens, no!"

Krystal plunked into the high-back desk chair and spun around, her eyes taking hold of the bright crescent moon illuminating the lazy waves of the harbor.

"I have had quite a bit on my mind lately." Goldie's voice was soft. *Too* soft.

"Is it something you can talk about?"

There was a pause. A long one. Krystal braced herself.

"Well, it's certainly nothing to concern yourself over, but I've been contending with some health issues is all."

Her empty stomach roiled once again, forcing her to spring from the chair and resume pacing.

"Well, anyway, I am sure this wasn't an easy phone call for you to make. I do hope we have squared away this silly squabble. We have, haven't we?"

"Yes, of course." Krystal tried to sound more upbeat than she felt.

Health issues. She would never breach the sacred boundary of Goldie's personal space in search of information that didn't belong to her. But this did not sit well, and her concern for her friend had now exponentiated.

)(

With Abe spending more time in the Maryland office while negotiating the details on a big case, Krystal and Pearl were left to face one another without their buffering neutral party. The offering of the late-night turkey sandwich, in all its simplicity, had opened up a small door in the wall between them. One thing Krystal had learned as a young girl was that life was much more pleasurable when there was harmony within the home. It's something she never had but knew existed when visiting friends' homes and witnessing their families in action—a father stealing a kiss from a mother stationed at the sink; the polite and even discourse at the dinner table between each family member; hands locked in a circle of love, heads bowed in prayer during grace. Her own experience at home consisted of yelling and swearing, in between reigns of eerie silence blanketing the house. These were not aspects of her former home life she wished to repeat in any fashion.

The following morning, she was greeted by another cloudless August day. By that point in the summer, Krystal had grown accustomed to the seemingly endless string of inviting beach days, the kind that remind you to be happy you're alive. Gliding across the hardwood floor and area rug of the master suite out onto the balcony, she marveled at the dance of waves as they peaked and valleyed. The harbor beach was a key launch site for kayaks, canoes, and paddle boards. The flurry of activity laced the air with a verve found only in the summer months. It was half past ten, right around the time Pearl would be taking a break from her morning chores to enjoy the view out on the veranda.

Normally, Krystal would have quickly wolfed down her breakfast alone at the island in the kitchen, but she was on a mission to foster a stronger connection. She carried her mug of green tea and a small plate of scrambled egg whites, placing them both onto the wrought-iron table on the patio. The scraping of the chair against the pavers caught Pearl's attention; she had been standing at the edge of the property, gazing in the direction of the Coast Guard tower.

"Good morning. I wanted to properly thank you for my late-night snack. It really hit the spot."

"I'm pleased to hear that," Pearl said. She approached the table and placed her hands delicately on the back of a chair, not quite ready to sit down. "Big day planned?"

"Join me." Krystal motioned toward the chair. "Please."

Pearl gingerly pulled out the chair and sat down, hands tented in her lap. She had never shown an interest before, yet there was an undeniable expression of curiosity in her eyes as Krystal spoke of some of the upcoming events she and Goldie had been collaborating on. She knew it didn't hurt that Goldie was in Pearl's age group, lending more credence to their alliance.

"We should do this every day." Krystal hoped for a positive reaction.

The lines across Pearl's forehead smoothed as she said, "I think that's a fine idea."

For the next two weeks, the women shared breakfast each morning. Pearl would brew the coffee and prepare the egg whites, while Krystal would steep her own tea and rinse the fresh berries from the farmers market. The two would meet together at ten thirty on the veranda for their shared feast.

One afternoon, Krystal was inspired to create a special necklace to solidify their newfound friendship. She sculpted the clay into a cylinder, adding a one-inch row of silver chain, and attached a piece of glass in seafoam green at the end. She was able to match the glaze to the glass—the perfect shade to accentuate Pearl's eyes. Since the necklace had come out so magnificently, she went ahead and made a pair of matching earrings to complete the set. It was some of her best work to date.

She remembered Goldie's wise words: "You're going to get what you put in. When you cook with love in your heart, the food tastes better. The same will be true of the pieces you craft." Goldie's advice had a way of sticking to her ribs, as she once heard Abe say of Pearl's beef chili. She was preparing to head over to Goldie's home, as she needed assistance with a few of the more challenging crafts she'd been working on.

With the tide moving in, the strip of sand of the modest harbor beach was rapidly disappearing beneath the curtain of foamy water. Krystal stood on the edge of her balcony, wrapped in her cotton robe. Her damp skin was prickled with chills from the constant wind as the sun dipped behind the trees to the west, casting a great shadow over the back of the house. She watched the last of the boaters returning from their day out on the water. A young mom with her daughter, maybe ten, looked up and waved. Having a home on the harbor was a dream come true. The Fisherman's Memorial was erected in 1988 and served as one of the most charming and nostalgic sights on the island. A mother carved in stone looked despondently out to the great blue with two small children at her waist. The boy looked up at his mother as if searching her face for answers. And sadly, as the years passed, more names were carved onto the stone wall.

Krystal dressed and headed to the mini transport van Abe had surprised her with to carry her goods to and from the studio. She needed to make a delivery over to Goldie's house. When Jocelyn first saw the new van, she teased her relentlessly.

"What's wrong with this picture? I'm technically the housewife over here, and the sexy blonde down the street with no kids is now the one in the signature vehicle designated for every soccer mom in America." Krystal loved the fact that Jocelyn could always get her to laugh at herself.

Within minutes, she was in Goldie's driveway. As she climbed the long front staircase, she spotted a lumpy ball of fur tucked into the corner next to one of the planters of the lemonade porch. She approached slowly, swatting off a swarm of black flies, and reached down to check the tag.

Shirley.

There was no movement in the cat's chest. Her eyes were sealed shut as if glued. Even her once bushy white mane was dull and lifeless. Krystal wondered how long the cat had been lying there, dead.

The thought of having to break the news to Goldie made her queasy. As she opened the screen door, her eardrums were pierced by the sound of a high-pitched mewl.

Laverne?

Their last point of contact was the night before. She wanted to shoot Goldie a text reminding her about their meeting, but she was not technologically savvy. She had a cellphone but was one of those people who kept it just to have but never used the damn thing.

Malcolm's unmistakable squawking grew so loud Krystal resisted the urge to plug her ears with her fingertips. It sounded as though he were trying to threaten an intruder. Either that or he was just yelling to himself. She wouldn't put anything past that crazy bird. Goldie mentioned he had a tendency to become irritable and demanding in the summertime when the business and studio kept her from the home.

She walked down the hallway and saw Laverne perched in her usual spot at the foot of the couch. For the first time, her eyes met Krystal's in what seemed to be a message of some sort. Was it a cry for help? Or a warning?

"I . . . said . . . leave! You have no business here. . . ." Goldie's voice boomed down the corridor.

Someone was in the house! Was she being attacked? Krystal's adrenaline spiked as she imagined the worst. She barreled down the hallway. The mewling was coming from Brutus, who was pacing the room, jumping on and off the couch. He poked his wet snoot against her hand. The house looked like the aftermath of a flood. It was in complete disarray, far worse than its usual disorganized state. It appeared unclean. Dirty. Birdseed was scattered across the floor. A mug of coffee on the side table appeared to have been sitting there for days by the filmy layer of curdled milk floating across the top.

"Shut up, Simon! Pretty boy! Pretty boy!" Malcolm was hysterical and completely out of control himself as he bobbed his head.

"Get out! Get out! Get out!" The darkness in Goldie's voice chilled her. Krystal could not believe those guttural, angry sounds of desperation were being emitted by her friend. As she entered the back room, she saw a woman sitting in the center of the room. Something was terribly wrong. Goldie was not in her right mind. She was unrecognizable: petrified, unmoored, visibly shaken.

"Hey. . . ." Krystal approached. "It's all gonna be okay, honey. I'm here now."

Krystal could see from her perplexed expression that her words were of no use. It reminded her of the few times she'd seen Goldie become transported to another place, a different dimension.

"It's me. Krystal. You are safe now." She gripped her shoulders gently, trying to make eye contact.

"Is . . . he . . . gone?"

"Is who gone, sweetheart? Who's bothering you?" Krystal cleared the papers and debris, taking a cross-legged seat on the floor.

"Simon. . . ."

Simon?

"Who is that, sweetie? Who is Simon?"

"Shut up, Simon! Pretty boy! Pretty boy!" Malcolm chimed in as if on cue.

His screeching made it impossible for her to think clearly. Goldie's head lobbed from side to side. With quaky hands, she shielded her wrinkled face. Brutus's whimpering, mingled with Malcolm's ranting, escalated the tension. She felt a paw on her thigh: Laverne. She had always been the more needy of the two cats, seeking constant affection. Reaching her one free arm out, she tried to stabilize her friend's gaunt and trembling limbs. The animals drew ever closer, begging for reassurance. Krystal became paralyzed with terror as a limp torso oozed from her embrace into a lifeless heap at her side.

21

Goldie

ELIZABETH CITY, NORTH CAROLINA,
DECEMBER 11, 1980

S he hadn't thrown a piece in three whole days and couldn't remember the last time she'd gone that long without working. Not only was her creativity stifled, she'd become emotionally crippled. *All he wanted was to get home so he could tuck in his little boy before bedtime.* And what was to become of young Sean?

The news of John Lennon's assassination landed on the heels of the ten-year anniversary of Patrick's death, triggering Goldie's grief all over again. She sat up to take a sip from her water glass, but as her head became too much for her knotted neck to bear, she promptly resumed position on the nest of sullied pillows. Sunlight filtered through a partially opened curtain, piercing her tender eyes. She had quarantined in the spare bedroom for the last few days. Every Tuesday, the linens were washed, but Winifred had failed at her attempts to remove the sheets two days prior.

Simon hired Winifred the year after Patrick died. As he

spent more time at the office, Simon worked himself up the ladder into a managerial position, nearly doubling his starting salary. With each promotion, he treated himself to many spoils and quite enjoyed having the status symbol of hiring a live-in. Over the years, the three had fallen into a rhythm: Simon headed to the office before sunrise, Goldie whittled away in her butterfly garden and threw pieces in her home studio, and Winifred tended to all the household chores from laundry to cleaning to meal preparation. On the many nights he would stay in a hotel near his office, Winifred still presented a gourmet feast for two, including a starter and dessert. Lovely as it was, it made Goldie feel even more alone in the colossal dining room, so she would insist Winifred join her at the table and share in the extravagance of her own creation.

It was now Thursday, and Goldie had neither the strength nor the will to strip the bed and haul wads of bedding down three flights of stairs to the laundry room in the basement. The one and only thing that drew her from her living quarters was a daily visit to the butterfly garden. It was the one place she felt whole, the one place she could still feel Patrick. His presence was there. Lingering. Observing. She would muster the strength to weed the flower beds, supplying fresh water and love to each of the plants, just as Patrick would have expected. Then she'd plop onto one of the Tuscan cast-stone benches where they would have their evening talks, once upon a time.

"You are going to make some lucky child very happy one day, Little Birdie."

All those years, his words had never left her. And yet a child of her own wasn't part of the hand life had dealt. The passion she and Simon once shared had waned over time. When they did make an attempt at intimacy, it was an awkward, unsatisfying fumble in the dark. The one time she tried to bring up her worries over the health of their sex life, he brushed it off, reminding her how hard he worked and how tired he was. Lately, their interactions were relegated to the dinner table—on the rare nights he came home for supper—and at the breakfast table each Sunday morning.

On the previous Saturday, Simon poked his head through the partially opened bedroom door. He swirled the amber liquid in his highball while leaning against the doorframe. The sour smell of alcohol made her empty belly roil.

"You ever plan on getting out of that bed?"

"Tomorrow. . . ." Her voice trailed off as her gaze wandered to a colony of dust bunnies huddled in a far corner.

"When was the last time you bathed?" His eyes were already dewy, which spoke to his second round. "This isn't sanitary, you know."

She blinked back at him.

"Or healthy."

An untimely yawn nudged its way out, demanding to be seen. What could she do? At least she managed to tuck her head to shield a wide-open mouth with the covers.

Simon narrowed his eyes in a withering glance. "In fact, it's downright concerning."

"Tomorrow. I'll get up tomorrow. And I'll take a long, hot shower. Don't worry." He seemed moderately satisfied by this response, as the tightness in his jowls loosened. "I picked up a quiche at the market. Spinach and mushroom."

In years past, he would stop off on his way home from work and surprise her with treats. Quiche had always been her favorite. It definitely wasn't Simon's, who was a bona fide carnivore, capable of single-handedly covering the utility bills on the butcher's home and place of business each week. It had been so long Goldie could not remember the last time he'd surprised her, and the gesture made her want to weep, if only she had the strength.

"Thank you."

"Yes. Well, I'll be in the dining room having supper if you care to join me."

And once again, the door was closed, shut tight, with Simon on the other side. He always showed his love through simple displays of affection. That was his way. There was still hope for them. Somewhere deep inside, the good parts of her husband may just still exist. Even if they were slightly buried beneath a blanket of insecurities and hurt.

She pulled back the sheets and swung one leg and then the other over the side of the bed. Her knees protested in pain as she stood. It was her chance to return the favor and graciously accept his dinner invitation. Taking careful and deliberate steps, she retrieved a fresh towel from the linen closet. As she headed toward the shower, Yoko Ono came to mind. It was nearly impossible not to be swept away and dazzled by the whirlwind romance between John and Yoko. Despite the speculation of many who ardently believed in her alleged hand in the breakup of The Beatles, Goldie had nothing against the woman. People could be so critical and heavy-handed—if only that's all they were.

22

Jocelyn

There was a touch more silver near his sideburns since the last time she saw him back in July. It wasn't that he looked older per se. More distinguished, perhaps. And was that a limp she detected or just her writerly imagination at play?

Watching Trevor cross the room in his khaki pants and golf shirt made her wonder how she wound up in the arms of this guy, who was so totally different from her rugged Bruce in weathered Levi's and worn construction boots.

"I realize you're upset about this. And yes, I understand. But you have to see things from my perspective. We weren't even together when Billy was born. You got physical custody, and I agreed. Now I have my own family and two more kids. I don't want Billy to think he is forgotten. He has a family here too. In Maryland, with me, Hannah, and the twins," Trevor said.

"I understand all that. What I don't agree with is you trying to take him away from me. I am his mother."

"Yes. And I am his father. And I never said I was trying to

take him away. Many people share custody. It's not uncommon these days."

"Keeping him from his mother for nine months out of the year is not sharing custody."

"It wouldn't be nine months."

A car door slammed in the driveway. Trevor didn't seem to hear it as he continued to blather on and on about how much fun Billy was having and how he knew this private school would challenge him in ways a public school could not. Bruce would have noticed someone arriving at the house. It was another thing that made the two men so different. Bruce was vigilant. Protective. On guard. It went with the territory of having been the man of the house at such a young age and for all those years. He was sweet but tough. Built to last, capable of withstanding the strongest of winds and highest of tides. Just like the houses he built from scratch.

"I've seen a lawyer," Jocelyn said.

"Hello there!" Hannah walked in carrying a canvas satchel across her back. "Jocelyn, it is so nice to see you! I had no idea you were coming!"

"That makes two of us," Trevor said humorlessly.

"Hold on. I'll be right back. I need to get this produce into the fridge. Don't go anywhere!"

Jocelyn had to hand it to her: There was something special about Hannah. She had been in the room for less than ten seconds and already made her feel welcomed.

Trevor and Jocelyn averted their attention from one another as their eyes danced around the room, waiting for Hannah to return.

"How are you?" Hannah approached with outspread arms, forcing Jocelyn to rise up off the couch. "You look beautiful. I wish I could tan like that."

Jocelyn hadn't realized just how desperate she was for a hug until she was swallowed into Hannah's embrace and held on for longer than she normally would have.

"The kids are all in camp. But I know Billy is going to be thrilled to see you," Hannah said. "How about a cup of herbal tea? Or Kombucha, maybe? I have cranberry, strawberry, and ginger."

"Thank you, but I'm fine."

"He sure does miss you, you know," Hannah said.

Had Trevor just shifted his body weight in the high-back chair, or was Jocelyn imagining things?

"How have the nightmares been?" Jocelyn asked.

"Much better. Oh, much. I've been letting him sleep with your books by his side. I told him no bad guys or monsters could get to him as long as he had his mommy's book for protection. And it worked!"

Jocelyn was so moved she could have cried. "Thank you for taking such good care of him."

"He brags to everyone he sees about the stories his mommy writes. Even the twins love the stories now." Hannah's clear blue eyes shifted to Trevor.

"Yes, that's true. All three kids can't seem to get enough." Trevor tucked in his bottom lip, nodding in agreement.

"I hope you plan on writing more children's books. You have a way. You know how to speak to them in a way that others cannot," Hannah said.

This was a strange turn of events: Supermom lauding Jocelyn's knack with kids. It wasn't exactly how she saw this trip playing out.

"And you have another book coming out, don't you? I almost forgot." Hannah's enthusiasm was genuine.

"I'm waiting to hear back from my agent to find out if my manuscript was accepted by the publisher."

"Agents, manuscripts, publishers. . . . You are big-time!" Hannah said.

"I wouldn't go that far." Jocelyn suddenly felt more humble than ever before.

"Honey, Jocelyn and I were just going over some stuff about Billy," Trevor said.

Hannah's bright smile deflated as she realized he was subtly suggesting she should leave them alone.

"Hannah, let me ask you: What do you think of this private school idea?" Jocelyn said.

"Oh, the school is simply wonderful. The campus, the teachers, the curriculum. It's one of the top-rated schools in the country."

"I'm sure it is. But, as a mother, how would you feel if someone wanted to take your child from you to go to school there?"

Hannah's mouth dropped open. She looked at Trevor. "I thought you said Jocelyn was in agreement?"

"She needed a little more persuading than I thought." Trevor shifted his eyes again; it was his signature move.

"Does Hannah know that you threatened to take me to court for custody of Billy?" Jocelyn said with a razor-sharp edge to her voice.

"What?!" Hannah's eyes grew ever wider. "Is this true?"

"Not *full* custody. Shared," Trevor said.

"Why drag this out in some courtroom? The only ones who will win will be our attorneys," Jocelyn said.

"I was under the impression this was something you both agreed was a good idea. I did not know that you've been pressuring Jocelyn into this. You just don't do that to a mother," Hannah said. She was shaking her head, arms akimbo. Jocelyn suddenly felt understood. Not alone.

"I don't want to be an absentee father!" Trevor said.

"Absentee father?" Jocelyn was shaking her head. "Of course you're not. Where did that come from?"

"I love my son. I need to be in his life. He has to know that he always has me. That I will always be there for him. Just like I am for my other two. I don't want to lose him."

"You could never lose Billy," Hannah said. "Why would you say such a thing? He has two beautiful families who love him to the moon and back. A lot of children don't have any family. Not even one person to count on. Billy is one of the luckiest kids around, to be surrounded by so much love." Hannah's rising emotion caught in her throat.

Jocelyn fought the urge to jump out of her seat and squeeze her to bits with love.

"If you really believe a private school would be better for Billy, then maybe we can find one in South Jersey near me."

Trevor shook his head and waved them off. "You win. I give up."

"There's nothing to give up on. Billy will always be your son. Our son. And we will always work out what is best for him. Together. As a team," Jocelyn said tenderly. "I would never try and keep him from you. It's important to me that you remain a prominent presence in his upbringing. Both of you."

Hannah was nodding and swiped a tear on the back of her sleeve while shooting her husband a subtle look of reproach.

Jocelyn left that afternoon before Billy returned home from camp. She didn't know how he would react to seeing her after all these weeks, and she couldn't take the chance that he would beg to go home with her. His visit with his father hadn't come to an end, and she certainly did not want to be responsible for cutting it short. Especially, in light of the peace she made with Trevor.

As Jocelyn returned home, the only thing hanging in the balance was the status of her book. She found herself losing an easy two hours scrolling Facebook and Instagram, then decided to check her email. In addition to the plethora of junk mail, there was one from her lawyer, Harrison Buck, with the subject:

INVOICE. Reluctantly, she clicked on the attachment. It was a four-page document, which puzzled her. Uninterested and dizzy from all the legal jargon, she scrolled to the last page for a tally of the damage.

$3,285.00

How could this be? Surely, they had sent her someone else's bill. Going back to the first page, Jocelyn saw the initial $600 consultation fee, two hefty charges for both phone calls, and thirty-six e-mails at $75 a pop. What?! They'd never said anything about being charged for *e-mails*. This was bullshit. The subtotal had reached over $3,600, but out of the kindness of his heart, Harrison Buck extended a ten percent professional discount to first-time clients. So Jocelyn saved over $300. And yet she still owed over $3,000! And for what? She'd heard lawyers could be as shady as mechanics, taking advantage of people (namely, women, the elderly, immigrants) who made easy targets. There was no way she was going to pay this bill as it stood.

She'd grabbed her phone to call Harrison Buck's office when she saw a pending voicemail from Jeannie Ball. Without hesitation, she pressed play to hear the message.

"Hello, Jocelyn. It's Jeannie. We need to talk. Call me, please."

Jeannie's voice was monotone. She spoke slowly, her words deliberate. Jocelyn played the message three more times. She didn't know why. Maybe she was in shock. Maybe she needed to hear it repeated in order to grasp what the words meant. What frightened her more than anything was the resignation that dripped from every one of Jeannie's words. As if she was surrendering. Her agent did not have good news to share.

Jocelyn was out of plays. There were no more moves for her to make. The only way out of this was to submit a book that was actually worthwhile. But books took time to write. Boatloads of time and energy and patience and sacrifice. How was she going to tell Bruce about the rejected book? How was she going to tell Bruce about the money she owed Harrison Buck?

She headed for the basement. There was one final journal entry from Daisy. She needed to see, now more than ever, how the story ended.

~Journal of Daisy Jane Anderson~
Summer 1981

Funny how time and distance will change your perspective on things. I can now see I was being used for sex. How naive and foolish I was to think that a man capable of deceiving his own wife would drop everything and run away with me. I've come to learn that men like him only end up doing the same thing to their mistresses, if they ever keep them around long enough to elevate them from "the other woman" status. I have done a great job of burying the past and forgetting about The Man Who Fathered My Son. That is what I call him now.

Tommy Myers (Laney's now ex-boyfriend) showed up yesterday unexpectedly with some news. (Tommy comes over almost every day to play with Brucie—the news was unexpected. Not the visit.) I don't know what I would ever do without him. He's been a loyal, sweet, and loving friend and provides a male role model for my baby. Funny how life works out. Laney and I don't even speak anymore. She was blinded by her jealousy. Last I heard she married some other musician and is moving to Tennessee. I hope she's happy. Despite what she may have thought and what she hears from the busybodies in town, my relationship with Tommy is and always was platonic. Nothing romantic, or otherwise, has ever happened between us. I just don't look at him in that way. I know he wants more from me, but I can't give it. I've been burned too brutally from what I thought was true love. Ha! True love. What is true love, anyway? The Man Who Fathered My Son didn't even tell me his real name. When

Tommy handed me the newspaper article, I couldn't believe my eyes. In fact, I still can't quite believe what I read. I only hope Tommy doesn't think this discovery will change my stance on being with him in any way. It doesn't. All it does is provide closure with The Man Who Fathered My Son.

This measly black-and-white newspaper photo is all I have left of him. A man who lied to my face. A man who told me his name was Frank Cooper. Why didn't you tell me your real name? I just keep staring at the picture as though suddenly the image of him will change, but it never does.

The article referenced his work and residence. It's him all right. I can't stop my finger from trailing the foreign name in print. Maybe I'm subconsciously trying to recognize this man I never knew. Maybe I'm trying to erase this name until it fades into nothingness.

He was found dead in his home last Sunday morning by his wife. *DEAD*. It appeared he had some sort of heart attack. I had no idea how much stress he must have been under between his wife's failing health and the demands of his corporate job.

Yesterday, without warning, that old wound was reopened. My pain and anger spilled from my eyes onto the flimsy paper. I swiped my finger one last time, stubbing out his image and the name I never knew. I will never have to see him or it again.

This concludes the story of The Man Who Fathered My Son. With this, my last journal entry in this notebook.

Goodbye, forever.

Whoever you were, Simon Knight.

Daisy Jane

Jocelyn flew to her desk. She had to find out more about this Simon Knight, that *creep*, whoever he was, for doing what he did to Daisy. And poor Bruce. To have such a man for a father. For the first time ever, she didn't replace the notebook in the safe. Somehow, she felt more secure having it with her than any-where else. And she didn't want to feel separated from Daisy. She needed her right there. At her side.

Her computer screen filled with an obituary from the *Daily Advance* in Elizabeth City, North Carolina. The article was written in 1981. There was a sketchy photo of a young gentle-man—early forties maybe? The headline read: *Man Found Dead in Home of Natural Causes.*

"On Sunday, July 5th, Simon Knight, age thirty-nine, was declared dead by the Elizabeth City Police in his home at 10:53 a.m. Knight had been a partner in the CPA firm of Stratford Accounting in Virginia Beach for the last ten years. His body was discovered by his wife of twelve years—"

"Hey, baby."

Jocelyn jumped up from her chair. She hadn't heard Bruce walk in. There was no time to throw the notebook into a drawer. Doing so now would only invite suspicion. She left it there, care-ful to keep her eyes from glancing at it.

"Whoa. Sorry. I didn't mean to scare you." He smiled, notic-ing the glass of wine. "You okay?"

She wasn't okay. She was anything but okay. And she needed him more than ever. Her Bruce. Her rock. But there had been so many secrets between them. There was no way for her to bridge that divide without coming clean—about everything.

"When did you get back? That was a quick trip. How is the little guy? I sure do miss him." Hearing the sun in Bruce's voice when she was filled with so much darkness made her feel even lower.

"He's had a great summer out there." She was unable to elab-orate. There was nothing else to add.

"I got some news." Bruce was smiling the way he did right before he was about to surprise her. "You ready?" he teased.

"I think so."

"I've secured a deal for an excavator. No more subcontractors for Anderson Contracting."

"Oh, wow. That's great news. How did you work it out?"

"Goldie Sparrows." Bruce folded his arms across his chest. One corner of his lips rose slightly. His cagey demeanor took her aback. "That woman knows everyone."

"Goldie?"

Jocelyn's mind spun. This good news was clouded in knowing Bruce had shared intimate details of his private business affairs with an outsider before her. It was a testament to how much he trusted and respected Goldie, and as much as she'd always been supportive of their friendship—even if she didn't fully understand it—Jocelyn was his wife and couldn't deny the pain she felt. More secrets between them.

"I have just about enough. With your book advance, we can cover this. No problem at all."

Jocelyn wanted to run from the house and scream until there was nothing left in her lungs. "I have something to tell you."

"Uh-oh. I don't think I like the sound of this," he said. The spirit in his voice from just a moment ago had already left. She missed it already. She wanted it back.

"They didn't accept the book."

"What are you saying? I thought this deal was as good as done."

"It wasn't my best work. I don't know. I just don't . . . I'm sorry."

"Not your best work? What the hell have you been doing at this desk for all these months? All this time on your own to write? This makes no sense at all. None at all."

"It's not as easy as people think to tie yourself to a chair all day long and try to concentrate and create something that's actually worthwhile, not knowing—"

"No job is easy! That's why it's called *work*. This was your end of the bargain. What would happen to our family if I didn't show up on job sites and stopped bringing home a paycheck?"

She rose from her chair in an attempt to embrace him, but he took two steps back and threw up a hand.

"Don't. This can't be fixed with a hug. Or sex. Just don't."

His voice had wrinkled. Not only was his anger apparent, so was his pain. The sound made her want to shrivel up and die right there.

"I'm sorry, Bruce." Her words, so weak and meaningless, popped like bubbles at his back as he stormed from the room.

His work boots—which he purposefully hadn't removed to spite her—punched each and every step to the second floor like gloved fists to a bag.

Jocelyn's toes and fingers tingled. Her tongue felt dry and heavy, her head woozy. Earlier that afternoon, she'd inhaled a granola bar, and the undigested oats and nuts threatened to splatter across her keyboard. She reverted to measured breathing just to maintain focus. Her system was breaking down. With her mind in such disarray, it was decaying every cell of her body.

No more lies. No more secrets. Not one more.

She climbed the stairs and entered their bedroom.

"Bruce. There is something else I have to tell you."

The loose letter tucked on the inside of the notebook crinkled in her unsteady hands.

"This belongs to you."

"What? What is it?" he said.

"It belonged to Daisy."

Bruce stopped blinking. "What do you mean?"

"It was your mother's journal. From long ago. Before she had you."

Confusion crossed his face as his eyebrows cinched, deepening the lines across his forehead.

"Where did you find it?"

"In the safe. It was stowed at the bottom beneath the felt."

"And you . . . read it?"

"Yes."

"You've been reading my mother's private journal. Why didn't you say anything? How could you keep this from me?"

I was afraid you'd snatch it from me. I needed to escape from my life into Daisy's world.

"I'm sorry."

"That's enough 'I'm sorrys' to last a lifetime."

She dropped her head in shame. With both hands, Jocelyn outstretched her arms to turn the notebook over to him. She knew Daisy would want him to have it, would want him to know everything. Daisy hadn't kept secrets; she'd written them all down for her son.

Jocelyn was the one who kept secrets.

23

Goldie

The sun blinked off the rapids of the Delaware Bay as the briny air tingled her lips. It had been over two decades since she was this far north up the East Coast, back when she would visit her aunt and uncle in Maryland before they passed. With Simon fully entrenched in his work, there had never been an opportunity to escape. Other than a few extended weekend trips to Nags Head, their Acapulco honeymoon back in 1969 was the last proper getaway they had as a couple. This would be her first trip without him. No one knew of her whereabouts, nor the reason for her mission. All she told Simon was that she'd be visiting a few cousins up north while he was away on a business conference in Denver.

Standing at the gunwale of the Cape May-Lewes Ferry, she tried to invoke the healing energy of the sea air to calm her spirit and troubled mind—Simon had caused enough damage, and she wouldn't allow him to steal the tranquility of the moment.

In the months following John Lennon's murder, the tension between them had mounted the way snow accumulates during a winter storm; at first, little by little, but as the hours pass, adding new layers, a powerlessness sets in with the awareness of the extraordinary effort, exertion, and teamwork that will be needed to dig through the icy mess.

She had never returned to their bedroom. She remained in the guest room so she could work and read and sketch as late into the night as she wished without complaint. Their estrangement took hold with afternoon phone calls to let her know he wouldn't be home for dinner. Then a few times a week, he'd call to say his partner's wife offered to let him crash in their family room so he didn't have to make the seventy-minute drive home only to have to return before dawn of the following day. Ultimately, they reached the point where Simon stopped letting her know he wouldn't be coming home. He just wouldn't show. There was no way for Goldie to know when she'd be dining alone—or spending the night in the enormous house with Winifred. The most startling realization was when she acknowledged just how little she cared one way or another of his whereabouts.

And then, Goldie made a discovery that would change their union forever. She found herself rummaging through his desk on the third consecutive night he hadn't made it home. Not quite sure of exactly what it was she was looking for, she sure got more than she bargained for. After finally tracking down the key to the one locked cabinet of his armoire, she retrieved an instant photo image of a young blonde with long braids taken on Simon's old Polaroid camera. She was wearing a long cotton skirt, a thin gold headband, and a white tunic with bell sleeves. Goldie was surprised to feel only a subtle twinge of jealousy, which was secondary to the pity she felt from looking into the girl's trusting eyes. The blind adoration she felt for her photographer was palpable. On the back, in Simon's handwriting: *Daisy*

Jane Anderson, Spring 1976, Virginia Beach. Her mind flipped back to that time as she tried to recall what was happening in their lives. That was right about the time he stopped reaching for her at night. Her thoughts of wanting a baby were dismissed by Simon, who would change the subject. Meanwhile, she now knew, he had been having an affair all the while. She inhaled sharply and held her breath for a beat, refusing to allow herself to come undone. Not yet, anyway. There was more to be seen in this cabinet, and she wanted the whole picture before determining how to proceed. As she flipped through the photographs, there was an oval mood ring set in sterling silver with an ornate leaf pattern placed upon Daisy's left index finger. It was a replica of the one Simon had bought Goldie five years earlier when the concept was first introduced to the market. At the bottom of the stack was a wallet-size photo of Daisy wearing a cap and gown. On the back: *Class of 1975—Lower Cape May Regional.* That dirty predator. This girl was only twenty-four years old, and who knows how young she was when Simon first got to her.

She searched through his *Encyclopedia Britannica* collection to read up on Cape May (also referred to as Cape Island). It seemed like a charmingly quaint area, wrought with history dating back to its inception in the seventeenth century. The town had a walking mall, as well as a five-star restaurant scene, boutiques, an arcade, ice cream parlors, mini golf, and a charming selection of bed and breakfast inns. Goldie paid a visit to the local library to see if she could learn more information. As luck would have it, Mrs. Briggs, the librarian, was from a small town just outside of Philadelphia and well acquainted with the shore town, which had recently added a zoo to their many tourist attractions. After ten minutes of listening to Mrs. Briggs speak of the many local farm stands and the Coast Guard base, Goldie needed no further convincing. She went home to pack and made her way up the coast to the special place known to host some of the most prominent leaders, activists, entertainers, and artists in our nation's history, including Ulysses S. Grant, Harriet Tubman, Frank Lloyd Wright, John Phillip Sousa, Henry Ford, Grace Kelly, Norman Rockwell, and Burgess Meredith. It was all so intriguing, and while she may have been completely unsure of what she'd find, there was one thing that was certain: Simon had been fully responsible for beguiling this unfortunate girl into trusting him. And she was determined to learn more.

Leaving the ferry station, she headed for the Chalfonte Hotel. Mrs. Briggs had given her some brochures on the classic structure, whose slogan was "Where the South Meets the North," historically, geographically, and culturally. It was built and established by Civil War Union colonel Henry Sawyer and later taken over and operated for more than sixty years by the Satterfields of Richmond, Virginia—a family with deep ties to the Confederate Army.

Geographically, the Chalfonte sat in Cape May below the Mason-Dixon Line, on the same latitude as Washington, DC. Its long-standing tradition of warm hospitality and nationally acclaimed Southern-style fare was an essential part of the Chalfonte experience. Meals were lovingly prepared by the third generation of Dickerson women, whose matriarch, Clementine, came with the Satterfield family every summer from their Virginia home. Clementine's daughter, Helen, soon followed and later Helen's daughters, Dot and Lucille, who continued the ninety-year tradition of sharing their beloved family recipes with Chalfonte guests.

She imagined herself in a Charles Dickens novel as she drove through the streets lined with brightly painted Victorians and impeccable landscaping. The desk clerk led her to a suite and offered to make a reservation in the Magnolia Room for supper that evening; he urged her to try their famous fried chicken and collard greens. It was a Wednesday evening, so Goldie opted for the catch of the day: blackened catfish served with buttered grits and Brussels sprouts sautéed with black-eyed peas. She capped her supper off at the King Edward Bar with an after-dinner cordial. A couple was canoodling in the love seat right outside the door on the wraparound porch. To give them privacy, she carried her cocktail over to a cushioned wicker rocker in the corner. During her research, Goldie had tracked down an Anderson family in the city directory; her plan was to enjoy the next few days acclimating to the town and then rent a bicycle to explore what she believed to be Daisy Jane Anderson's neighborhood, located within six blocks of the Chalfonte.

The next morning, after a hearty breakfast of two eggs sunny side up, a scoop of yogurt with nectarines from the local farm, and freshly squeezed grapefruit juice, Goldie found herself standing before the African lions' cage at the Cape May Zoo. Such lazy, nocturnal, majestic beasts. She had always loved mammals from the Felidae family of cats and longed for a variety of pets, but Simon was allergic to anything with fur, feathers, or gills. In the beginning of their marriage, he would quip to dinner guests, *"If I ever kick the bucket, this one over here will be fixin' to recreate Noah's Ark out of my place. You just watch."* Goldie would politely smile against the backdrop of hushed tittering, unable to shake his reference to their home as being *his* place.

As she turned to treat herself to an iced tea at the snack bar, her blood turned cold. She couldn't feel her extremities. It was as if her system were trying to regulate her body temperature from a delirium in the sweltering sun. Sitting on a bench just outside the comfort station was a young blonde who looked like a twin to the one in Simon's photograph. Immediately, Goldie recognized the forest-green mood ring on the girl's left hand and the thin gold headband. *Daisy Jane.* In her lap sat a child. Just past his toddler years. Three, maybe four. He was running his fingers through her hair as they rubbed the tips of their noses together. *"Eskimo kisses . . . Eskimo kisses . . . that's my good boy, Brucie."*

As she moved in for a closer look, the little boy stopped, taking notice of her. Patrick's eyes stared back at her. She nearly gasped seeing her late father-in-law in the face of a child.

Daisy looked up. "Hello."

"Your little boy is precious."

Daisy smiled with all the pride of a lioness. She looked down at the cub bundled in her arms, addressing him directly. "Bruce, the nice lady just paid you a compliment. What do you say? We say *thank you.*"

"Tank-oooo." He even had the same cowlick as Patrick in the front right-hand side of his part.

A *father.* Simon was a father. Goldie was heartsick. Not only because her husband had been unfaithful, she was married to a man who had impregnated a young girl and deserted her.

Daisy stood to tuck in Bruce's shirt and dab his cheek with her wet thumb. "Well, have a nice day." And off they went as if nothing happened. As if Goldie's whole world hadn't just been spun right off its orbit.

For days, she tried to make sense of this new information and wondered if Simon knew about this perfect child he had a hand in creating. On yet another brilliantly sunny afternoon, Goldie spent her last day browsing the shops and boutiques before treating herself to a late lunch at one of the local seafood joints. She scooted into the last booth against the back wall. Just as the server delivered a plump set of fresh crab cakes along with a chilled glass of Chablis, a family settled into the next booth. In an instant, she recognized the cascading sunshine hair. And then, the honey-pitched gentle baby voice—Brucie. It was inconceivable that Simon could produce such a lovingly sweet child. Patrick's DNA had somehow skipped a generation. And how he would have adored his grandson. Fate could be a fickle and cruel beast, as these two would never come to know one another in this lifetime. The sentiment tugged on the deepest part of her soul.

She tuned in to the conversation between Daisy and the people she presumed were her parents, who seemed to be grilling her over something.

"I just don't understand. What is wrong with Thomas Myers? He is a lovely young man," said the woman.

"I didn't say anything was wrong with him. Did I say that? Did you *hear* me say those words?" Daisy's insolence was on par with that of a disgruntled teen. "You cannot go around picking out boyfriends for me. That's not how this works."

She sure could identify with struggling to break free from the rein of her folks and be respected. There was a time, not all that long ago, when Goldie had worn those very same slippers.

"Every woman requires a male companion to offer stability and protection. With Thomas, you'd have a complete family."

"We already are a family. My son and I don't need a man to complete us," Daisy said, growing ever more defensive.

"You need to tell this fellow, whoever he is, that he has a son to provide for. It ain't right that a man doesn't provide for his kids. It just ain't right, God damn it," the man, who was presumably Daisy's father, boomed.

"We've been over this a thousand timesss . . ." Daisy dragged out the last word with listless impatience, like a mother lacking sleep. "He already knows. He knew I was pregnant. I looked for him. It's been years. He obviously doesn't want to be found."

"It's just that . . . *you know who* will be attending school soon, sweetheart," her mother whispered. "It was one thing when he was a baby. All a baby needs is his mother, after all. But the time has come for him to have a real male role model."

"What's this guy's full name? Frank something?" her father chimed in with minimal enthusiasm.

"Oh, dear, for heaven's sake. His name is Cooper." Her mother was ruffled. "Frank Cooper. Isn't that right, Daisy?"

Frank Cooper? That was Simon's old college roommate from Harvard, who had moved to Santa Monica. She hadn't heard that name in over a decade. Was this a lie Daisy was telling her parents—or one that she was fed by Simon?

"Yes, Mother. That's his name."

Goldie was eavesdropping so intently she hadn't noticed the server standing by her side.

"Pardon me. Did you say something?"

She approved the second glass of wine while trying to keep an ear tapped into the next booth. From what she was able to ascertain from their conversation, Daisy occupied the bedroom she grew up in, which she now shared with Bruce. Money— or lack thereof—was of top concern, and she was being urged to find work to lighten the financial burden on her parents. It sounded as if her mother, who had never worked outside the home, was now working as a cashier in the Wawa convenience mart. Daisy's biggest concern seemed to be finding suitable day care for Bruce.

As the family gathered their belongings to leave, Daisy spotted Goldie.

"Oh, hey. I remember you. From the zoo, right?"

The rebellious teenage voice evaporated, replaced by the free-spirited young mother she'd met at the park. Daisy's beauty was striking. And even a bit intimidating, at first glance. Yet her genuine disposition surfaced and made her all the more endearing. Goldie wondered how such a pretty and vivacious young woman had become mixed up with the likes of Simon—but then, she had married him.

"Yes, hello. Nice to see you again," Goldie said.

"I'm Daisy, by the way."

Daisy's mother excused herself to the ladies' room as her

father pored over the check and headed toward the front of the restaurant. Goldie seized the opportunity.

"How old is your son?"

"He turned four in March." She turned to her boy. "Brucie, do you remember meeting Miss Goldie at the zoo the other day?"

He nodded.

"Well, hello again, Mr. Bruce. Fancy meeting you here." She crouched to meet him at eye level. It was as if Patrick was staring back at her. His eyes, his essence. If only she could capture the moment, drink in the sound and smell from this precious child.

"Sweetheart, what do you say?" Daisy prompted. "We say *hello*."

To that, Bruce released the monkey-hold he had around his mother's waist and lunged over to Goldie, flopping into her arms as if he had been doing so every day for the four years of his existence. It felt natural. Familiar. At once, she was flooded with comfort and pressed her hand to the middle of his back, feeling his ribcage gently expand and contract on each heaving breath.

"You are going to make some lucky child very happy one day, Little Birdie."

"Wow! He really likes you." Daisy was awestruck.

Bruce planted a sloppy wet kiss on Goldie's cheek. As he pulled away, a strand of saliva bridged her skin to his mouth. She was struck with a wave of nostalgia as Bruce was pulled from her arms.

"I'm sorry." Daisy was fussing. "He slobbered you. He does that when he gets excited." She handed Goldie a napkin. "He's kind of like a beagle that way. My little Snoopy."

Both women laughed, which caused Bruce to watch in wonderment before he began laughing too.

"No apology necessary." Goldie gently blotted her cheek.

The whole situation began to feel weird. What if Daisy discovered she was Simon's wife? Would she think her some kind of a creep? It was time for her to move on. Checkout was tomorrow, and she needed to arrive at the ferry station early.

As she exited the restaurant and passed in front of the picture window, the sound of rapid tapping on the glass stopped her. Daisy and Bruce were vigorously waving. *Goodbye.* Bruce mimicked his mommy, who was demonstrating how to blow kisses through the window. Something unforeseen lodged in Goldie's throat. She pretended to catch his kisses in the air, placing them on her lips just before her final wave. The smile on her face belied the turmoil and inexplicable melancholy now pervading her core.

On the walk back to the hotel, she knew what she needed to do. There was no way she would sit idle as a young woman and her baby struggled in vain while Simon sat on his father's massive treasure trove. It wasn't right. And it wasn't what Patrick would have wanted for his grandson. Her father-in-law intended that money to provide for his family, and Bruce Anderson was part of Patrick's bloodline. Long as the trek home would be, she knew the greatest feat of all still awaited.

Goldie selected the juiciest twenty-four-ounce porterhouse steak the butcher had to offer. She used a few extra dollops of whipped butter cream and liberal amounts of salt and pepper for the garlic mashed potatoes. Carefully, she peeled and sliced two bunches of carrots from her garden, simmering them in butter, brown sugar, and honey, just the way he preferred. For dessert, an English toffee pudding and double fudge brownies with walnuts, all made from scratch. She hadn't prepared such an elaborate meal in an age, but the thorniness of the subject matter required extra padding.

Earlier that afternoon, she'd polished the pewter candelabra, which was handed down from Simon's paternal great-grandmother, Lillian. He would often question why she never used his family heirlooms, so it was validation as he warmed to the sight of this old family favorite centered on the table. In each of the twelve holders sat an ivory tapered candle. Goldie selected *Bach's Violin Sonatas* from their vast collection of albums, placed the record on the turntable, and delicately dropped the needle. The rich sounds coupled with the soft lighting created an intoxicating atmosphere.

The Knights' dining room was not unlike a ballroom. It had enough space for a wood fireplace set in stone, a grand piano, and a hand-carved table made of cherry wood with sixteen high-backed chairs upholstered with jacquard-woven damask in deep burgundy. In all of the nearly twelve years since Patrick had gifted them the home, there was not one instance, not one dinner at which every seat had ever been filled. Simon sat at the head of the table next to the fireplace, while Goldie occupied the spot to his right—it was preposterous for her to be positioned down at the other end. If a home represented the family unit as an entity unto itself, the dinner table served as a place holder for each of its members. Despite their proximity, the long vacant table was indicative of the emptiness within their marriage and the ever-growing distance between them. Having pristinely elegant, untenanted chairs didn't provide the comfort of an ordinary round kitchen table just large enough to accommodate each family member in a cramped but cozy space.

Simon didn't offer much in the way of praise for her culinary efforts, but that didn't deter her. His satisfied smile as he stuffed tobacco into his pipe while humming along to Bach was confirmation enough that she had accomplished her mission (at least the first part of her mission).

He shared anecdote after anecdote, quipping about his work, colleagues, and clients—how foolish and unintelligent they all were, unlike him. Much as she tried to feign interest, she was riddled with unnerving thoughts about how he might handle what she had to say. He began to take note of her unease, pausing every so often to inquire, "Everything okay?" Each time there was a lull between stories, she felt as though she were teetering on the edge of a dive platform from the stern of a boat. The anticipation of the jump paralyzed her from being able to follow through, and so she kept stalling. The record started to skip, and she welcomed the opportunity to cross the room to blow dust from the vinyl. As she returned to her seat, Simon's countenance had taken on an element of spiciness. His yellow eyes danced in the flickering candlelight as he leered in her direction. Not having seen that look from him in so long, she almost forgot the meaning behind it until he reached for her hand, tendering a firm and all-telling squeeze. Much to her dismay, her efforts to please him through food had only ended up whetting his primal urges, and she knew having his hand on hers was a direct message that Simon had intentions of capping the evening in their marital bed. The thought of his hands peeling her clothes from her body and looking for homes in her most tender and private of spots filled her with disgust, sending a shiver from her low back into the floor beams beneath her feet. She smiled nervously. The words she longed to say were now trapped in her throat, festering like a virus. They needed to be emitted, if only to free herself from captivity.

Simon released her hand. His posture stiffened as he pushed himself away from the table. The temperature in the room seemed to plummet.

"What did you just say?" There was a silver-sharp edge to his tone that hadn't been there a moment ago.

I know about you and that Daisy Anderson girl.

Goldie ultimately did squeeze the words out but was blinded from the stress and could hardly remember uttering them.

Suddenly, the room seemed darker, as each candle burned closer to its base.

"I'm not looking to upset you, Simon. All I am asking is that you do the right thing."

"The right thing?" He snickered.

"You have a son, Simon. A little boy."

He took a hard drag off his pipe, ignoring her. He regarded the snifter in his hand with deference, as if it and he were the only living entities in the room.

"Did you hear what I said?" Her words prompted him to stand abruptly and head for the exit.

She called after him. "Would you like to know his name?"

Simon froze halfway across the room. He did not turn around. She couldn't imagine what he was thinking. She was not going to just give in. He should humble himself enough to ask for the boy's name.

"He's your son, Simon. Would you even care to know what she named him?"

No response. He continued to walk out of the room. A moment later, she could hear the sliding glass doors open, leading to the back patio. Goldie was numb. She sat transfixed as gobs of ivory candle wax pelleted the mauve tablecloth like acid rain.

She spent the following week unable to sleep for more than ten minutes at a clip. Images of Daisy and Bruce camped on the side of the road with a rusty tin can and frayed clothing haunted her dreams. During the day, imagining what would become of young Bruce with no father figure and no financial backing distressed her. She'd known all about troubled teens looking to make a quick buck from selling drugs, which often led to gang violence. Harsh realities didn't just exist among inner-city kids; suburbia had its share of corruption and violence. She knew she needed to try to speak to him again. There was nothing to lose, even if their mutual resentment was a wall neither of them wished to scale.

That Saturday afternoon, Goldie was on her knees in the butterfly garden. She heard the squeak of the Sutherlands' door in the next yard and dropped her trowel. Simon was surreptitiously slipping out the back door of their neighbor's home. There was a young girl in his arms he was kissing on the neck. Ginny and Kurt had been in Sarasota for the last two weeks visiting Ginny's elderly mom. Their daughter, Maryann, was home on summer break from North Carolina State. The Knights had dined with the Sutherlands every month or so for the last ten years. They'd share tidings at Christmas and barbecue together on the warm-weather holidays: Memorial Day, July Fourth, Labor Day. What would they think if they knew what Simon was up to? How could he live with himself? What kind of a man on the verge of forty has sex with his next-door neighbors' college-age daughter? He couldn't keep his trysts relegated to his office temps?

For years, she ignored the untoward glances he'd make at other women. From the voluptuous to the narrow-waisted, the blondes to the ravens, the buxom to the modest, Simon relished variety. She never paid much mind, hoping most men his age behaved much the same way. It wasn't until she learned of Daisy Anderson that Goldie had proof just how far and dangerous his pursuits could get. But seeing Simon's tongue in Maryann Sutherland's mouth, whom they'd known since she splashed around her round plastic pool in diapers and came trick-or-treating in her Bugs Bunny costume, was far too much to bear.

She rinsed off her shoes and hands with the hose before entering the house. She looked like a sow that had spent the day wrestling with hens in the mud. Removing her apron and sunhat, she entered the parlor, where Simon sat wearing a smug look, as if he'd just pulled off the heist of the decade.

"I suppose you don't give a God damn who you hurt. I can only imagine what the Sutherlands would think of the scoundrel living next door."

Simon stared back at her defiantly from over his full glass of scotch, as if daring her to make a scene. He was the man of the house, and he could do as he chose, including, but not limited to, sleeping with the pretty young girl next door. Goldie was a mere housewife. Nothing more than a "glorified maid," as he had so eloquently mentioned to her on several occasions.

"If you don't like these arrangements, then try your luck at finding another man who will want you now that you're past your expiration date."

She held strong and tried to remain impervious to his insults. "I may not have given you a child, but seeing how you treat the son you have, I'm glad I didn't. I can only wonder what Patrick would think if he were here now."

"Don't you dare speak of my father. You know nothing about him."

It was a ludicrous remark, and they both knew it. Goldie was the one with the connection to Patrick—not Simon with his seething jealousy. He could never measure up to that larger-than-life man, and Simon harbored all sorts of insecurities of his own, which he vehemently tried to safeguard behind the barbed wire of his irascible exterior.

"Simon, please. I implore you to do the right thing. This is not how you were raised."

"I've heard all I am willing to hear on the matter. Perhaps young women should exercise proper decorum instead of spreading their legs for married men. Daisy Anderson needed to learn a lesson. She was an ingenue. Clingy. Vacuous. You take any of the Johns out there and they may not have treated her as kindly in the bedroom, if you know what I mean. I did that tramp a favor by cutting her loose. At least now the kid will ground her, and maybe she can pull that wreck of a life together."

"Simon. Please—"

"No more! Not another word from you."

He stormed off, thrusting the French oak front door on its

hinges with such force a family portrait was thrown from the wall of the foyer. Jagged shards of glass blanketed the floor. She could go no further. The situation was no longer safe. She was left with one overriding thought: *He's left me no choice.*

Goldie spent the hour just before dusk strolling through the butterfly garden to water, tend, and prune. As she retreated into the house, she was unable to shake the hatred she now felt for Simon. She didn't know what brought her more anguish: his poor behavior and ill-treatment of others or that she had been one of those unfortunate women to marry such a man, which on some level made her an accomplice. Unable to process the many voices in her head clamoring for attention like recalcitrant children, she knew only one thing: her rebuffed attempts to right his wrongs had been too feeble, too passive. It was a mistake she was not willing to repeat. Situating herself at the epicenter of an imminent storm, Goldie would be the one commanding the punishing winds, the unforgiving rains, and the fury of the tides.

On Sundays, Winifred spent her day off visiting family. It afforded Goldie an opportunity to smooth the tension with Simon, alone. As she entered the kitchen, she found him propped at their breakfast nook with the newspaper blocking his face. She poured his coffee, making light, innocuous inquiries as to the lineup of the workweek ahead, hoping to calm the choppy waters between them.

She shared some thoughts on the big project she'd be tackling that afternoon: a new set of dessert dishes for the church raffle with a matching pitcher and teacups with saucers. Simon folded down the edge of the paper, if only for a moment. He nodded, then returned to his article. It was all the acknowledgment he would offer, and that was more than adequate. She hadn't coveted his acceptance for a long while now.

After refilling their mugs, she returned the carafe to the

burner, opened the refrigerator, and reached for the sealed plastic container tucked far back in the dark recesses of the bottom shelf.

In all the decades that would follow that final Sunday morning at their cozy breakfast nook in their North Carolina home, Goldie would never forget the sheer anticipation of what she was about to do. Awash with an eerie sense of calm, she became mesmerized by the spinning of the dripper in its jar. Methodically, she drizzled golden honey over the dark purple berries.

Simon awaited with the jumpy impatience of a child. His sweet tooth ignited; his eyes widened in wonderment.

"Looks delicious," he said. "You've made quite a fuss."

"Enjoy," she said tenderly.

Goldie slowly slid the ceramic bowl of granola closer to him. "They're from the butterfly garden."

24

Krystal

Krystal kicked off her shoes, curled her legs into her chest, and dropped her forehead to her knees. For the last eight hours she'd been in the chair at Goldie's bedside, who was now fast asleep with an IV in her arm and oxygen tubes running through her nose. The monitor displayed her heart rate and blood pressure, both of which had finally stabilized. Still, Krystal could not dispel the hopelessness pervading her mind like a cancer.

When she reached the hospital hours earlier, she called Abe in a panic. He arrived twenty minutes later and spent the evening by her side, holding her close. Together, they read in silence on his iPad.

"Creutzfeldt-Jakob disease is characterized by rapidly progressive dementia. Initially, individuals experience problems with muscular coordination; personality changes, including impaired memory, judgment, thinking; impaired vision. People with the disease may also experience insomnia, depression, or unusual sensations."

She thought back to the many instances over the last few

months when Goldie's behavior had changed without warning. How she had lost grip on her awareness as her mind floated off to another dimension.

"There is no treatment that can cure or control CJD. Researchers have tested many drugs, including amantadine, steroids, interferon, acyclovir, antiviral agents, and antibiotics. Studies of a variety of other drugs are now in progress. However, so far none of these treatments have shown any consistent benefit in humans."

Krystal hadn't realized she was holding her breath until she was forced to release an exhale.

"Current treatment for CJD is aimed at alleviating symptoms and making the individual as comfortable as possible. Opiate drugs can help relieve pain if it occurs, and the drugs clonazepam and sodium valproate may help relieve myoclonus. During later stages of the disease, changing the person's position frequently can keep him or her comfortable and help prevent bedsores. A catheter can be used to drain urine if the individual cannot control bladder function, and intravenous fluids and artificial feeding may also be used."

Abe just shook his head and squeezed his eyes shut, rubbing his brow vigorously with stiff fingers as he did the night before receiving a verdict on a big case. As bad as this news was, the moment of truth slapped Krystal hard in the face, as if her mother's angry hand had returned from beyond to deliver one last blow.

"Ninety percent of those diagnosed will die within the first year."

She looked at Abe. He threw a protective arm across her back and pulled her in. "Oh, sweetheart."

Krystal fled the room, not wanting to come undone next to her sleeping friend, and covered her mouth as tears spilled, streaking her cheeks with day-old mascara. Abe led her to the cafeteria and brought her a warm cup of tea.

"Baby. We will do whatever it takes to see that Goldie gets the best care possible. I'll make some phone calls."

If anyone had the money to pay out of pocket for sufficient healthcare, it was Abe. But not every husband would be willing to do such a thing all in the name of love for his wife. After an hour, he left for home to prepare for a business trip to New York City. Krystal assured him she would be fine, encouraging him to tend to his work.

"I promise you, angel. I will not rest until we find the best neurologist in this country."

She tried to let Abe's parting words soothe her while the ticking of machines and monitors lulled her into a trance. . . .

She was walking down the hallway of her childhood home. The house was never all that tidy or clean but somehow appeared even more unkempt than she remembered. The deep stench of cigarette ash permeated every crevice. Taking slow and deliberate steps, she reached the kitchen and found her father. He was lying on the ground like a heap of soiled clothing. The wall phone, which he'd managed to grab before crashing onto the linoleum, was glued to his damp and sickly hand. Of course, Krystal hadn't actually witnessed any of this in real life. But her mind took her to the place she'd never been before. Envisioning her father's last moments, suffering and dying alone in that old house.

Jocelyn arrived at the hospital just minutes after Krystal's text.

"How did you get here so fast?"

"I was on my way out," Jocelyn said. She looked frazzled and worn, unlike her typically more polished and fresh appearance.

"I'm sorry for dragging you over here like this. I didn't mean to make you worry. I just . . . I didn't know who else to call."

"Please do not apologize. I would have been insulted if you hadn't called me." Jocelyn squeezed her upper arm reassuringly.

Krystal shared the information on Goldie's illness.

"This is going to kill him," Jocelyn whispered. "Bruce loves her so much."

"Are you okay? Because . . . you don't seem like yourself."

"I'm not, Krystal. I'm not myself at all. I've screwed things up. Big time. With Bruce."

Krystal must have looked shocked, because Jocelyn quickly added, "Oh. It wasn't another man or anything like that. God, no. Can you imagine anyone being foolish enough to cheat on Bruce Anderson? It was something else. Something I was keeping from him. A couple of things I was keeping from him, actually. And . . . well, he's sort of not speaking to me."

"I'm so sorry. You're so great together. I'd hate to think of you guys having issues. I'm sure things will work themselves out."

Krystal could not believe what she was seeing and hearing. She thought Jocelyn had the near-perfect life, marriage, career. Everything was off-kilter. Maybe there was a full moon at play.

Hours later, she woke to the sound of a female clearing her throat and looked up to find Pearl framed by the doorway. She was peering into the room, as if awaiting permission to enter. Fluorescent lights tracked the ceiling of the long hallway, illuminating her from behind, creating a shadow effect across her face that concealed her expression.

Pearl walked stealthily over to the side table and gently slid a small canvas bag from her shoulder. Krystal was touched to see that Pearl hadn't taken off the green necklace and earring set since the day she gave them to her.

"It's important for you to eat a proper breakfast," Pearl said. "Hospital food can be dreadful."

"Breakfast?"

One of the nurses must have lifted the blinds while Krystal was asleep. A new day had arrived without warning. She watched Pearl remove the contents from the bag: a sizable plastic container with four compartments filled with egg whites, sautéed mushrooms, strawberries, and beach plums. She handed over Krystal's favorite pink cardigan sweater, the one she kept on the back of her chair for those late nights spent working in her study, and a toiletry case filled with makeup remover, press powder, lotions, and gloss.

"I thought you could use some freshening."

On impulse, Krystal stood. Her knees screamed in protest from having remained in a bent position all night. Without allowing the fear of rejection to creep its way into the moment, Krystal followed her instincts and embraced the dear lady.

"He told me," Pearl said ever so softly. "He told me everything. I am sorry, love."

Hearing such tenderness in Pearl's voice caused Krystal to come undone.

"There, there. . . ." Pearl made soothing circles across her back.

The unexpected comfort brought her back to the time she was being picked on by some kids during recess. Her second-grade teacher, Mrs. Roy, put Krystal on her lap, stroking her back to keep her calm. For a kid who was ignored at home and never knew what genuine affection felt like, Mrs. Roy quickly became the most important adult in her young life. From then on, she didn't mind as much when the kids were mean to her—it gave her a chance to steal the doting and coddling she'd been starving for. How she wished she could go back and thank Mrs. Roy. But that was thirty-six years ago. Thinking of her now, she wondered if her special teacher was still alive or how long had she lived and how she may have passed. Did she suffer? Was she alone? The thoughts were too much to bear. She began to tremble.

"Come. Let's take a minute." Pearl ushered Krystal from the room as she grabbed the container of food.

As they passed the bed, Goldie's head lobbed to the side; she seemed to be floating on a cloud of peaceful oblivion, completely unaware of the strife swirling around her.

"I don't know what to do," Krystal said, once they reached the cafeteria.

Pearl opened the container, scooped a few egg whites onto the fork, and handed it over. "Please. You must eat. You need to keep up your strength right now."

Krystal obeyed. It wasn't until Pearl secured a tuft of hair behind her ear that she noticed a slight tremor to her hand.

She swallowed her first bite. "Are you doing okay?"

"Certainly. I am fine. Just fine."

The room was filled with doctors in scrubs topping off their super-sized coffees to wash down their baskets of fried chicken, alongside weary visitors picking their way through the salad bar and deli counter. Suddenly filled with concern, she continued eating her cold egg whites while keeping a careful watch on Pearl. Now that they had bonded, she could not imagine losing her too. She just couldn't. Pearl rubbed the sea glass of her necklace.

"Well . . ." She seemed self-conscious with Krystal's eyes on her. "It's just that your friend, Goldie, is nearly ten years younger than me. It was hard enough watching the older generation drop off one by one. Then your peers start falling ill, and reality bites you on the rear but hard. It can be . . ." She was searching for the word.

"Scary?" Krystal said.

"Petrifying!" Her outburst caught both of them off guard.

Krystal was beginning to understand Pearl. She was unsure of herself and terrified of what the future held. Just like any other woman out there. Just like Krystal.

Pearl used both hands to smooth down the back of her bob.

"Once the younger generation starts to go, you stop counting how many years you have left and begin wondering when your own phone is going to ring with fatal test results."

She placed a hand on Pearl's arm.

"Look at me going on like this." Pearl straightened in her chair, letting Krystal's hand slide onto the table. "I am sorry for your friend. She deserves better. We all do." Pearl coughed, as if to cover a brew of emotions. She knew better than to call attention to it and changed the subject.

"So. Did he leave for New York?"

"First thing this morning. Even beat the robins, who didn't make a peep until he was out of the driveway."

"I guess I should get back in there. See what's going on." Krystal rose from her seat and closed up the plastic container. "Thank you, Pearl. For coming here and bringing me this delicious food. I really appreciate it."

"I know you do, dear. I know you do."

The women walked down the hallway next to one another as they made their trek back to Goldie's room. The whirring of the monitors and machines was hypnotizing. Krystal felt herself slump into the chair she'd spent the night in. Pearl took the seat next to her.

Softly she whispered into Krystal's ear, "Look." She was pointing to the windowsill. "Do you see them?"

As if on command, a kaleidoscope of monarchs fluttered just outside the windows.

"It's a miracle." Pearl sat in awe of the phenomenon. She raised her hand as if under a spell. Her index finger sailed through the air in an arc before landing on Goldie fast asleep in the bed.

"They're here for her."

25

Goldie

Her eyelids fluttered. She was back in time. She could still hear the celebratory jingles streaming from the carousel and the buttery decadence wafting from the popcorn truck.

"The earth gives us sweeter wines 'round these parts." The vintner's smile was the width of a yard stick; his sun-beaten lips curled back, revealing a rickety set of wine-stained teeth. "Please, young lady. Allow me." He handed her a flimsy plastic cup as he reached for a glass jug.

It was the summer of '68. The year the carnival arrived in town. Goldie drew a sip from the cup of strawberry wine, and her taste buds sprang into a jig from the sugary tartness. In her twenty-three years, she had never tasted anything as tantalizing or refreshing. As the minutes passed, the midday sun worked in tandem with the alcohol, warming her skin. She continued to take delicate sips, feigning polite interest while the vintner crowed over the technicalities and intricacies of the fermentation process. The frayed edge of the cheap cup pierced her lip like a warning as she rounded the corner on her third helping of the blush brew.

Goldie couldn't recall which clique of girls she was in back then, but the overriding sentiment from that afternoon was the satisfaction of running her hands down the silky-smooth flank of her white go-go boots. For a handful of years, she'd worked as a candy striper, saving her pennies for the lavish purchase, longing to emulate Nancy Sinatra's groovy on-stage performance of her hit song. Of course, North Carolina in July was not the appropriate season for such apparel, but she rebuffed her mother's attempts to dissuade her, unable to resist an opportunity to show off her sexy new footwear. With each and every step of the half-mile walk to town, she was reminded of the burden that accompanied breaking in a new pair of shoes. The tender skin just below her Achilles heel was rubbed raw, leaving her with a pesky blister—her fashionable badge of honor.

She continued to retreat into this long-forgotten footage being played back to her like a silent movie. It struck her as interesting how certain recollections remained untouched by time. She vividly saw herself toddling back home on bare and bloodied feet with her precious go-go boots cradled in one arm, lugging a bottle of strawberry wine in the other. The following morning, she was greeted with a roomful of sunshine, a monstrous headache, and a sour stomach, causing her to wonder why on earth anyone in her right mind would foolishly drink to excess more than once. Too much of a good thing was exactly that: too much and not so good, after all.

That scorching summer day at the carnival back in 1968 was the beginning and end of Goldie Sparrows's short-lived romance with strawberry wine. Like most mementos from the past, she wondered whatever became of those beloved go-go boots, but more importantly, she pondered the whereabouts of that long-gone innocent girl with a headful of dreams and a seemingly endless stretch of roadway at her blistered feet in the decades she had yet to travel.

A crusty set of lids slowly rose like a window that had been shut for years as her consciousness returned from the astral plane. Brutus grunted. He blinked up at her, a heavy head planted on her belly, mooring her to the mattress. His drippy snout saturated her grey knit top as if marking his turf by way of doggy fluids. He had missed her so. She could feel the love emanating from his doleful brown eyes, which spoke to her: *I'm not letting you out of my sight. Please don't leave me again.*" She knew Krystal had been by several times to walk, feed, and shower love and attention for each member of her pack, but it wasn't the same and she knew it; they were attached to their mommy.

Goldie observed the bedroom she'd slept in for decades. The world was askew. While she recognized all the parts—her fur babies camped all around her on the bed, the faux-finished armoire she'd spent weeks distressing by hand, the semi-opened louvres of the white plantation shutters—the room was somehow tilted on an invisible axis. The angles were off. It was as if the earth had cracked in certain spots. She felt misplaced as if she and the room and all its components no longer belonged to one another. Something life-changing had occurred during that extended hospital stay where she'd battled to survive like a beach plum tree in late October. It was an insidiously unyielding force, and she hadn't been prepared for the profound and startling alteration of her perspective.

Malcolm cawed from down the hallway.

"Pretty boy, Malcolm. Goldie's home."

He only "spoke" in the presence of a human. Adrenaline poured into her veins. Her heart thumped in her chest like a dog's tail against a hardwood floor. And then she remembered: *in-home nurse.* It had been so many years since she'd shared her living space with someone other than her animals. Under different circumstances, she may have warmed to the idea of having another person around to carry on a legitimate conversation with. But the nurse was there to administer her meds, regulate her temperature, and monitor her vitals—the whole process made her feel decrepit and useless. Oh, how soon Father Time in all his wickedness shoved one to the seemingly elusive threshold between autonomy and dependency.

On the day she was discharged, Goldie was too woozy to grasp the doctor's parting words about the nurse who would be accompanying her home. One thing she was pretty well certain of was that her healthcare plan wasn't sophisticated enough to cover such an exorbitant expense as in-home care. She had a sneaking suspicion Abe Axelrod had something to do with the RN occupying the guest bedroom at the end of her hallway.

Krystal had saved her life. If she hadn't arrived at the house that evening, Goldie would have been left to suffer and die alone, surrounded by her traumatized animals. She had not been coherent enough to call for assistance. The last thing she remembered was the harrowing news she'd received from Dr. Carroway and then waking up in the emergency room in the middle of the night. Everything in between was a complete blank. Krystal was unflappable and present through the entire ordeal from what Goldie had been told by the nurses.

In the middle of her ten-night stay, she was awakened from a nightmare. Her dressing gown was saturated through, as were the bedsheets and pillow cases, like she'd been soaking in a tub and jumped right into the bed without toweling off first. She'd drunk the last of the ice water and was so parched it hurt to swallow. She reached out her finger to press the call button and was startled to see she was not alone. A female was curled into a tight ball in one of the visitors' chairs. Blonde hair cascaded down her shins. She couldn't see her face, but those sultry and alluring Rapunzel tresses were unmistakable. The nurse filled a pitcher with water and caught Goldie watching her sleeping friend.

"Hard to believe you're not related. That young lady hasn't left your side. You must be a pretty special person," the nurse said.

Goldie's throat was so raw from dehydration she had a difficult time speaking, but she felt compelled to return the sentiments. She wagged a finger at her devoted young friend.

"She's the special one."

"It sure is refreshing to see sisters having each other's back this day and age. I'd say you're both pretty special."

If speaking didn't feel as though her throat were being scraped with fifty-grit sandpaper, she would have whispered to the nurse, *Would you look at that: only a woman her age can spend a whole damn night in such an uncomfortable position. If I tried that, we'd have to add an orthopedist to my team of specialists.* The thought made her smile. The nurse smiled back, wishing her a peaceful return to sleep. Goldie said nothing of the drenched fabric, not wanting to risk waking Krystal with all the hoopla of having to swap out her linens and dressing gown.

Brutus let out a lazy half bark as the nurse tapped on the open door to Goldie's bedroom.

"You knock that off, Mister. That's not how we treat a guest in our home." She stroked his neck.

"How are you today, Missus?" The nurse had an inscrutable countenance and a thick Jamaican accent.

"Still kicking." Goldie wished she could remember the nurse's name.

"Do you have any hunger?"

Jezebel? Janice? She believed it started with a *J* but wouldn't bet the ranch on that. How could she forget the woman's name?

"I suppose I might be able to sip on some broth, perhaps," Goldie said reluctantly. The nurse nodded. "But with nothing in it. No vegetables or noodles or meat or anything of the sort. Just good old-fashioned plain broth. Please."

"Yes, Missus."

The nurse crossed the room to collect the serving tray from last night's snack: pureed carrots and a ramekin of jarred applesauce with a sprinkle of cinnamon and sugar. Baby food. Her journey through life had brought her to the piteous valley of baby food. It was true what they said about coming full circle: you entered the world under the auspices of a caregiver charged with stuffing you into diapers and spoon-feeding you, and lo and behold, that's exactly how you would exit if fortunate to live long enough to experience such humiliation.

"Pardon me. I seem to be having an awful time remembering much of anything these days. What is—"

"Jasmine. My name is Jasmine, ma'am."

"*Jasmine.* Such a pretty name."

Now she remembered. When they were first introduced, she complimented the young woman on the rarity and beauty of her name. At the time, the nurse's face brightened in gratitude. Now, she just nodded slightly before taking her leave. Goldie wondered how many times they'd had that same exchange and felt the urge to hide her face in hot shame. Why was this happening to her?

The places her mind took her didn't make much sense. But then, not much of anything did these days. Long-forgotten memories were resurfacing like seaweed along the shoreline of her mind. Allowing her eyes to rest, her thoughts took her on another journey to the past, where she sat quietly in the butterfly garden she built with Patrick. It was the night before that last breakfast with Simon, all those years ago.

"You're looking especially dapper this evening, gentlemen." Goldie addressed her fleet of Black Knights waving in the light breeze as if in salutation to their queen.

She entered the center enclosure where she kept her latest addition to the crew—*belladonna*. Beautiful woman. She also quite liked the other monikers: devil's cherry or deadly night-shade. According to the encyclopedia, when ingested, the glossy black-purple berries would lead to fever, rapid pulse, difficulty swallowing, burning throat, dilation of the pupils, headache, dry mouth, hallucinations, hot and dry flushed skin, burning of the throat, and subsequently, death.

It hadn't taken long. As Simon swallowed his last bit of granola, the belladonna was busy working her magic. Goldie stood over him. She could see the life slipping from his eyes. It was like watching him fall down a well with no way to rescue him. By the time emergency services arrived, he was pronounced dead. Cause of death: congestive heart failure. With a long family history of heart disease, no autopsy was called for. Simon was cremated the next day.

Goldie opened her eyes, remembering the astonished look on Krystal's face upon first discovering the plant in the butterfly garden. Of course, she hadn't been able to properly explain why she kept such a lethal plant there. The presence of the belladonna was a comfort of sorts, reminding her that Simon was gone for good, no matter how many times he appeared at her darkest moments. His voice, his words, filled with contempt. His sardonic smile, the cruel yellow eyes. And the scotch. That pungent, offensive odor. All hallucinations. Every bit of it. Nothing was real. Simon was dead. And he was never coming back. (The belladonna was standing guard to make sure of that.)

"Your soup is ready, Missus."

"And by soup you mean broth, correct? Broth only?"

"Yes, Missus. Broth only."

Jasmine assisted her on the staircase while Goldie pondered what had brought this fine woman from the pristine sandy beaches of Jamaica to South Jersey—of course, she dared not ask, as she had most likely already been given the answer. Her self-consciousness was amped up, and she couldn't shake the feeling that Jasmine might well view her as just another finicky, spoiled old lady with her many requests and demands. But Goldie didn't feel deserving of such an assessment; it was only a matter of not wasting food, and she cringed at the thought of having to throw out a perfectly decent bowl of soup because her teeth and mouth had weakened (along with the rest of her), protesting in searing pain with every forced bite.

Goldie slid into one of the cushioned chairs at the kitchen table and faced the steaming broth, waiting for it to cool before she would even consider bringing the spoon to her mouth. A large takeout bag from the Salt Water Café sat atop the counter. She eyed it curiously.

"That handsome lumberjack fellow visited while you were in the shower," Jasmine said.

Lumberjack fellow? She was nonplussed.

"The one married to that writer lady. Mr. Bruce?"

Bruce!

"He said this was your favorite meal."

Jasmine removed the contents to store in the refrigerator.

"He really is a nice-looking fellow, isn't he?"

Clearly, Jasmine had wonderful taste in men, and Goldie couldn't help the pride she felt hearing such praise. He had picked up three servings of the homemade cabbage soup she worshipped. He had often teased her for being able to consume large bowls of soup in the summer months.

"Soup is for the wintertime. It's gonna hit ninety-five today. I could cut the air with my circular saw. What the heck do you take to the beach? Hot porridge?"

She missed the sound of her own laughter and their mornings together. Coffee hadn't tasted the same since. Would it ever again? Maybe that was the way the world worked: the simple moments captured throughout one's lifetime—like that first cup of morning coffee shared with a friend—wound up being the priceless treasures you knew you would miss the most.

Brutus was getting antsy and bumped his head into Jasmine's hand. Goldie was too weak to take him for a walk and sensed the old boy knew as much; canines were remarkably astute and very much tuned-in to the needs of their caregivers. On the occasions when she felt sad, he would console her. He'd burrow his entire face in the crook of her neck, placing his brisket across her torso, making it clear in no uncertain terms that she would never have to suffer alone. It wasn't an easy proposition to be seated at her own kitchen table watching Brutus circle someone else.

"Jasmine?"

"Yes?" She bent down to clip the hook onto Brutus's collar, and he dutifully thanked her with a slobbery tongue against her cheek.

"I wasn't always like this, you know." Goldie cursed the person she had become. One who had to wipe the emotion from her eyes with a paper napkin like some fool with no control over her feelings.

Jasmine's chin dropped an inch in reverence. She had kind brown eyes capable of embracing another from across a room. "Only fools grasp fistfuls of sand expecting them to stay put."

As she retreated from the kitchen, Goldie called to her back, "I want you to know, I appreciate you being here . . . with me. If I haven't thanked you yet—"

"Only about seven times, Missus. You are quite welcome. It is my pleasure." A flash of bright white winked at her from slightly parted lips.

Seven times. Goldie was simultaneously relieved and dismayed—her floundering memory had become a vicious enemy.

Later in the day, she propped herself into the wicker rocking chair on the front porch, with Laverne nestled on her lap and

Brutus sitting protectively in front, as her attention was drawn to the butterfly garden. She realized now why her heart was splitting into pieces. It wasn't for the conversations and experiences at her back that she may or may not forget. It was the ones she'd never come to know. The ones she wouldn't be here for.

In one year's time, she wouldn't see that Krystal would come into her own, as she took the reins with the demureness of a lady and the poise of an esteemed business owner. She wouldn't live to see the fruits of her friend's labor as she spent her entire winter feverishly learning the art of pottery. She wouldn't be in attendance at the thirtieth anniversary celebration of Little Birdie Studio that Krystal would throw next spring to introduce the pieces she'd created. While retaining her striking beauty, Krystal's appearance would slowly transform into a more sophisticated, almost regal presence. And Goldie would see none of it. But she could certainly picture it all, now.

She envisioned the moment she would never have, watching Bruce Anderson as he straggled into the studio at the end of the party with a bouquet of flowers he had picked just for her, and the awkward yet loving exchange that would have unfolded.

"I hope you like these," he would say, holding a large vase of flowers covered in shiny foil paper.

"How lovely. What a kind gesture." Goldie would be unable to conceal the blush on her face.

"I'm not exactly a flower expert, and my wife told me roses were too romantic and cliché, or something. I didn't know what you liked, so I called the florist asking for sunflowers, since those are Jocelyn's favorite. I figured most women must like them. But these sure don't look like the real thing to me. They might be a miniature version or something. Anyway, I hope they're okay. Whatever they are. . . ." Bruce would fumble with the wrapping until the flowers bobbed to and fro in greeting.

"I love daisies."

SUZANNE SIMONETTI

"They're daisies?" Bruce would ask like a spellbound child.

"Indeed. They represent purity and innocence, and they're extra special for sure. Some people consider daisies to be two flowers in one. Look here . . . the white petals count as one flower, and this cluster of tiny yellow discs that form the eye is another. Technically speaking, of course."

Bruce's eyes would expand as he processed her words. And then his facial muscles would contort as if he were ready to share more. And Goldie would brace herself.

"My mornings aren't the same without you." He would cough after getting out the last word, unable to hide his unease from sharing such a raw sentiment with her for the first time.

His words, both precious and dreadful, would gnaw at her rawest parts. She'd know better than to attempt a response and risk the loss of composure she prided herself on. Instead, she'd fall into his embrace while placing her head where it longed to rest: against his solid shoulder.

Goldie's mind shifted gears and took her on a journey back through time to the Cape May Zoo, when she first looked into the eyes of that little boy. He had never left. He'd been there all along, hiding behind the great man he'd become. Both the child she wanted to protect and the man she helped create.

My Little Birdie.

How much she wanted to believe Patrick was there with her now. His loving and patient eyes on her, providing more comfort than she'd ever known. But her mind was her most despised betrayer.

I'm right here, Little Birdie.

Patrick's voice was soothing to her ears, like the thrum of a soft spring rain. In all those years, she had never fully acknowledged the tread marks dug on her soul from losing him. How her heart splintered with cracks, knowing Bruce would never know his grandfather.

You saw them. The monarchs. I was right by your side the whole time. In our butterfly garden.

She still lamented the grandchild he longed for, the grandchild she had never given him. His words were like a lullaby sent on golden drops of sunshine. . . .

My sweet Little Birdie. I always said you were going to make some lucky child very happy one day. I knew you would find him. I knew you would find each other. And I knew you would take care of what needed to be done. None of this will make any sense to you now, and that's okay. One day, it will.

Goldie's eyes rolled from side to side beneath her eyelids, waiting for more.

My precious grandson. Our Bruce. He was my gift to you.

Epilogue

Jocelyn

ONE YEAR LATER

J ocelyn must have paced the house two dozen times in a half hour. Finally, she couldn't resist and charged into the kitchen.

"It's perfect!" Hannah's exuberance was contagious as she turned the last page of Jocelyn's latest manuscript.

"Oh, really? You think?" She topped off Hannah's mug of green tea.

"Yes. You fixed all the tangles and unclear spots. It's so much stronger. It's wonderful. I even love it more the second time around."

With Trevor's parents in California visiting his brother's family, he and Hannah began a yearly tradition celebrating the season in Cape May after Thanksgiving and through Christmas while the twins were on extended break from their private school. For Jocelyn, it was a bonus to have another woman around to be silly with and one who had become a dear friend and loyal reader.

Watching Billy with his whole family around him—Mom, Dad, stepparents, and siblings—was an absolute joy. It was most extraordinary, and she knew if not now, one day Billy would look back in gratitude that she and Trevor had reached this place, providing him with such a stable and united parental team.

"How has Bruce been handling everything?" Hannah asked tenderly.

"He's going to miss her. They had their own special bond, as you know."

Hannah's eyes widened with concern and empathy.

"He'll be okay, though. She went peacefully, from what Krystal told me. It was a blessing the way it happened. Goldie was a special person."

In the weeks following Jocelyn's admission to Bruce about the money she spent for the lawyer, her botched book deal, and Daisy's journal, an insidious silence fell over the house. For Billy's sake, they feigned some level of normalcy. Home life became a sloppy dance of awkward goodbye kisses in the morning and stilted conversations at the dinner table.

One evening, she found Bruce in the garage tinkering with his old bicycle. It was the first big present his mother had ever given him. She stood behind him in silence. He must have felt her there, because he stopped working and started speaking.

"The snow was falling that morning. It was the first and last birthday I can ever remember seeing snow on the grass just days before April," he said.

"It sure is beautiful."

That night in bed, Bruce pulled Daisy's journal from the nightstand.

"I read it," he said.

Jocelyn curled up closer to him.

"I didn't realize how much I miss her. I really do. More than ever." Bruce tucked his bottom lip as his eyes pooled. "I wish you two had met."

Jocelyn ran her finger over a tear that had escaped. "I feel like we have met," she said, crying with him. "Through her words, I've come to know her heart and mind. She was a good mother and person. You were a lucky little boy."

Bruce nodded and smiled. Jocelyn kissed him softly on the mouth.

"I have something to show you." She ran downstairs to retrieve the first hundred pages of her manuscript.

"I've been writing her story. Daisy's."

Jocelyn watched carefully as he read through the pages. His eyes flickered. And a few times, he paused to look up at her. It reminded her of the times she had flipped a book to the back cover for a glance at the author's face while reading her words. It was the first time she had ever shared her work with him this early in the process.

The hardcover release for *Daisy Jane* was set for that October. Now that Daisy's story had been brought to life, Jocelyn started journaling. She left nothing out. One day her words, her story, may just comfort her own son.

On a cool September morning as Jocelyn returned home after dropping Billy at school, she sat at her desk sipping coffee while sifting through the mail. There was a letter addressed to Bruce. It was on stationery from Little Birdie Studio. Jocelyn suspected it was not from Krystal Axelrod.

Bruce

As he pierced the seal, a faded black-and-white photograph of a middle-aged man and a young woman with white-blonde hair fell out. They were standing in what appeared to be the center of a garden surrounded by butterflies. Bruce stared at the photograph, trying to discern who he was looking at. He could feel Jocelyn inching closer. She sat in silence as Bruce began reading the letter out loud.

My Dearest Bruce,

I am hoping this letter finds you as happy as you were the last time we had coffee together at the café. You may not remember that day, but I shall never forget it. In all my years, I can't remember seeing a man as filled with love and joy for the future as you were then.

My late husband's name was Simon Knight. And he was your father. Our marriage was never built to last. Simon met your mother at a time when our marriage was just beginning to unravel. Daisy was a symptom of a much larger disease that had been brewing within the cells of our union since its inception.

After learning of Simon's affair, I tracked down your mother in Cape May. She wasn't easy to find, but I managed to pull it off. You cannot imagine my surprise when she turned up with a little boy in tow. How adorable you were! You had just reached your fourth birthday when I saw you for the very first time at the zoo.

When I returned to Elizabeth City, I confronted Simon about you and Daisy, imploring him to do the right thing. He was a very wealthy man. He had more money than he needed and far more than he ever deserved. I knew myself well enough to know my spirit would never be at peace knowing there was a young girl with a baby who was struggling to survive while the man responsible for their predicament was living like a king with no responsibilities. Much as I begged, he refused to budge on the matter. And Simon continued his trysts with other women; only this time, he was flagrantly throwing his dirty deeds in my face.

After Simon's untimely demise, I mailed your mother a package of cash from Simon's estate every month. I moved up to Cape May because I fell in love with the town and because it allowed me to keep a closer watch over you and Daisy. Being able to follow you over the years was a joy. Even from the proverbial nosebleed seats, I could see the man you were becoming, and it warmed my heart. Your mother was far more scrupulous than I ever imagined she'd be. Another person may have spent it all on folly. What a magnificent woman she was.

It's important that you know you are nothing like your father. You are nothing like Simon. That's not to say you are not a Knight. Oh, but you are! Through and through. You are the very essence of your late grandfather, Patrick Knight, the man whom I loved more than anyone in the world. You have probably heard that certain traits tend to skip a generation, and in your case, that rings true. Patrick's goodness skipped his own son and was passed on to you. As were his striking blue eyes. I've enclosed a picture of us taken in 1969. It was the day of our wedding. Patrick, your grandfather, was forty-nine years old at the time. The fair maiden with the flaxen hair on his arm is yours truly. I was twenty-four. But I won't bog you down with my own sappy memories of yesteryear. I only wish you and Patrick could have met. I don't know what I believe or don't about the afterlife, but I have hope that eventually we will all be reunited.

I know I am dying. And it isn't fair or just for these secrets to be buried with me. You have a right to know the truth. All of it. I am sorry I didn't tell you more about who I was, Bruce, but I enjoyed our exchanges so much and feared you may not understand the nature of my intentions.

I only ask one favor of you: Remember me. Remember all our mornings together and our lovely conversations. Being close to you and seeing how much you were like your grandfather made me feel like we were related in some sort of strange way.

Take care of that beautiful boy, Billy, who is now in your care. If Jocelyn were to search the globe, she would not find a better husband to stand by her side or man to father her son.

I know how special Jocelyn is to you, a woman whom I have grown to love and respect as well. Please tell her that for me.

I want you to look at this photograph if you ever feel lost or alone. This is how I wish to be remembered. Smiling. Happy. Young. At your Grandpa Patrick's side.

We will be watching over you from our butterfly garden.

Goldie

Bruce folded the letter and placed it on the table. While he couldn't make out Jocelyn's face through the reservoir of tears in his eyes, he could hear her weeping.

"She saved your life."

"Yes, she did."

Bruce picked up the photograph. He could see the strong resemblance he had with his grandfather. Even though he'd never met the man, Bruce could feel his love. His protection. And he owed it all to Goldie Sparrows.

Krystal

The harbor winds had become a familiar and cherished companion. Krystal sat at the wrought-iron table on the patio, holding her morning mug of tea with both hands as her eyelids fell. The cool and salty air enlivened her skin. A few stray pieces of hair had fallen from the bun at the nape of her neck, teasing her bare shoulders. She spent far less time looking into mirrors these days and slipped into a simple cotton sundress, tying her hair up without much of a fuss.

The Andersons would be joining them for dinner that evening. Pearl was in the kitchen putting the finishing touches on her famous Cornish game hens and rosemary roasted potatoes. The whole house smelled sensational. Abe was in the wine cellar selecting the perfect vintages to pair with the feast and preparing his humidor for post-dinner brandy and cigars for him and Bruce.

Billy goat was everything Jocelyn had described: a handsome and exuberant child with a penchant for blondes and breasts, as she soon found out. One afternoon, she was leaning over the counter to add some milk to Billy's cereal, and he gently poked her flesh with the tip of his index finger and laughed. Jocelyn was slightly horrified and disciplined him immediately. Krystal had to leave the room to hide her amusement from Billy, lest he think such behavior was acceptable. Silly as he could be, he was a good boy, and even Pearl grew fond of the little guy. There was something to be said for having a child in the home who lightened the air, adding pep and giddiness to the atmosphere.

The thud of the chair broke Krystal's reverie. She opened her eyes to see Pearl sitting by her side. The women had continued their breakfast ritual, no matter the season. All winter long, they'd set up at the granite island in the kitchen, but once the spring returned, they shifted their operation back outside to the veranda. Pearl's affections for Abe had been transferred to Krystal, and while she'd never get used to the idea of being waited on, she knew how detrimental it was for a woman not to feel valued for her contributions. Pearl's solicitousness was more for her than anyone, and it brought her great joy to be able to tend to Abe's wife in his stead; Krystal cared too much for Pearl to ever take that from her.

There was a stirring at her feet.

"She's claiming you for her territory, you know," Pearl said.

"Her territory?"

"She's frightened you may leave her too." Pearl motioned to the Himalayan now brushing her wet pink nose at Krystal's ankles.

"I'd never leave this princess."

She reached down to stroke Laverne and felt the purring against her open palm, resisting the urge to scoop up the ball of fluff while seated at the table. It was no secret that Pearl warmed to a scarce selection of things in the world, including house pets. Normally, she'd have bristled being asked to permit a cat to enter their domain, but under the circumstances, she acquiesced.

The only thing Goldie had loved as much as her craft was her babies, and she saw to it that they would land in what she considered to be the right hands after her passing. Krystal was the one who had scribbled her instructions as to where she wanted each of the animals to be placed. Brutus was to be given to Goldie's neighbor, Mary, who already had two German Shepherds and was no stranger to the upkeep and demands of a larger dog. Krystal knew she'd visit Mary regularly to see the old boy.

Malcolm wasn't an easy decision. He was boisterous and finicky. According to Goldie, he was about ten years old, and African greys could live up to six decades, so there was a chance he would outlive his next owner. She delicately told Krystal she couldn't trust just anyone with her precious bird, who required ample amounts of TLC, but she had been too polite to come right out and ask her to assume such a role after everything she had done.

"I cannot see Abe's governess permitting you to take on both a Himalayan and a parrot," Goldie said. She was in such a weakened state by then, Krystal would have said anything to set her mind at ease.

"Would it be okay with you if I keep Malcolm in the studio?

I'm there every day anyway. It's my second home. He'll never be
left to fend for himself. Just think of all the attention he'll get
from the customers."

Goldie closed her eyes. "Perfect. Simply perfect."

Watching her friend leave this world had been excruciating for
Krystal. But oddly, not for Goldie. An inexplicable sense of
peace washed over her. There was no movement save for a flut-
ter in her eyes. Her lips parted as she drew in one final breath.
And then she was gone.

In the weeks that followed, Krystal acquired that same sense
of peace and could feel Goldie in almost everything she did.
From working at the studio and her days with Malcolm to her
morning walks along the shoreline, gathering shells and sea
glass.

As she looked across the harbor from the veranda, she could
feel her now.

You are worthy. You have a voice. Never be afraid to use it.

In the quiet moments, as Krystal pondered her future, life
was full of unexpected and wondrous surprises. And it was
Goldie who taught her how to look for them.

As she made her way back toward the house, the loose wisps
of hair resumed their dance across her bare flesh. Once she
reached the sliding glass doors, she reached for the handle and
froze at her own reflection. She'd recognize that bright orange
and black piping anywhere. A monarch butterfly had alighted
on her shoulder as tenderly as a kiss.

The End

Acknowledgments

For nearly ten years I have had the great fortune of working with Caroline Leavitt, who quickly became a friend, mentor, and sister. Years ago she told me I was the *real thing*, and with that, a future I had never dared to imagine unfolded before me. To have received such profound validation from this tried-and-true professional was a life-altering moment. Caroline has the power to turn my angst and despair into tears of sweet relief with only a few words.

A loving thank-you to Patti Davis, a writer I always admired who became a friend I now cherish. She so effortlessly titled this debut. In countless ways, Patti bolsters my strength and motivation—professionally, personally, spiritually—with her gentle wit and unassuming guidance. As I stumble to find my footing and voice along the many dark and lonely detours, my bond with Patti remains a great treasure and source of comfort.

A huge hug of gratitude to Mary Morris, who is one of the most warm-hearted and fun people I know. Her generosity and brilliant advice have guided and calmed me in immeasurable ways. Listening to Mary and Caroline share ideas and thoughts over lunch is like being invited to a slumber party with the "cool" kids.

Thanks to my fabulous publicist, Caitlin Hamilton Summie, who is also a talented writer. Her diligence, effort, and know-how were a balm along the journey. I will never forget how she held my hand and walked me through this dream like a long-lost friend. Woot!

Gratitude to the fantastic team at She Writes Press: my publishers, Brooke Warner and Crystal Patriarche; my steadfast project manager, Shannon Green; Julie Metz, for giving me the book cover of my dreams; editor Krissa Lagos; and countless others. And to all of my SWP sisters, with our many Zoom sessions and exchanges of information—I am honored to share in this journey with this talented pack.

Big love to my beta readers and dear friends Teresa Camara Pugh, Sally Lomanno, Daryl Brown Morris, Gail Rosen, Jan Schmidt, and Hillary Strong for their honest feedback, and for filling me with the courage to keep going.

A special thank-you to my first Cape May friend, Wesley Laudeman, whom I met in 2013. She enthusiastically provided me with colorful pages of typed information on the town of Cape May and life therein from her unique perspective as a born-and-bred local. Wesley remains one of my most favorite people and best reasons for living here.

A shout-out to fellow writers, artists, and dreamers within my community and beyond who have been wonderfully supportive through the years: Alexia LaFortune, Amy Rosen Cooper, Amy Ferris, Barbara Dreyfuss, Bob Dreyfuss, Cathy Williams, Dan Twork, Daryl Richardson, Debra Lynn Shelton, Dennis Flanagan, Elissa Diener, Eryk Hanut, Evie Maxfield, Frank Fiorino, Gale Hampson, Gina Heron, Heather McQueen, Jenai Fitzpatrick, Jim Silvestri, Karen Ramsey, Kate Conley Chadwick, Kathy Radigan, Kerry Murphy-Hammond, Kimberly Engebrigsten, Lindy Michaels, Loretta Nyhan, Manish Patel, Maria Reda Fiorino, Nadia Reda, Pamela Singer, Robert

DiCarlo, Sally Beth Edelstein, Susan Henderson, Suzanne Pattison, Suzanne Kulpberger, Tammy Hetrick, Terence Turner, Terry Lynn Thomas, Tina Giaimo, Tom Sokat, Tricia Alexandro, and William R. Sutton.

Thanks to my family—Maggie, Papa Joe, Elizabeth, Steven, Jameson, Brody, Scott, Justin, Adeline, Jerry, Joey, Justine, and Pat—and their belief in me despite the disappointments along the way.

To my sweet husband, Joe, for never once giving up on me, and for his candid feedback at every bend in the road: this achievement is ours to share.

A heartfelt tribute to my late aunt, Patricia Marie Pringle, who was wickedly stolen from us in June 2018 by Parkinson's disease. She visits me in my dreams. There have been times the veil between us is so thin, I can feel her presence and even smell her as I sit at my desk deep in thought, or when I trail the shoreline the way we once did together. I breathe a little easier knowing she was able to read the first draft of this tale before her last sunset.

Reading Group Guide

1. How does this book's title work in relation to the book's contents?

2. How do the creative arts matter to this book as a whole?

3. Part of this novel turns on secrets. Discuss.

4. Which scene from this narrative stuck with you the most?

5. A theme of this novel is self-determination—discovering and being true to oneself. Discuss.

6. Would you visit Cape May? What about the events taking place in a tourist town affects the story?

7. Butterflies, plants, and animals are critical to this tale. How?

8. Who of the narrators would you be friends with? Why?

9. What do you think will happen to Krystal and Jocelyn as people? What about as friends?

10. What surprised you most about this book?

11. Are there lingering questions from the story that you're still thinking about?

12. If you could ask the author anything, what would it be?

About the Author

Suzanne Simonetti grew up in the New York suburbs just outside of the city. After earning a BS in marketing, she spent several years writing press releases, until she left her corporate job to focus on her passion for crafting fiction. She lives on Cape May Harbor with her husband. When not on her paddle board or yoga mat, she can be found at the beach trailing the shoreline for seashells, scribbling in her notebook, and channeling dolphins for meaningful conversation.

SELECTED TITLES FROM SHE WRITES PRESS

She Writes Press is an independent publishing company founded to serve women writers everywhere. Visit us at www.shewritespress.com.

Center Ring by Nicole Waggoner. $17.95, 978-1-63152-034-1. When a startling confession rattles a group of tightly knit women to its core, the friends are left analyzing their own roads not taken and the vastly different choices they've made in life and love.

A Cup of Redemption by Carole Bumpus. $16.95, 978-1-938314-90-2. Three women, each with their own secrets and shames, seek to make peace with their pasts and carve out new identities for themselves.

Stella Rose by Tammy Flanders Hetrick. $16.95, 978-1-63152-921-4. When her dying best friend asks her to take care of her sixteen-year-old daughter, Abby says yes—but as she grapples with raising a grieving teenager, she realizes she didn't know her best friend as well as she thought she did.

Again and Again by Ellen Bravo. $16.95, 978-1-63152-939-9. When the man who raped her roommate in college becomes a Senate candidate, women's rights leader Deborah Borenstein must make a choice—one that could determine control of the Senate, the course of a friendship, and the fate of a marriage.

The Moon Always Rising by Alice C. Early. $16.95, 978-1-63152-683-1. When Eleanor "Els" Gordon's life cracks apart, she exiles herself to a derelict plantation house on the Caribbean island of Nevis—and discovers, with the help of her resident ghost, that only through love and forgiveness can she untangle years-old family secrets and set herself free to love again.

Magic Flute by Patricia Minger. $16.95, 978-1-63152-093-8. When a car accident puts an end to ambitious flutist Liz Morgan's dreams, she returns to her childhood hometown in Wales in an effort to reinvent her path.